HOT
ADDICTION

A *HOSTILE OPERATIONS TEAM* Novel

LYNN RAYE
NEW YORK TIMES & USA TODAY BESTSELLING AUTHOR
HARRIS

www.**lynnrayeharris**.com

First Edition: April 2017
Library of Congress Cataloging-in-Publication Data

Harris, Lynn Raye
    Hot Addiction / Lynn Raye Harris – 1st ed
        ISBN-13: 978-1-941002-17-9

1. Hot Addiction—Fiction
2. Fiction—Romance
3. Fiction—Contemporary Romance

OTHER BOOKS IN
THE *HOSTILE OPERATIONS TEAM* SERIES

PROLOGUE

Five years ago…

DEXTER DAVIDSON CHECKED HIS WATCH for the thousandth time that morning. It was nearing noon and his bride-to-be was over an hour late. His father stood in the chancel, his rented tuxedo making him appear distinguished and genteel rather than rough and worn like the farmer he was. But the look on his face was what killed Dex the most. It was one of pity and a growing resignation.

"Fuck this," Dex growled as he clenched his jaw tight and walked down the aisle, between the rows of pews where the guests waited for the ceremony to start. The chapel doors were open to the outside because it was springtime and warm. But it was also raining. A soft, gentle rain, but rain nonetheless.

Perhaps the rain had caused a delay. Dex stood in the open door and took his phone from his pocket. Annabelle still hadn't answered his texts. He sent another one, just in case, and felt his heart shrivel just a little bit more when no answer came.

He tried calling, but it went to voice mail without even ringing. "Belle," he said, his throat tight and his eyes burning, "where are you, baby? I'm worried. Please let me know you're safe. If you've changed your mind, it's okay. Just let me know."

It wasn't okay if she'd changed her mind, but what else could he say? Annabelle Quinn had been his girl for the past four years. He'd fallen madly in love with her in an instant. He'd known her most of his life, had ignored her for much of it because she was his little sister's best friend, but one day, *pow!* She'd smiled at him the way she had a million times before—and he was done for. He'd been hers from that moment forward.

And now they were supposed to be getting married. He'd come home on leave from the Army at Christmas and asked her to marry him. She'd said yes. She and his sister had planned everything while he went back to Afghanistan and did his best to stay alive. He didn't know how long he stood there before he felt a presence beside him.

"I'm sorry, Dex." Katie put a hand on his arm. "She's not coming."

He wanted to deny it, but the look on Katie's face told him all he needed to know. He felt hollow inside. Empty. Because he knew she was right. He'd known it deep in his gut for the past twenty minutes.

His sister's eyes were shiny. He took the phone from her hand and stared at the text message on the screen until the words blurred together and his heart burned away, turning to ash.

Belle: *I can't, Katie. Please don't hate me, but I can't. Tell Dex I'm sorry. I shouldn't have let it go this far. I've thought for a while that marrying him wasn't right, that I'm not the woman for him—I should have been brave enough to say so. He deserves more than this. Tell him.*

Dex stood there for a long moment, his gut roiling with emotions he didn't know how to process. He dropped the phone and strode out into the rain while Katie called after him. He put his uniform hat on, shoved his hands into his pockets, and kept walking down the muddy road, away from the country church that Annabelle had insisted was the place she wanted to be married.

He didn't know where he was going or what he was going to do when he got there. All he knew was that his life would never be the same again.

ONE

ANNABELLE QUINN-ARCHER COULDN'T GET OVER the feeling she was being followed. She swiveled her head to look up and down the street but saw nothing out of the ordinary. She'd had that feeling a lot in the past month, ever since Eric had died in Africa, but there was never anyone waiting in the bushes to jump out at her. She'd varied her routine, never doing the same thing long enough to get predictable, and she'd hired a private detective to check for anomalies.

He'd found nothing. She'd paid him and sent him on his way, feeling like an idiot for being paranoid. But still, there was something that didn't feel quite right to her. Maybe she was overworked as her friend Molly had suggested, or maybe she was still reeling from the fact her husband was dead and there'd been almost nothing left of him once the animals were finished with his body.

A mixture of emotions rained down on her, like always, when she thought of Eric. She hadn't wished him dead, but she also couldn't be sorry he was out of her life. Guilt sat like a stone in her belly at her inability to care that he was gone. All she could feel was relief that she was finally out from under his thumb. For the first time in five years, she could breathe.

Guilty, guilty, guilty.

Maybe that's why she thought she was being followed. Maybe it was just the truckload of guilt perched on her shoulder like a malevolent gargoyle that was wearing her down and making her paranoid.

Annabelle ducked into the Archer Industries building and headed for her office, greeting people with a smile that shook at the corners. They were worried about what would happen to their jobs now that Eric was dead, but she intended to fight for their future. They still had a team of talented engineers, and they had a revolutionary—though flawed—product. Development would continue.

When she got inside her office, she shut the door and sagged against it, closing her eyes and taking a deep breath. Life over the past month had been chaotic. Stress lived with her these days.

As if she didn't feel guilty enough, there was also the fact that *he* was back in town. Dex. She'd seen him from a distance just two days ago, walking into the Briar City Diner with his sister and her family. Annabelle's stomach had twisted hard at the sight of him. Of them, actually, since she and Katie were no longer on speaking terms.

She missed her best friend—but she'd had no idea how much she'd missed the man she'd once planned to marry until she saw him again. Dexter Davidson, six foot three inches of pure muscle with dark hair, a five-day scruff, and deep brown eyes. Her first love.

Her first *lover*.

What would life have been like if she'd married him that day?

"Dammit," she muttered before opening her eyes and going over to her desk. She had work to do and no time to get lost in maudlin thoughts about Dex. He hated her. And why wouldn't he? She'd skipped out on their wedding and then married another man three weeks later. And not just any man, but his fiercest rival.

It didn't matter that she'd had to do it. It only mattered that she *had* done it. He would never forgive her for it. Katie had tried, bless her, but when Annabelle married Eric so soon after she'd left Dex at the altar—well, that was the end of that.

Her gaze strayed to the photo of the little girl on her desk. Charlotte was her world, her reason for existing. So long as she had her daughter, life would be okay. That's why she had to fight for Archer Industries and why she had to succeed. Eric's estate wasn't as big as people thought. He'd mortgaged everything to the hilt in order to live the lifestyle of a successful CEO.

He'd been counting on this latest technology to make a fortune for the company and for himself. Unfortunately, the Helios project had national-security implications, which meant he couldn't sell it to foreign governments or entities. But the US government wanted to buy it and they'd offered a very handsome price on delivery. In the meantime, they would fund development.

Eric should have been happy, but he hadn't been. He'd raged and complained for days, swearing the technology was worth five times what the US was buying it for. She'd stopped listening to his diatribes. Eventually he'd calmed down, and work returned to normal.

But now he was dead, and the project had veered off schedule. Annabelle took a determined breath and started to pick up her desk phone to call the lead engineer, Marshall Porter.

The phone buzzed before she could make the call. "Yes?"

Her secretary was on the other end. "Mrs. Archer, there's a call for you from a Mr. Lyon. He says it's in regard to the contract with Washington."

Her belly sank. "Thank you, Lucy. Oh, and can you call Charlotte's preschool and see what it is they need for the party next week?"

"Of course, Mrs. Archer."

Annabelle clicked the button to connect the call while also pulling up a spreadsheet on the Helios timeline and numbers. She didn't remember a Mr. Lyon from Washington, but she had to be ready for anything. "This is Annabelle Quinn-Archer," she said as she tapped a couple of keys. "What can I do for you, Mr. Lyon?"

There was a long moment of silence on the other end of the line. Annabelle was already getting lost in the numbers on her screen, formulating her answers to any potential questions, when the voice came through, hard and cold and so menacing it made the hair on her neck stand up.

"You can tell me where the money is, Mrs. Archer. Or you can die like your husband."

4

Dex shoved a hand through his hair and gazed out at the farmland. It was time to cut hay for the livestock, but Dad wasn't going to be harvesting anything this year. Not after his open-heart surgery last month and the fall he'd taken just a few days ago. He'd hit his head and been knocked out cold. It was hours before the neighboring farmer had found him in the barn, disoriented and in pain from the broken leg he'd suffered in the fall.

The cows were being taken care of by that same farmer for now, and there was a For Sale sign at the end of the drive. The sign was especially jarring, but there was nothing to be done for it. Dad wasn't getting any younger, and the farm took too much work. It was time for him to retire.

Katie ambled into the room, her eyes red-rimmed as she clutched a framed photo. "I can't believe it's come down to this."

Dex shrugged. "It's life, Katie. Time moves on and so do we."

"You could take over the farm—"

"No. I can't." His voice snapped into the air between them, and she sucked in a breath. "It's not me," he said, softer this time. "It's never been me. Even if I wanted to, I still have another couple of years on my enlistment. Besides, there's no future here and you know it. If there was, you'd have had Jessie give up his job at the bank and learn to farm so *you* could take over when it was time."

She dropped her chin. They both remembered the lean times growing up, the beans and cornbread every night because there was nothing else. The early mornings feeding livestock, the days in the saddle when it was time to cull the herd, the millions of backbreaking tasks that went with raising cattle. "You're right."

He went over and put his hands on her shoulders. "He'll be all right. Once the stress of this place is gone, he'll be able to enjoy life again."

"Farming *is* Daddy's life."

"Not anymore. The doctors say it's time he stopped or he won't live another year."

"I just wish he could stay here in the home he knows."

"He needs to be closer to town and his doctors."

"I know." Katie sighed. "When Jessie and I bought a house with a mother-in-law apartment, we thought it would be for his parents when they came to visit. I never dreamed of Daddy living there."

"It'll be an adjustment for everyone, I'm sure."

Katie's eyes were shining. "Don't misunderstand me, Dex. I *want* Daddy there. I just don't know if he wants to be there." She swiped her fingers beneath her eyes. "I need to get back to the rehab facility and see how he's doing."

"I'll be along in a bit."

"Okay." She grabbed her purse and headed for the door. "The kids are looking forward to seeing more of their Uncle Dex, by the way."

Dex laughed. "They're three and one. I doubt that very much."

Katie smiled. "Fine, it's me who wants to see you. So don't forget I'm cooking dinner tonight, okay?"

"I'll be there."

Katie went outside and climbed into her Lexus SUV. She waved brightly before backing out and heading up the driveway. Dex watched her go and then took out his phone and scrolled through e-mail. This was the second time in a month he'd gone on emergency leave from the job, but his team was still in DC and waiting for their next assignment. He hoped it didn't come before he got back. He wanted to be in the action, risking his life protecting his country and its ideals, rather than here watching the death of the life he used to know.

He might not want to be a cattle farmer, but seeing the old house sold wasn't as easy as he'd thought it would be. He'd grown up here. Fallen in love here. He hardened his heart at that thought. No good ever came of thinking about Annabelle Quinn—Annabelle *Archer* now. The thought that she was a widow echoed through his mind, but he shoved it away. He didn't care. Didn't care what she did or how she was doing.

Fuck her and all the false promises that had ever issued from her cherry lips.

He put his phone away and let his gaze slide over the worn living room—the ratty couch and rattier recliner, the huge flat-screen television he'd bought his dad for Christmas, the dated wallpaper and creaky floors of the old house. He didn't know why he was standing here, reluctant to leave. He'd seen this place often enough to have every crack in the wall memorized. He despised and loved this house in equal measure. Once his mother had died, it had gotten even sadder and more worn than it had been when they were still a family.

He gritted his teeth and headed for the door. Time to lock up and get back to his hotel in town. He'd just turned the key in the lock and started across the porch when a blue Mercedes turned into the driveway and rolled toward him.

It was a nice car, an AMG sports car, low-slung and sleek, which meant it had cost the driver a pretty penny. There was no reason for a car like that to be here—unless it was the real estate agent.

Dex leaned against the porch railing and waited for the agent to pull up. Whatever she wanted—and he knew it was a she because he'd paid attention to the name on the sign—it wouldn't take long because he wasn't going to let it.

The car stopped but the driver didn't get out. Dex started to get annoyed, but then he saw the woman's hands on the wheel, clenching and unclenching like she was thinking about what she wanted to do. He couldn't see her face because of the reflection off the glass and the angle he stood at. Before he could start down the stairs, she must have made up her mind because the car shut off and the door swung open.

A second later she emerged, blond hair shining in the sunlight, cherry lips glistening with gloss. Dex's heart was a dead thing, and yet it still managed a hard throb at the sight of her.

Fortunately, that throb went away and anger filled him instead. Hot, hard, swelling anger. "What the fuck do you want, Annabelle?"

TWO

SERGEI TUROV INHERITED A MESS when his boss died. To be fair, he'd been the one to order a bullet put into Grigori's head, but still. A mess.

The empire he and Grigori had built together was in tatters after the Americans swept in and halted their trafficking operations across the globe. That created much ill will among their partners. He still had Zoprava, the technology firm that was the legitimate arm of his empire. He also had the other interests they'd built. He would make everything better with time.

His business acumen was superior to Grigori's. Grigori had gotten wound up over a girl—Sophie Nash—and let himself be robbed of vital information that had been used to take him down. Sergei did not blame Miss Nash. It was no use shutting the barn door after the horse had escaped.

Not to mention, he had no intention of attracting the scrutiny of the organization Miss Nash had brought to bear against Grigori. HOT, aka the Hostile Operations Team. He should not know their name, but he did.

It was information to be tucked away. Used when it would do him the most good. He would not pull the trigger a moment sooner than necessary. He was a patient man. Usually.

Right now he had other fish to fry. He picked up the phone on his sleek glass-and-chrome desk and dialed a number.

"*Privyet*, Sergei," a voice said after two rings.

The city skyline twinkled. The Kremlin rose tall and proud above the Moskva River, its walls shining with light. He never tired of the sight. "Dmitri. What is your progress?"

The man on the other end snorted. Sergei did not like him. He was former KGB, a toady of Grigori's. He was also unpredictable—but Grigori had gotten them into this mess, and Dmitri had been his instrument for the transaction. Sergei didn't like it, but no sense in starting over when Dmitri knew all the players and the stakes.

"I am working on it. You will get your money back. And I will get my fee."

"Yes, you will get your fee."

"I have been thinking… twenty percent," Dmitri said.

Sergei ground his teeth. *Of course.* "The deal was ten."

"Yes, but I am worth more."

"Get the money in a week and you'll get twenty percent. Longer than that—the original ten. Take it or leave it."

Dmitri scoffed. "If I leave it, you will get nothing."

"There are others willing to do the job. Take it or leave it."

Silence sat heavy on the other end. "You drive a hard bargain, Sergei Alexeiovich."

The line went dead. Sergei sat back and propped his Italian loafers on the desk. Yes, he did drive a hard bargain. He had plans far bigger than any Grigori could have conceived of.

He slid a cigarette from the mahogany box on his desk and lit it with the gold lighter Grigori had given him years ago. He blew out a breath and studied the skyline.

Patience would get him everything he desired. And far more besides.

Annabelle's nerves danced a tango in her belly. The afternoon sun slanted at the perfect angle, illuminating Dex in a golden glow that did nothing to hide his perfection. As if anything could mask that raw male beauty. He'd always looked amazing, no matter what the environment, and so tempting that he made her insides flutter.

His brows were drawn low and thunderclouds dominated his expression. He was angry, of course he was—but she'd had no choice about coming here today. He was the only person she could think of who would know what to do.

"No police, Mrs. Archer. I will know if you call them."

She held the car door like a shield, her heart beating a disjointed rhythm as she searched for words. The *right* words. The words that would make Dex Davidson's hard expression melt away. If she could just tap into the tender concern he'd once had for her, she could make him understand. Not an easy task since she hadn't spoken to him in five long years.

Good luck with that, girlie.

"I need your help." Forced past the tightness in her throat, the words were little more than a croak.

He stared at her for a long moment. And then he laughed. A wonderful belly laugh that startled her. It took a second to realize he was laughing *at* her.

She stepped out from behind the car door and took a step toward the porch. She'd spent many nights in this house, hanging with Katie in her room, playing in the fields and creeks, riding horses, and having so much fun she never wanted to go back to her staid, boring life in town.

It was a wonder her parents had let her hang out with Katie Davidson, considering how they were always grasping at the social ladder. Though perhaps it had gotten her out of the way often enough that they didn't feel guilty attending so many functions. Her staying with Katie had been free babysitting for them. And for people who'd always pretended to have far more money than they had, free was too good a bargain to pass up.

"You've come to the wrong place," Dex said, his voice a growl that reverberated down her spine and into all the warm, tingly places it should not. Places that had been dead for so long now that their sudden reawakening stunned her.

"I know you have no reason to help me." She forced herself to move toward where he stood. It wasn't easy, not only because of the *here be dragons* look on his face but also because her stilettos weren't meant for gravel. All she needed was to go down in a hard sprawl to make her humiliation complete. "I have nowhere else to turn. I'm in trouble, Dex. Big trouble."

Considering she now knew that Eric's death hadn't been an accident, *big trouble* was an understatement.

"Not my concern, Annabelle. You stopped being my concern when you didn't show up for our wedding. A wedding you planned, a wedding you insisted you wanted right down to the day you left me standing there with a church full of guests and a heart that broke in two and kept on breaking for months after."

His words gouged into her chest, leaving soul-deep grooves. Of course he'd been hurt. She had too. But he wouldn't believe her if she told him that.

She staggered to a halt at the bottom of the steps. He looked about as welcoming as a grizzly. "I'm sorry."

"Not good enough. Not nearly good enough, lady." His fists flexed at his sides and his entire body was plank-stiff. Angry didn't begin to describe it.

Annabelle sucked in a breath. Her vision blurred as she thought about her little girl. *For Charlotte.* She had to get through this for her baby. Had to face this man and beg him. There were some things she couldn't tell him—things she couldn't tell anyone—but she'd do whatever it took to get him to help her.

"I have a daughter—"

"Congratulations. Still don't care."

"I'm all she has left. Eric is dead, and if anything happens to me—" She couldn't quite stop the sob that broke free. But she choked it down and kept her eyes on his. She was shaking like a leaf, but she couldn't stop.

Dex's dark eyes were unreadable. His jaw clenched tight. "She has grandparents, I assume. They'll take care of her."

Pain stabbed into her. Eric's parents were dead, killed in a small-plane crash three years ago. And her parents? God no. She'd planned to make Molly her daughter's guardian if anything happened to her, but the past month had been too chaotic to get that done. And if something happened to her right now?

Her parents would get Charlotte. Annabelle shuddered to think it. Her child would be cared for, because her parents *did* love their granddaughter, but she wouldn't blossom in their care. And no way did Annabelle want her daughter to wonder, the way she had, why she hadn't been enough for her parents. Why they'd always wanted more. They were still social climbers, still wannabe jet-setters, and that was no way to raise a child.

"That's cruel of you to say."

"You taught me how to be cruel. Or don't you remember?"

"You hated Eric," she said, stiffening her spine and hardening her heart against his anger. She had to regain control of this situation, had to make him understand.

"Yeah, well he hated me too. Don't make it seem like I'm the only one."

"He hated you because you were so good at everything you did. He wanted to be quarterback of the football team, but you were. He wanted to be homecoming king, but that went to you as well. Everything he wanted, you had."

Dex's face grew harder if that were possible. "You're kidding, right? His parents had money. He had everything he could have desired that meant anything. So what the fuck did he hate me for? He was always going to have an easier time in life than I was. But I didn't care because I had you, and that was all I needed." He snorted. "Except he got you too in the end, didn't he? You married him three weeks after you left me at the altar. Were you seeing him behind my back, Belle?"

For a moment she couldn't breathe. Whether because of the accusation or the fact he'd used the nickname he'd once had for her, she didn't know. Maybe a bit of both. "No," she bit out. "I never cheated on you. Never."

"Jesus Christ, you're a fucking liar."

Her eyes blurred as his words hit her square in the chest. "I'm not lying."

"Honey, you could swear on a stack of Bibles and I still wouldn't believe you. You were seeing him while I was off risking my life in the Army. But instead of telling the truth and coming clean, you planned a wedding. Were you going to break it off with him? Or maybe you decided that his money was far more attractive than anything as pitiful as my love was ever going to be."

His gaze skipped over to her car—a car that she knew had a six-figure price tag—and then back again. The disgust on his face was almost enough to break her. What could she say that he would believe? No matter how many truths she unearthed or how many sins she confessed to, Dex Davidson wasn't going to change his mind about who she was or how she felt about what she'd done.

And yet she couldn't give up. She knew what kind of man he was, and he was precisely what she needed right now. He'd been Special Forces five years ago. An Army Ranger. She'd heard whispers of his exploits in town over the years—missions, medals. Dex could help her.

He *had* to help her. And right now, she'd say anything to get him on her side. Even the truth, no matter how humiliating it was.

"Eric was a bastard. I hated him. I wanted a divorce, but he wouldn't agree to it. We slept in separate bedrooms and I focused on Charlotte and work. It probably would have continued that way for years if he hadn't been killed in Africa last month."

He studied her and she tumbled on, encouraged.

"Eric stole some money from someone and they think I know where he stashed it. They're going to kill me if I don't give it to them. But I have no idea where it is or how to find it—I need help." She said everything in a rush before he could stop her, and now she gulped in a breath and prayed it was enough.

Dex's eyes narrowed, and for a moment she felt a flicker of hope. But then he shook his head, a slow wag from side to side, as he took the steps down to her level. Even in high heels, she had to tilt her head back to look up at him. Heat emanated from him like from sun-baked asphalt. She could smell the familiar scent of his body, that manly pine-and-leather smell that used to wrap around her senses. She ached for the days when he would put those arms around her and pull her close. The days when she'd been his girl and the future had seemed bright and full.

His mouth curled into a smile. Relief skimmed up her spine. She'd gotten through to him. The Dex she'd known and loved still had a heart as big as the ocean.

"Sorry, Annabelle—but I just don't fucking care. Call the police if someone is threatening you. But don't ask me to get involved. You aren't my responsibility."

Air punched from her lungs. "He said no police. Dex, please—"

"Have a nice life." He strolled away and climbed into the big Ford truck sitting near her car. After he started it, he revved the engine. Then he spun the big vehicle around and shot down the driveway. Gravel plinked against the metal of her Mercedes like small-arms fire. Annabelle jumped onto the porch, heart racing. She narrowly missed getting hit by the barrage. Her left shoe lay in the dirt like a casualty.

Her throat was so tight she could barely breathe as Dex disappeared in a cloud of angry dust. When he was gone, when she was certain he wasn't coming back, she screamed her frustration to the empty air. Then she sank down on the steps and gave in to the hot tears welling behind her eyes. She'd never felt so alone or so hopeless as she did right now.

Dex had been her world once. Now he didn't care if she lived or died.

THREE

DEX FELT LIKE AN ASSHOLE. The farther he drove from the farm, the more he wanted to turn around and go back. Just to make sure she was okay. Nothing else. Not to say he was sorry or to ask her to tell him more about the threat against her.

He flexed his fingers on the wheel and gritted his teeth. He didn't know Annabelle anymore, didn't know what she was capable of. Hell, he'd never known. That much was clear.

So why wasn't he as certain as he wanted to be that she was only trying to get his attention? That she was overreacting to some perceived threat that was probably nothing more than an angry customer blowing off steam?

Dex snatched up his cell phone and brought up his contacts. Then he hit the one he wanted.

"Girard," came the answer. "What's up, Double Dee? Everything okay with your dad?"

"Yeah, Dad's fine. Thanks for asking." Anger and doubt rode him hard. "Look, can you get some information about Archer Industries in Briar City, Kentucky? They're a small firm making computer parts or something. I don't really know."

"Sure. Why?"

"The CEO was killed last month and his wife just told me she's gotten a death threat." He could feel the curiosity burning through the phone. "We were engaged once. Didn't work out and she married this guy—Eric Archer. She said someone claimed her husband stole their money and they think she knows where it is."

"What do you think?"

Dex focused on the road in front of him. "I think I don't want anything to do with this—but I also think I need to know if she's in real danger. Could be she's blowing it out of proportion. I just wanna be sure."

Because no matter how much he despised Annabelle, he didn't walk away when someone needed help. It wasn't who he was or what he did. If she was in real danger, he'd recommend a good protective service for her and extract himself from the situation with a clear conscience.

"All right, let me check into it. I'll let you know what I find."

"Thanks. I appreciate it." He ended the call and continued on his way into town. Tension vibrated through his body. He hadn't anticipated seeing Annabelle today, hadn't been prepared for that kind of confrontation at all. It was always possible while he was in town to run into her somewhere, but he'd spent most of his time going between his hotel, the rehab facility, Katie's house, and the farm— places Annabelle wasn't likely to be.

Except when she made it a point to seek him out. He tried to push her image from his mind, but it didn't work. She'd looked so pretty and sad. Her hair had been scraped back in a ponytail, and she'd worn tall heels with cropped pants that revealed her delicate ankles. He couldn't help but notice she still had a body designed to drive a man wild.

Rage surged at the idea that Eric Archer had touched that silky skin. Dex had been her first. He'd once thought he'd be her only. But holy shit, she'd had a kid with Eric. A frickin' kid.

The interesting part came when she'd said she hated Eric. Why? Was she trying to win his sympathy?

Dex growled. Dammit, he didn't need to keep thinking about this. He didn't care if she hated Eric, didn't care why, didn't care that she had a kid or thought someone wanted to kill her. He couldn't afford to care after what she'd done to him, after the dark path she'd sent him down.

When he reached the turn that would lead him into town, he idled for a minute, thinking. And then he took a right and drove toward the shooting range instead. He had to burn off some of this tension. He needed Jane cradled in his arms. He needed to caress her metal body, squeeze her smooth trigger, feel her explosive energy. Somewhere between the slow, steady breaths, the rhythmic heartbeats, and the utter stillness long-distance shots required, he could burn off the rage and find peace again.

To hell with Annabelle Quinn and her drama.

Annabelle waited for about twenty minutes. Part of her knew it was in vain. Part of her hoped Dex's innate protectiveness would take over and he'd return to help her.

Get up, Annabelle.

He'd abandoned her and he wasn't coming back. She didn't have time for a pity party. With a quick look around, she slipped over to her car and jumped inside, hitting the lock button while her heart hammered. Her cell phone lay on the seat. She'd missed a call.

Marshall Porter. She didn't have time to talk to him right now. She started the car and smashed the gas while in reverse. Then she slammed it into drive and flew down the gravel road.

She didn't care about the rocks hitting her car, didn't care if there were dings or scratches. Her life was falling apart, and there was nothing more important than protecting her daughter. She thought again about calling the police, but it was too dangerous. She was in this alone. Mr. Lyon was waiting and time was running out. His voice still twisted in her ear like a snake's skin sloughing away.

"What do you want from me?"

"The money, Mrs. Archer. You have twenty-four hours to locate the account numbers. When I call again, you will transfer the money—or you will die."

"I don't have it. I don't even know what you're talking about."

"You will find it. It is your only choice."

"How will I know I've found it?"

"You will know."

He'd hung up and she'd started shaking. She had no idea what he was talking about, but she decided it had to be a lot of money. *You will know.*

She'd logged into the Archer Industries' server. She'd gone through everything, looking for any clues to a secret account, but there'd been nothing. If Eric had hidden money from her, he'd been very thorough. He'd have had to be since the company finances were her responsibility as chief financial officer. It was all in order, so she'd turned to their personal accounts. They had separate accounts, but she had access to his. There was nothing other than a few auto-pay bills that had drafted out since he died.

She'd checked back through the months, looking for big deposits or drafts. There'd been nothing suspicious.

Annabelle hit the button on the steering wheel to activate her phone. "Dial Molly," she said when the computer voice asked for a command.

"Hiya, Annabelle," came the cheery voice on the other end of the line.

"Hey, Mol. Need a favor. Can you keep Charlotte for a few days?" It was the last thing in the world she wanted to do, but it was also the thing she *had* to do. She glanced in her rearview mirror, that niggling feeling still eating at her. There was no one following her. But what if she was wrong?

If she did what she really wanted, which was to whisk Charlotte from school and keep her close, she could very well be putting her child in danger. Her lungs constricted at the thought. Her eyes burned.

No, I won't do that. Even if I'm desperate to see my baby one more time.

"Sure. Is something wrong?"

Annabelle licked dry lips as her heart punched her in the ribs. "No, nothing's wrong. I just need to go to DC. Contract negotiations. Very last minute."

Molly was used to her chaotic life this past month, so she wasn't likely to question Annabelle's lie.

"All right, honey. Are you bringing her over or do you need me to pick her up?"

"Could you get her from preschool? Just buy her whatever she needs. Don't go to the house, okay?"

There was a moment's hesitation on the other end. "That's a weird request, Belle. You're scaring me. Is everything all right?"

Please don't grill me, Mol. Please. "I'm sorry. I don't mean to. But there's been some weird stuff happening in the neighborhood and I'd prefer if you don't go over there alone."

"Weird stuff? What kind of weird stuff? Did you call the police?"

"Attempted burglary I think. A neighbor told me yesterday. He called the police. They're doing extra patrols, that kind of thing." It was the only thing she could think of, and she cringed that Molly would see through the bullshit.

"I didn't hear anything about it on the news," Molly said. "Wow."

"Well, you know how it is. The country club is probably asking for discretion on the issue. Don't want to start a panic."

"Seems a bit extreme, but whatever. I doubt anyone's going to bop me over the head in broad daylight in a neighborhood like yours."

"You never know," Annabelle said. "Just buy her whatever she needs for a few days. You can use my credit card."

Annabelle had long ago set up Molly as the person who could take Charlotte in any emergency, which meant she had credit cards and authorization to pick Charlotte up from school as well as get any medical treatments necessary. If Katie Davidson was the best friend of Annabelle's childhood, Molly Carter was the best friend of her adult life. They'd met in college when they were both pregnant and trying to finish up their senior year. They'd been tight since.

"Okie doke. Not a problem."

"I'm sorry to ask, Molly. I know it's short notice—and you've got your own daughter to take care of."

"It's okay, babes. I can handle two little munchkins. In fact, having Charlotte around means that Becca will have someone to play with after school—which means I can get some graphics work done on the computer."

Annabelle wasn't sure how much work Molly could get done with two four-year-olds running around, but she wasn't going to question it. "Thank you so much. You have no idea how much this means to me."

"You can pay me back in chocolate cakes."

Annabelle laughed even though her nerves were shot. "Deal. And hey, I'm sorry if this causes trouble with the new guy."

Molly scoffed. "It'll be fine. We've only been on a couple of dates. If he's got a problem with me watching my best friend's daughter on short notice, then he's not the guy for me."

Annabelle felt guilty but she also loved Molly fiercely right now. There was so much more she wanted to say, but she couldn't. Molly would get suspicious and Annabelle would have to tell her what was happening—and that would put Molly and the kids in danger.

They spoke for a few more seconds. It was excruciating to pretend everything was okay, but somehow she made it through. After she ended the call, she squeezed the wheel and told herself she'd done the right thing. Her heart disagreed, but her brain was determined.

Okay, so getting Charlotte tucked away somewhere safe was done. That was step one. Step two was... what?

Go through the financials again? Search for any anomalies? Except there *were* no anomalies. She would know if there were.

She shook her head. *Think. THINK.*

She needed to go home and search the house. Maybe Eric had left something there. She'd been planning to hire someone to clear out his room but she hadn't done it yet. Thank God.

She raced home and darted her gaze up and down the street before driving into her garage and powering down the door. She entered the house, disarming the alarm and then resetting it. It gave her a measure of comfort that it was still on because that meant no one had broken in while she was away.

She kicked off her shoes and ran up the stairs to Eric's room. It was a large room, a suite with a bedroom, sitting room, and huge bath. It looked exactly as he'd left it, not an item out of place. The maid had been in here to dust, but otherwise nothing had changed.

Annabelle rushed over to the desk containing Eric's personal computer. She stabbed the button to turn it on and went through the drawers and the filing cabinet while it booted up. Eric didn't have much in the desk or the cabinet.

The computer screen blinked, asking for a password, and her heart dived to her toes. Of course he would password protect his computer. Who wouldn't?

She tugged out the chair and sat down, tapping in a password she thought he might use. But the computer wouldn't open. She tried again and still got nothing. One more time and she'd be locked out for a few hours. She shoved the chair back and chewed her lip, thinking hard. What would Eric use? It wouldn't be Charlotte's name. God no. She closed her eyes and tilted her head back.

Nothing came to her.

With a growl, she slapped the lid closed and undocked the laptop from the monitor. She could take the computer to her tech department and get one of the software geeks to unlock it.

Covering all the bases, she went over to Eric's bed, bending down to check beneath the mattress. She rifled through his drawers, his closet, his vanity, looking for anything out of the ordinary. There was nothing. He had financial magazines, tech magazines, and car magazines. He didn't have an address book, but then Eric had been a techie. Everything he did would be digital, and there would be backups. But where? His cell phone had gone missing in the attack, and there'd been no activity on it since.

She stopped in the middle of the room and turned around, looking at everything. The only thing that called to her was the computer, and she couldn't get into that. Eric had more than one computer, but this was the one he'd used at home. He didn't like carrying computers with him. Knowing him, everything was in the cloud. But which cloud? Which service? He hadn't hidden it in AI's servers. All his files there had been business related.

Annabelle snatched up the laptop and pivoted. She needed to go over to Archer Industries right now and get someone to break into it. She rushed into her room and opened the safe, taking out her pistol and loading it. She hadn't shot a gun in years, but Dex had taught her how, and she used to be good at it. Her heart pinched at the thought of Dex, but she shoved a mental wall up, blocking him from view before she ran to the garage and fired up the Mercedes. The door powered up slowly. She didn't wait for it to finish before she pressed the gas and shot backward onto the street. Before she could accelerate, a truck pulled in front of her, blocking her escape.

She scrambled for her purse and the pistol she'd stuffed inside it—but the truck door opened and a familiar figure got out. He sauntered over to the passenger side of her car and her temperature shot up a hundred degrees at that smooth, rolling gait.

"You need to put the car back in the garage, Annabelle," Dex drawled, his voice utterly calm through the glass. "And then you need to come with me."

FOUR

DEX HAD NEVER GOTTEN A chance to shoot. He'd been setting up Jane when his phone rang. His team leader, Matt "Richie Rich" Girard, had been on the other end.

"Eric Archer's company was developing a revolutionary technology that the US government wanted in the worst way," Richie had said. "They've been doing tests on the battery life of drones and have found a way to recharge using radio waves. The drone doesn't have to land to do it. It's midair, free, and prolongs the mission indefinitely."

Dex had been impressed. Who knew Eric Archer had it in him? He'd been a decent student but not a genius. Then again, the dude came from money—and that got you a lot in life. Including, apparently, high-tech companies with revolutionary products. When Dex had been growing up, Archer Industries made computer parts and electrical circuits. Looks like they'd branched out.

"Wow."

"Yeah, the implications are huge—but Archer never delivered."

"And?" Dex asked, his mind reeling.

"He died in Africa. The story is that he was torn apart by animals on a safari, but the truth is he went to meet with a Russian, presumably to sell the technology to him. We don't know if he delivered it or not. But Archer took the Russian's money—and something went wrong. CIA intel indicates the Russian shot Archer and threw him to the animals."

"And he wants his money back."

"Yep."

"Seems like it would have been smarter to get it back before killing Eric."

"You'd think. Probably more going on here than the CIA knows."

Dex sighed. "I'm going to guess the money's not at the local branch office."

"Nope, definitely not. The Archer accounts aren't exactly flush."

"What does that mean?"

"Means that Annabelle Quinn-Archer is on a budget. A healthy budget at the moment, but still a budget. There's no fortune in any of their accounts."

"Do we know who this Russian is? Or where he is? Or why it's taken him a month to come looking for Annabelle?"

"We're working on it. But at the moment, no to all questions."

"So Annabelle probably is in danger."

"Yeah, I'd say so."

Which was why Dex was now standing there looking at a frantic Annabelle. It was possible she knew more than she was letting on about Eric and the Russian, but her fear was real. Her eyes were saucers and her hands trembled as she pushed her blond hair from her face. He could see the butt of a pistol in her purse, and there was a laptop on the passenger seat.

She powered down the window. "I need to go to the office."

"We can talk about that after you get in the truck with me."

Her brows arrowed down. "Why should I? You told me you didn't care earlier. What's changed?"

For someone who'd been so desperate this afternoon, she sure was reluctant to trust him now. Because something had happened? Because she'd found where the money was and she was planning to leave town?

"I was pissed off. I shouldn't have said that." He was still pissed, but now he was concerned. He didn't have to like Annabelle to want to keep her safe. Even if she was more involved in Eric's dirty dealings than she let on, she was still in danger. Why come to him otherwise?

Her eyes narrowed. "How did you find me? I didn't tell you where I live."

"Honey, everyone knows where the Archers live. It's hardly a secret." He lifted his head and studied the house for a moment—the huge, white stucco house with the circular drive and the six-car garage. "Not very subtle, is it?"

Her pretty blue eyes clouded. "It's what Eric wanted."

"And Eric always got what Eric wanted," he murmured.

Annabelle sat up a little straighter, her prim nose in the air. "Not always. I think I mentioned that earlier."

Dex snorted. "High school and life are two entirely different things. Now park the car in the garage and let's get out of here."

She hesitated for only a moment before she did as he said. He got into his truck and pulled it into her driveway, darting a glance around as he did so. The houses here were huge and easy to find. The community was gated, but that was a joke since he'd gotten through with no trouble.

There was another car on the street about a block away. A black Chrysler sedan with tinted windows, it looked exactly like something the government would send an agent in. Not that they had, but Dex wouldn't take it for granted. He eased his sidearm from the glove compartment and tucked it into the hidden holster at the back of his jeans. Then he opened the door and got out just as Annabelle emerged from inside the garage.

"I have to go in the house to close the garage. I'll come out the front door."

He took a step forward. "Going with you."

"I'll only be a moment."

"Do you want my help or not, Annabelle?"

She blinked. "Yes."

"Then I'm coming with you." He ducked beneath the garage door, and she went over to the wall and pressed a button. The door glided down as she unlocked the interior entry to the house. He could hear her punch in a code to silence the alarm. Once inside, he closed the door and locked it.

She'd shouldered her purse and tucked the laptop under her arm. Not hers, most likely. If it had been, she'd have had a bag for it. Probably Eric's.

Dex strode over to the front window and eased the curtain back. No movement from the car on the street. He looked over his shoulder at Annabelle.

"Can you pack a bag real quick?"

"I... Yes, I suppose I can."

"Then go. Double-time, Annabelle."

She dropped her purse and the laptop and trotted across the massive living area and into a hallway. He divided his attention between the street and the interior of the house, which was spectacular. Every lottery winner's dream come true. A house with giant rooms, tall ceilings, copious wood moldings, and furnishings that cost more than he made in a year.

Matt Girard had said Annabelle was on a budget, but it must be a sizable one.

A few moments later, she came racing out of the bedroom with a black leather duffel. She'd slipped on flat shoes with her cropped trousers, and she looked no less stylish than she had with high heels. She stuffed the laptop into the duffel, then shouldered her purse.

"Ready."

With a last look at the street, he went over and took her bag. She was so much shorter without the heels, and her head tilted back sharply as she met his gaze. He had a sudden urge to press his mouth to hers, which made him angry. He took a step back.

"Then let's go," he clipped out.

She fished her keys from her pocket and hit a button to set the alarm. Then she went and jerked the door open. They strode to his truck and he held the door for her. He slung her bag onto the back seat and went around to get in the driver's side.

After he started the engine, he turned to her. "You're going to need to hold on, Annabelle. It might get bumpy."

"Why? What are you talking about?"

He didn't bother answering as he backed out of the drive and headed toward the road that led out of the subdivision. The black sedan also pulled away from the curb.

He let them follow him through the neighborhood, but when he reached the highway, he flicked on the signal to turn right—and then went left, jamming the accelerator and rocketing into traffic. Annabelle let out a scream.

"Are you crazy?" she demanded.

"Yeah." He glanced in the rearview and saw the sedan leap into traffic. He gave the truck another shot of gas. "Where's your daughter, Annabelle?"

She'd grabbed the overhead handle for support. "W-with a friend. I didn't want her anywhere near me right now."

"That's probably wise. Can you trust the friend?"

"Of course I can! Molly would protect Charlotte with her life if she had to."

Dex shot her a look. "And do you really want her to have to do that?"

"What are you suggesting?"

He took a hard right at the last second, and Annabelle squeaked as the seat belt anchored her in place.

"Fucking hell," she yelled when she got her voice back. "Are you trying to kill us both?"

"Nope. Trying to lose a tail."

She gasped. "A tail? Someone's following you?"

"Actually, they're following you. You didn't see the black car down the street?"

She'd gone pale. "Cars park on the street sometimes. I didn't think anything of it."

"Why? You have fucking circular driveways and shit. There's room for visitors in those massive drives."

"It's just the way it is. Nobody wants to get blocked in, so visitors sometimes park on the street." She lowered her gaze to her lap. "Dammit, I should have known. I've felt like someone was following me—but I was never sure."

"As soon as we're clear of this, I want you to call your friend and have her take Charlotte somewhere."

"Where?"

"I'll make arrangements for a safe house."

"Molly has a daughter of her own."

"She can take them both. It'll be safer that way."

He didn't think it possible for her to grow any paler, but she did. "Okay. I'll call her. Anything else?"

He yanked the truck into another sharp turn and then drove into an abandoned warehouse in the commercial district. He killed the engine. It was dark inside and their breathing filled the silence to bursting. He didn't think their tail had managed to follow all his turns, but they needed to wait it out for a few minutes before they could leave. He was already planning his next move, but her last question hung in the air between them. He said the first thing that sprang to mind.

"Yeah, there is… Tell me why you wouldn't marry me but you married Eric Archer only three weeks later."

FIVE

ANNABELLE'S PULSE DRUMMED IN HER veins. Not only from the grand prix race through the streets, but also from worrying about Charlotte, Molly, and Becca.

And then boom, Dex asked *that* question.

When she'd gone looking for him at his dad's farm, she'd considered the possibility that he would ask it. Until today, they hadn't spoken since the night before the wedding. She'd thought about what she'd tell him if he did. She'd thought about telling him the truth, but what did it matter? Whatever she said, he'd still be angry and she'd still be the woman who'd betrayed him. Didn't matter if she'd done it to save her father's miserable skin or if she'd done it because she was a coldhearted bitch. The result was the same.

Now the question was here and she still didn't know what to say. The truth was complicated.

"I wanted to marry you, Dex. With all my heart, I wanted to. But I wasn't brave enough." That much was true. Instead of defying her father and letting him face the consequences of his actions, she'd caved into pressure and stayed home on the day she should have been saying "I do" to this man.

"So you didn't show up. Didn't call, didn't answer my texts. Just stayed home and let me wait for you. You could have had the decency to send a text to *me*, but you said nothing for almost two hours. Until you texted Katie that bullshit excuse."

Her heart pulsed a wave of pain into her belly, her brain. It was as fresh now as if it had happened yesterday. He would never know how much she'd cried or how afraid she'd been once he was gone and she'd realized he wasn't coming back.

A couple of nights later, Eric had come over to talk to her about *their* wedding. The memory of that night was seared into her brain. She wasn't ever telling Dex—or anyone—about the things Eric had done.

She hardened her resolve. It did no good to let herself remember. Charlotte was her priority. She would do whatever it took to keep her daughter safe.

"I was afraid to tell you I'd changed my mind." It wasn't a good excuse and she knew it. She *had* been afraid, but not of telling Dex she'd changed her mind. She hadn't changed her mind; she'd let it be changed. And she'd been afraid that if she had any communication with him, she'd fly out the door and race to the church. She'd been a sobbing, angry mess that morning. Her mother had cried too, but her tears were more about self-preservation than any tender feelings for Annabelle's heartbreak.

"You have to help us, Annabelle. You have to marry Eric or your father and I will be ruined. I don't know what will happen to us."

The heat of Dex's anger flared bright. "That's what I don't get, Annabelle. You didn't seem in the least bit conflicted when you were fucking me two nights before the wedding."

She dragged in a breath, both at the vulgarity and at the way it sent a little sizzle of lightning into her sex. She wasn't a dirty talker, didn't get off on hearing it, but there was something about that word on his lips that made her breathe a little faster.

"Don't talk like that. I don't like it."

He snorted. "Because you're such a lady, right? Living in a fancy-ass neighborhood and driving a fancy-ass car. You've ended up exactly where your parents wanted you to be, haven't you? Guess you started thinking about life with me, living in cramped housing on Army posts around the world, and got cold feet, huh?"

"That's not what happened!"

"How did Eric feel about that last pity fuck you gave me, huh? Or didn't he know about it?"

Fury and hurt twined together, rolling through her like lightning, sparking and crashing against the walls of her heart. But what right did she have to get upset? She'd left him and she'd married Eric. From his perspective, what else could it be?

"I don't want to talk about this." Because she couldn't breathe if she had to talk about it.

"Of course you don't." His voice was like iron—hard and unyielding. He twisted the key with a jerk of his wrist. The engine roared awake, startling her.

"Is it safe?" she asked when he eased the truck backward.

He threw a glance at her. "We'll find out."

37

It was dusk now and the streetlights popped on around town. Dex eased onto the road running parallel to the warehouse and accelerated in the opposite direction of downtown. He put his phone to his ear. When he started talking, she knew he must have dialed someone.

"Need to get a little girl and her babysitter to a safe house," he said. "The sitter also has a daughter, so room for two kids and an adult."

Annabelle's spine melted into a puddle of relief. Her child would be safe. Molly and Becca would be safe too. Guilt tapped a beat in her brain at getting Molly into this mess though. There weren't enough chocolate cakes on earth to pay Molly back this time.

"Yeah, thanks. Send me the coordinates when you get them. I'm taking Annabelle to a different location." He paused and then laughed, a sharp burst that wasn't real amusement. She thought he glanced at her but she didn't turn her head to find out. "Nope, nothing to worry about, boss. It'll be a cold day in hell before that happens again."

He tossed the phone into the console and pressed his foot down. As the truck picked up speed, she rubbed her hands over her arms. They were in Briar Creek's commercial district, and the buildings were starting to thin.

"Wait," she said, and he turned his head casually, his gaze dripping over her like hot syrup.

"Yeah?"

"Eric's computer. I need to get someone at Archer Industries to crack the password."

"No can do, sweetheart. We're going somewhere safe. I'll take a look when we get there."

She tried not to get angry, but that was hard to do when her emotions were already on edge. "Are you a programmer, Dex? I didn't think that was what you went into the Army to do."

She knew he hadn't. Unless he'd changed jobs. Possible, she supposed.

"Nope, not a programmer. But I have a guy who can crack it."

"Is that where we're going?"

"Not tonight."

Fear was a pit in her belly that grew bigger with each passing minute. "He gave me twenty-four hours. Time's running out."

"You're with me, and your daughter will soon be in protective custody. It'll be all right."

"Look, I know this is probably no big deal to you, but someone threatened to kill me—and if I don't give him what he wants and he can't get to me, who knows what he might do? I have friends, family, a company to run—this person could be capable of anything, and we can't put *eve-ry*one in protective custody!"

"I said I was going to help you, and I will. I may not like you, but I'll do everything I can to keep you safe."

She crossed her arms and tried not to feel the pinprick of hurt in her soul. "I need to let my secretary know I won't be in tomorrow."

"You can't call anyone."

Her stomach churned. Lucy needed to know where she was. Maybe not right now, but definitely by tomorrow morning when Annabelle didn't show up. "I have responsibilities. I can't ignore them."

He glanced at her. "This guy gave you twenty-four hours. What were you planning to do for those hours anyway? Run your company and search for the money on your off time? Or dedicate every minute to finding it? Or *have* you found it?"

She whipped around to stare at him. "What? No, I have no idea where it is! Why would you ask that?"

He shrugged. "You didn't exactly seem happy to see me. Maybe you found it and don't need me anymore."

"I didn't. I was hoping I'd know where it is as soon as I get into Eric's computer. Then I could go back to work and forget any of this ever happened."

He snorted. "Do you really think you're going to be able to forget? Even if you found the money and transferred it where this guy wants you to, do you honestly think he's going to let you off the hook? Or will he keep demanding more?"

Her throat went dry. She didn't even know who this Mr. Lyon was or what Eric had done to him. He hadn't given her the chance to ask either. He'd said Eric had his money and he wanted it. End of story. "More? What else could he want?"

"Yeah, Annabelle—more. People like that don't typically get what they want and disappear. Once he knows you'll respond to the trigger, he'll keep pulling it until there's nothing left. He'll bleed you dry—and he may kill you anyway. This is war, honey. All-out war—and this guy has to be stopped."

SIX

SHE WAS LOOKING AT HIM like he'd just told her she had terminal cancer. If she was a part of what Eric had been up to, she was doing a damned good job of being shocked. He had to consider it though. Maybe she knew exactly what Eric had been doing and she needed Dex's help because the chickens were coming home to roost. If she *was* involved, it was treason. Dex wouldn't stick his neck out for her. He'd keep her alive, but he'd turn her over to face the consequences when this was over. No questions asked.

"How do you know you can stop him?" she asked.

"Because it's what I do. You just need to hang in there and let me do it. Isn't that why you came to me?"

She nodded. "So can you call my secretary? Tell her I'll be back in a day or two?"

"I'll make sure it's done."

She reached out and squeezed his arm. A lightning bolt of electricity zipped through him. "Thank you," she said.

"Sure." He shifted in his seat as his groin throbbed to life. It had always been thrilling whenever they touched. Seemed as if time hadn't changed a thing. He wasn't so out of control of his body that he had a raging hard-on from a simple touch, but he wasn't as in control as he'd like to be.

He could still remember the last time with Annabelle. They'd torn at each other's clothes, kissing and tasting and moaning as they worked to get naked. He'd entered her without finesse and pumped until he exploded.

He'd been away in Afghanistan and she'd been in Briar City, and he'd missed her like hell. She'd claimed to miss him too. He'd believed every sweet word that came from her lips. They'd been lies.

Even after she'd abandoned him at the altar, he hadn't stopped believing all at once. He'd been trying to make sense of what had happened, trying to think of what he could say or do to get her back—and then he'd called home and his father had told him that Annabelle was married. He'd been downrange for two months at that point.

When he'd found out she'd married Eric three weeks after she'd been supposed to marry him—well, he'd gone a little nuts. He'd applied to Delta selection. He hadn't made it the first time, but he'd applied again. He'd gotten in and life had turned into one dangerous mission after another. When the Hostile Operations Team came calling, he didn't hesitate to throw himself into the job.

He'd thought he wouldn't have time to think about Annabelle, but he'd been wrong. Being part of a sniper team meant he had nothing *but* time while waiting for the enemy to arrive so he could take the kill shot. During those quiet hours when speech was too dangerous to engage in, he'd thought about the girl he'd loved and what her betrayal had done to him.

He hadn't been celibate, far from it, but he hadn't entered into any relationships either. He hadn't found anyone who'd made him want to try. He'd pictured Annabelle smiling at Eric the way she'd once smiled at him, and everything inside him stayed dead and cold.

His phone startled him out of his thoughts. He picked it up to glance at the screen. It was Katie. *Shit.*

His sister's bright voice filled his ear. "How's spaghetti for dinner? Kyle wants it, and I said I'd ask you first since you were the guest of honor."

Dex pulled in a breath. "Katie, I'm sorry—"

"You forgot, didn't you? Well, it's not going to be ready for another two hours, so you've still got time."

Guilt pricked him. "Honey, I'm really sorry but something came up. I can't make it."

Katie sighed heavily. "Oh, Dex, the kids will be so disappointed."

"Yeah, I know. Well, the three-year-old might be, but I'm going to bet you can distract him with a Minion movie or something."

"Fine, I'll distract him. But who's going to distract me?"

"It's work, Katie, or I'd be there. Swear. How was Dad?" he asked, changing the subject.

"He's good. Tired, but rehab is going well. They think he'll be out in a couple of days. He says he's happy to come stay with me, but I don't know that he is. He's going to miss those cows after a while."

Dex laughed, but it was a sad laugh. "So take him to the farm. He can talk to Bob and get his fill of cows." Bob had been their neighbor for as long as Dex could remember. When Dad had his accident, Bob stepped in.

"Are you headed back to DC?"

Dex's eyes felt gritty. "I might have to, yeah. But I'll be back just as soon as this job is finished. I've got leave saved up."

"We never see you, Dexie. You're always out of the country on some job or other. I thought the Army might send you to Fort Knox one of these days and then you'd at least be in Kentucky."

"Maybe," he told her, but the real answer was never. Not unless he left HOT and asked to be transferred. Even then, it might not happen.

Except he wasn't leaving HOT. Not until he got sent home in a box.

"All right," she said. "Well, call when you can. Let me know when you're coming back."

"I will."

Annabelle sniffed and he shot her a glance, wondering if she was crying. Not that he cared. He couldn't see her eyes, so he didn't know. He flexed his hands on the wheel and threw up a prayer to the heavens that she wasn't. He didn't want to deal with a crying woman—most particularly not *this* woman.

"I'm sorry I ruined your plans," she said.

Okay, so not crying. Good.

"I've been in town for a few days. It's fine."

"You asked Katie how your dad was—did something happen?"

"He had open-heart surgery last month, and just a few days ago he fell and broke his leg pretty badly. The doctors put it back together, but he's in rehab."

"Oh." She sounded surprised. "I didn't know. I hope he'll be okay."

Dex shrugged. "As well as he can be, I guess. He's being forced to retire, which is why the farm is for sale. He can't manage it anymore."

"I'm sorry to hear that. I didn't realize the farm was on the market." She made a bitter sound. "I haven't realized much of anything in the past month, quite honestly."

"You drove past the sign earlier."

"I didn't see it."

"I thought you were the real estate agent when you turned into the driveway."

She laughed, but it wasn't a very happy sound. A few moments later she asked, "How's Katie?"

"Fine. She's married, has two kids. You probably know that, living in the same town."

"I do. We never talk though."

He knew why that was, and even though he loved his sister for taking his side, he knew she had to miss her best friend. Katie and Annabelle had been friends since kindergarten. They'd known each other's secrets, their hopes and dreams. He sometimes thought that if he'd never fallen for Annabelle, it would have been better for his sister. He'd cost her a best friend, and he still felt guilty for that even if he'd suffered too.

Annabelle didn't say anything else as the miles ticked by. After a while, he could see her dip her head and lift her hand to her eyes. *Dammit.*

"You okay?" he asked.

"Sure, why wouldn't I be?"

Her words were bright, but he didn't quite believe it. "No reason."

"I mean, being threatened by a crazy person and being here with you is a lot to process," she said, her voice still artificially bright, "but I'll be okay."

She curled a fist in her lap. He could feel the emotion vibrating from her, the sense that she was working to keep it all together.

"After Eric died I thought the worst thing was dealing with the business and keeping the contracts on schedule. Which I've done to the best of my ability. But now this. Jesus, what the fuck was he doing?"

Her voice had grown hard and angry. It wasn't something he was accustomed to hearing out of Annabelle. She'd always been optimistic and hopeful. It was one of the things he'd adored about her. Yet he couldn't let sympathy for her cloud his judgement. She sounded like she had no idea what Eric had been doing, but she could be trying to throw him off the scent.

"Tell me about the radio wave recharging system," he said.

Her head whipped around. Her eyes bored into him. "How do you know about Helios?"

"It's my job."

"You've said that a couple of times already, but exactly what *is* your job? I thought you were an Army Ranger and that you'd done tours in a war zone. But now you can arrange safe houses and you know about our top secret project when you shouldn't. What's going on, Dex?"

"That's why you came to me for help? Because I'd done tours in a war zone?"

"I thought you could protect me. I didn't know where else to turn. Mr. Lyon said no police, and I saw you in town the other day…"

Mr. Lyon? What a sick fuck. Eric's body had been mauled by lions, which the caller surely knew. "You wanted a bodyguard? You could have called up any protection firm for that."

"I don't know them. I know you."

"And you trusted me not to throw you to the wolves? Brave, Annabelle."

"You wouldn't. You might hate me, but you wouldn't let someone hurt me if you could stop it."

"I said no at first."

"I know—but you changed your mind or you wouldn't be here now."

"I changed my mind because I found out you were involved in some serious shit."

"Did you think I'd lie?"

"I have no idea what you'll do. I don't know you anymore."

She dragged in a breath. "Seeing you again isn't any easier for me, you know. It's not something I'd have done on purpose if I wasn't desperate."

"Eric was making a deal to sell the technology to someone in Africa. What do you know about that?" Might as well hit her with it and see what happened.

"What?" She had that deer-in-the-headlights look again. If she was faking it, she was damned good. "He couldn't do that. We have a contract with the military."

"He did, Annabelle. He met with someone and received money, but either he didn't deliver on the product or it doesn't work."

"Oh my god." She rocked back and forth in the seat until he thought she might explode. "It's not even ready—

or at least that's what Eric and Marshall said. They needed more time."

"Who's Marshall?"

"Marshall Porter, the lead engineer. He and Eric were developing the technology together. It's not a new idea, but it's never been used for something this big. Eric and Marshall figured out how to do it though. We've tested it —it works as it should in the laboratory tests. But when we've tried live tests, it's not consistent."

The hairs on Dex's neck stood at attention. Was Eric that stupid? Had he really sold a faulty technology on the black market? And how faulty was it? Was it something a foreign government could finish if they had the basic idea to work with?

"It's treason, isn't it?" Annabelle asked, making the leap to the heart of the matter. "Eric committed treason against the United States."

Dex wasn't going to sugarcoat it. "Yeah, that's pretty much the definition of treason. He conspired to sell a top secret military project to a foreign agent. And if you knew anything about what he was doing, you're guilty too."

She sat up ramrod straight. He could feel the angry energy vibrating from her. She was shocked—and he'd bet his left nut it was genuine.

"No. No way in *hell* would I do such a thing. If you think that— My god, do you really think I could do that? If you do, then *fuck you*, Dexter Davidson. Fuck you and your smug superiority!"

"Calm down, Belle."

"I will *not!* How dare you? You think just because you went off to the military that you're so much better than I am? You have no idea what I've been through—

what I've endured over the past five years—and I won't sit here and let you accuse me of something so heinous—"

"Enough," he barked. "I believe you." What she'd endured? What the fuck did that mean?

She subsided, arms folding over her middle, but she still crackled with energy. He thought if he touched her, he might suffer a lethal shock.

"Asshole," she muttered.

Dex scowled into the darkening sky. Yeah, he'd fucked this one up. "You were his wife. It's no stretch to think you might be involved."

"Fuck you."

"Jesus, Belle. I've heard you cuss more in the last few miles than I've ever heard you cuss in your life."

"You bring out the best in me. And before you harass me another second, don't forget I have a pistol in my purse. A traitor like me might just shoot your ass with it."

No question in his mind now. She wasn't guilty of treason, and she hadn't been helping Eric. "You aren't a traitor."

"No, I'm not. But I still might shoot you if you mouth off to me one more time."

"Fine. I'm sorry I suggested you might be involved. But Belle, I won't be the only one who thinks it. Clearly this Mr. Lyon believes it or he wouldn't be after you for the money. There'll be others who reach the same conclusion. Unless we get to the bottom of this."

She huffed. "Then we need to get to the bottom, don't we?"

SEVEN

EXHAUSTION AND WORRY CLAWED AT Annabelle. They'd been driving for two hours, and though she shouldn't be so worn out since it was still early, she was. Her life had been threatened, she'd been involved in a car chase, her child was being taken to a safe house, and the man she'd once loved had accused her of treason.

Just your average day.

Thinking about Eric made her stomach turn inside out. She'd already despised him, but this? My god. He'd planned to commit treason. She'd known he didn't care about her or Charlotte—but what about his country? How much money did it take to make someone sell out their nation and all the people in it?

And what about the people at Archer Industries? All those people who depended on him and the company, and he'd been willing to betray them like that—their hard work, their dreams, their jobs. Because the US government would come down hard if Eric had sold the technology to a foreign agent. Archer Industries would lose their contracts, their livelihood.

A cold finger of dread skated up her spine. Dex was right. People would think she'd been involved. She could go to jail. Or did they execute traitors?

Nausea swam in her blood, twisted her stomach. She hauled in a breath and tried to tamp down the sickness. Dex would help her. She hadn't done anything wrong. The truth would come out when they found the money.

She had to believe that or she'd sink into a pool of despair.

She forced herself to concentrate on the good stuff. Charlotte, Molly, and Becca were out of harm's way. They'd made it to a safe house and they were being guarded by a government agent. They had nothing to worry about. Annabelle pictured the three of them—Molly on her computer, Charlotte and Becca playing—and felt immensely better.

Her eyes grew heavy after a while and she closed them. When the truck jerked hard, she bolted upright, heart pounding. She blinked in confusion. Had she slept? She must have. They'd turned off the main road and seemed to be on a dirt track running through a forest. She hooked a hand into the strap over the door while her insides churned.

"Sorry to wake you," Dex said.

"Where are we?"

"West Virginia."

"Why?"

"Because Mr. Lyon won't think to look here. Because it's safe."

"Why couldn't we have gone with Molly and the girls?"

"Best to separate you for now."

A structure materialized out of the gloom. "Is that where we're going?"

It was a small log cabin, plain, with two rockers on a porch that ran the length of the building, and a door with two windows, one on either side of the door.

"Yeah. It's a hunting cabin, so don't expect anything fancy."

"Is it yours?"

"Nope. Belongs to a buddy."

"What if he's here?"

"He isn't."

"And if he shows up?"

"He won't."

"Dammit, Dex, could you speak in complete sentences?"

"Pretty sure I was."

Annabelle wanted to scream. "Fine. So why here? We're in the middle of nowhere."

"Precisely."

"That's not how they do it on *NCIS*."

He chuckled. She didn't think he'd meant to. "This isn't *NCIS*. But tell me, what do they do?"

The heat of embarrassment surged through her. What had she been thinking to tell a military guy how the military worked in Hollywood?

"They usually have an apartment somewhere in the city. The agents take turns watching whoever needs protecting. Someone delivers food."

"Yeah, and I'm gonna bet that the bad guys always find the civilian at some point, am I right? They bust in and take the poor bastard—or it happens when the agents are moving to another location. Then someone has to rescue the same guy all over again."

Annabelle cleared her throat. "Fine, yes, that's usually what happens. But *NCIS* saves the day in the end."

"I'll save the day, but the goal is for you to stay right here. No surprise visits from the bad guys if we can help it."

"How long are we staying?"

"As long as we have to."

"That's not an answer."

"It's the best one I have."

He pulled around and parked the truck in a carport behind the house. Then he shut off the engine and studied her. Her heart skipped like it always had when Dex Davidson looked at her, but there was no emotion in his expression. Not anymore. She was no more important to him than the average stranger.

And that was a disheartening thing to know.

"I didn't bring much," she said. "I didn't realize we'd be away for more than a day or so."

"Doesn't matter. The place is stocked with essentials. There's a washer and dryer. Hand me your phone, Annabelle."

"Why? I turned it off like you told me—"

"Hand it to me."

She did. He pocketed the phone. Then he threw open the door and climbed out. After a moment of staring after him, she followed.

"Hey," she called, "give me back my phone!"

"Sorry, no can do. You can't use it out here. There's no signal anyway."

She folded her arms over her chest. "Then why take it?"

He turned to her, his dark eyes unreadable in the dim light from the exterior lantern. "Because I wanted to see if you'd still do what I said."

Anger twisted in her belly. Heat skipped from her lips to her breasts, melting downward when she thought about the kinds of things he'd once told her to do. *Kiss me, Belle... Spread your legs, Belle...*

She forced herself to breathe. "This isn't a contest, Dex. I trust your expertise to keep me safe and help me find the money. But if you're going to play games with me, I'll think twice about following orders."

"Best not to," he deadpanned. "I'm the one keeping you alive."

And that was the crux of the matter. Without him, she would die.

"Can we go inside? I'm hungry."

"Give me a minute to clear the place."

"I thought you said no one was here."

He reached behind him. The click of his trigger echoed in the night. "Still have to check."

He disappeared in the shadow of the house. A door creaked open. Then a small light appeared in front of him and Dex went inside. He was back soon after, switching on the interior lights and holstering his weapon.

"It's clear." He came down the steps and sauntered over to the truck. After he opened the rear door, he shouldered a bag. Not her bag. She reached inside and grabbed hers, shutting the door with a kick and following him into the house.

It was almost like that time they'd gone camping—except for the good parts. They'd pitched a tent in the woods and spent the entire weekend fishing, grilling out, roasting marshmallows, and making love. She'd emerged sore but happy, and so in love she'd thought nothing would ever change.

That was before she'd realized how cruel the world could be or how the actions of others could change your life forever. If she'd refused to help her parents, what would have happened?

She'd be married to Dex, but her father would be in jail or dead. Her mother would be alone and broke. She'd done the only thing she could do—and she was still paying for it.

The cabin was small and stuffy from being closed up. The living room and kitchen were all one room. There were three doors on the far wall and a loft. A ladder leaned against the wall.

"Middle door's the bathroom," Dex said, pointing. "The other two are bedrooms. Take whichever one you want."

She opened the door to the first room. It was narrow and cramped and she threw her bag in. Dex arched an eyebrow when she emerged.

"You don't want to see the other one?"

"Not really."

"It might be bigger. Or have a better bed."

"I don't care. I just want to find the money and get rid of it so I can have my life back." She went back into the room to dig out Eric's computer. "And speaking of getting my life back, you're going to need this."

Dex took the computer when she handed it over. He set it on the table in the kitchen and fired it up. The screen saver blinked at him with that same blank box, daring him to sign in.

"Any ideas?" he asked.

"No. I tried, but I didn't want to get locked out, so I stopped."

He snapped the lid closed. "I'll call my guys in a little while. First, food."

He opened the cabinets and pulled out a box of macaroni and cheese. She went over to the fridge and opened it. There was milk, cheese, meat, hot dogs, and some veggies and butter. There was also cream, thank God. She could drink black coffee, but she preferred cream.

The freezer revealed a few frozen dinners, some pizza rolls, and ice cream. There was also some steak and chicken and something labeled *deer sausage*. When she turned around, Dex had ripped into the macaroni box.

"Is that for you or do you plan to share?"

He shrugged. "We can share if you fix some hot dogs."

"I can do that."

They worked in silence. When the food was done, they sat at the table with their paper plates and plastic forks. Annabelle forked creamy macaroni into her mouth and wanted to moan. She never ate macaroni and cheese these days. Too fattening.

But it was heavenly even if it came from a box. She could eat the whole damned pan if she were alone and had no one to judge her.

"A bit of a letdown, isn't it?"

Dex was watching her. It never failed to amaze her how beautiful he was. Her belly clenched with longing as she let her gaze wander over those sensual lips. Lips she'd never get to kiss again.

Oh my, you so fucked this up for yourself, girl.

His gaze narrowed and she fixed her eyes on his, refusing to let them stray again. Then she shrugged. "I like macaroni and cheese. And I like hot dogs. You forget that I have a four-year-old."

He went still. "Four? Your daughter is four?"

Liquid fear rolled through her. He could do math as well as anyone. "Yes," she said, her throat tight. "She is."

"You and Eric didn't waste any time. But I guess that shouldn't surprise me."

Annabelle's stomach turned over and she set the fork down. "It happens sometimes."

"Guess so."

There were so many things she wanted to say, but her throat was too tight. Besides, none of it was a good idea.

I think she's yours, Dex. But I don't know for certain, and I'm too scared to find out. Because what will you think of me then?

She couldn't add that kind of uncertainty to her child's life. To the world, Charlotte was Eric's daughter—even if he'd questioned it himself from time to time. She dropped her gaze, unable to handle the flood of bitter memories just now. The ugliness when Eric went into his rages. The accusations. The nights when she took Charlotte and went to Molly's because Eric was so volatile.

"You stopped eating," Dex said. "Why?"

Leave it to Dex to notice the things she didn't want him to see. "Full, I guess."

"You didn't touch the hot dog and you took about three bites of macaroni."

"Then I guess I've lost my appetite," she snapped. "Maybe if you'd leave the past alone—" She couldn't finish the sentence. She choked it off and dropped her head to the side, staring at the linoleum and willing herself not to cry. It wasn't his fault. It was hers.

"I'm sorry."

Her head came up. That wasn't what she'd expected. She met his gaze. His dark eyes were troubled. She wanted to run her palm over his jaw, feel the scruff and his warm skin. She wanted to close her eyes and press her lips to his, wanted to go back in time.

Impossible.

"I'm over you, Annabelle," he said, and she felt as if he'd shoved a dagger into her chest. "But I'm not over what happened. It was… pivotal in my life. And seeing you now, well, I wonder where we'd be if you'd showed up that day. It's not hard to imagine we'd have a kid of our own."

Her heart was breaking. Simply breaking. She wanted to throw herself on his mercy and tell him everything. But it wouldn't solve a damned thing. She'd made this bed and she had to lie in it.

"I didn't know you wanted kids," she said softly.

"We talked about it. Did you forget?"

"No. But it was always a someday kind of thing. Not right now. And who knows if it would have happened? Some people never have kids."

She didn't add that some people probably *shouldn't* have kids. Her parents, for instance. Oh, they'd never been cruel, but they'd been more focused on themselves than her. So long as she was fed and clothed and alive, they didn't bother putting her needs first.

Which was why she'd vowed to be different. Charlotte was her world and always would be. She could bear the loss of this man with her daughter in her life. If she never married again, never kissed a man or felt any tenderness for a partner—she could live with it. She didn't miss sex at all—strike that. She didn't miss sex with Eric. With Dex?

Well, she was no doubt remembering it with rose-colored glasses. It couldn't have been as fantastic as she'd thought it was. That was youth and nostalgia, right?

"Yeah, who knows?" He leaned back and folded his arms over his chest. She tried not to notice how his biceps popped out or how broad his chest was. Dex had always been fit. But now? Holy wow. He looked like he could bench-press the refrigerator.

"Kids don't fit into my life right now anyway," he added.

It occurred to her that she didn't know if there was anyone in his life. Oh God, did she want to know? Could she take it?

"Are you married?"

He snorted. "Are you kidding? Think I learned my lesson about weddings." He got to his feet and grabbed his plate, going over and dumping it in the trash. "Look, there's no need to talk about this stuff anymore. Eat your dinner, and I'll see what I can do about the computer."

"I'm not hungry."

A shadow fell over her. He stood above her, hands on hips, looking big and bad and prickly as hell. "Eat your dinner or I'll force it down your throat."

"You wouldn't."

He nodded. "I sure as hell would. You're hungry, but you're worried about your daughter and that's screwing with your appetite. But she's safe, Annabelle. If you won't eat for you, eat for her. She's going to need you strong and healthy."

She picked up her fork and shoved it into the macaroni. "You don't play fair," she said when she'd swallowed a mouthful.

He didn't crack a smile. "Neither do you."

EIGHT

COLONEL JOHN MENDEZ STALKED INTO his office and threw his hat on the desk. Then he loosened his tie and went into the attached bathroom. The sooner he got out of this Army Service Uniform and back into his ACUs, the better. He jerked the tie loose, shrugged out of the jacket, and attacked the buttons. When he'd finished removing everything, he yanked on the digital camouflage he preferred and left the dress uniform with all its medals hanging on a hook.

There was a knock at the door when he returned to his office.

"Enter," he barked.

His deputy commander, Lieutenant Colonel Alex "Ghost" Bishop, walked in. "How'd it go on the Hill, sir?"

Mendez flung himself into his chair. "As expected. Congressman DeWitt has a hard-on for HOT—or maybe it's just me he wants to fuck."

Ghost snorted. "You'd think he'd be too busy trying to get elected president."

"He's a dangerously delusional man who got elected to Congress because his parents have more money than God. Why the hell he thinks that qualifies him to be president, I have no idea."

"He's been giving Senator Campbell a run for his money."

Mendez shoved a hand through his hair. It was starting to feel a little long. Didn't look it, but it felt that way to him. Time for a haircut. Just as soon as he could find a spare minute to get it done.

"Campbell's the front-runner for the nomination. I doubt DeWitt will be a serious impediment. Besides, Campbell's been a senator for years, and his approval ratings are high."

"DeWitt has a strange sort of appeal to some."

Mendez frowned at his deputy. "Unfortunately for us. If he somehow gets elected, he'll gut programs like ours. He wants more tanks and guns—but he lacks the ability to understand why sending us in first helps keep the world stable."

DeWitt had no respect for the work that organizations like HOT did, as evidenced by the pressure he was bringing to bear for investigations into Special Operations

Not that HOT had anything to worry about. Mendez did everything by the book.

Well, almost everything. He thought of former operator Jack "Hawk" Hunter's call last month. Chase "Fiddler" Daniels had gotten involved in some tricky shit involving Grigori Androv and his band of merry Russians. Mendez had called Ian Black in—unofficially, of course—and everything had turned out fine in the end.

But Androv took a dirt nap shortly after HOT released him from their custody, and they still didn't know who'd pulled the trigger. DeWitt was asking questions about that, among other things.

"You'd think we'd be more concerned about the threats staring us in the face than the phantom ones DeWitt conjures up in his mind." Mendez flipped through the papers on his desk. Nothing leaped out at him.

"People are easily led by their more immediate fears. Prey on that fear, and you have them in your pocket."

"PsyOps 101," Mendez said. "The Russians were the masters of that during the Cold War."

"Unfortunately, propaganda works. Even in the US."

His phone buzzed and he slid it from his pocket. It was a text from Samantha Spencer, the CIA operative he'd been seeing lately.

Sam: *You've been a bad boy, Johnny. Congressman DeWitt was raging at the director on the phone just now.*

He had no idea what the congressman could possibly be saying to the CIA director about HOT.

Mendez: *Not my problem.*
Sam: *Dinner tonight?*
Mendez: *Sure.*
Sam: *My place or yours?*

Mendez hesitated. It was always her place. She'd pointed that out recently and asked why he never brought her to his house for sex. He'd thought about it. But, truthfully, he preferred going to her house. He could leave when he wanted and there was no danger of her forgetting her toothbrush in his holder.

Mendez: *Yours is nicer.*

He could almost hear her sigh.

Sam: *Fine. Eight?*
Mendez: *That works.*

He put the phone away and looked up to find Ghost waiting patiently. "Got a situation, sir," he began.

Mendez sighed. "Don't we always? What is it this time?"

"An Alpha Squad operator. Dex 'Double Dee' Davidson. He currently has the CFO of Archer Industries, Annabelle Quinn-Archer, in protective custody."

"Archer Industries?" Mendez frowned. "The Helios radio wave project, right?"

"Yes, sir. The CEO was killed in a lion attack in Jorwani last month. According to the CIA, he was trying to sell the technology to a foreign agent. Money exchanged hands, though there's no evidence the technology did. The alleged buyer wants their money back."

"Well, fuck. There goes my quiet evening."

Ghost snorted. "Sir, you don't like quiet evenings."

Mendez laughed. "Not really. All right, let's get down to the command center and see what's happening."

It was hell being cooped up in this small cabin with Annabelle. She smelled like sweet summer memories and looked like his every wet dream come true. She was petite and pretty. Not stunning, not the kind of woman who turned every head when she walked into a room, but the kind who, once you looked at her, you couldn't stop looking.

Dex had ignored her for years. All those sleepovers with Katie. All those years of being annoying little girls and then, later, giggly teenagers. He'd caught Annabelle looking at him sometimes from beneath her lashes, her cheeks pink and her pretty eyes sparkling. He'd had a girlfriend the first time he noticed it, but he'd been intrigued nonetheless.

She looked at him like that for a year. And then one day she smiled, just like always, and his heart thumped extra hard in his chest. It had been at football practice, and she'd been on the cheerleading squad. The cheerleaders were doing their own practice, and Annabelle was on top of the formation. She'd tumbled down perfectly and then lifted her head and smiled.

He'd kissed her that weekend, a hot, desperate kiss at midnight in the hallway of his house. She'd been staying overnight with Katie, and when he'd stumbled in after a night out with the guys, she'd been in the hall in her little shorts and tank top.

He'd walked right up to her and stood toe to toe with her.

"Do you know what you're doing to me, Annabelle?"

She'd shaken her head.

He'd dropped his mouth to her neck, tasted her sweet skin. She'd moaned—and then he'd tugged her into his arms and kissed her until they'd both been so hot they'd had to shove each other away or wake his father and sister with the noise they were making.

Shit.

He didn't need to think about that or he'd be hard right this minute.

Dex grabbed the laptop and carried it over to the couch. He opened the lid, then took out his phone and made a call.

"Double Dee," Richie said. "Whatcha got?"

"Need Billy the Kid," Dex said. "Got a computer here that belonged to Eric Archer, but Annabelle doesn't know the password."

"Putting you on speaker."

"How's it going, son?"

Dex jerked. That was the colonel's voice. He hadn't expected the commanding officer. "As well as can be expected, sir."

Mendez was legend in spec ops. Truth be told, he made Dex a little nervous. And nothing made Dex nervous. He was usually as cool under pressure as a block of ice. As a Special Operator, as a sniper, he had to be. He'd literally stared death in the face and hadn't blinked.

Mendez made him blink.

"How's your father?" the colonel asked.

"Recovering, sir. Thank you."

"Good. All right, tell the Kid what you've got. Let's see if we can't crack this computer."

"Hey, Double Dee." It was Billy's voice now. "I'm gonna have you start the computer in safe mode, then we'll see if we can change the password."

"And if we can't?"

There was a moment's hesitation. "Then I'll need to lay hands on it myself."

"Copy that. All right, tell me what to do. Let's bust this baby open."

NINE

ANNABELLE FINISHED HER FOOD AND cleaned up the pan Dex had used. He was on the phone with someone, grunting and saying things like "Copy that" and "Negative, Kid. What now?"

He tapped the keys on Eric's computer and cussed from time to time. Finally he expelled a frustrated breath and snapped the lid closed.

"Yeah, copy. Over and out."

She turned as he threw his phone down on the couch and raked both hands through his hair. Muscles popped and flexed, putting on their own after-dinner show. He leaned back, eyes closed, and she wished she still had the right to go over and push her hands into his hair and massage his temples before pressing her lips to his.

"Problem?" she asked as she walked over and perched on the arm of a chair.

He cracked an eye open. "Billy Blake is one of the best programmers in the business. He couldn't get me in. We have to take the computer to him. He has more resources back at HQ."

She swallowed. "Where's HQ?"

"DC."

"When?"

"In the morning." He rubbed a hand over his eyes. "It's still a long drive, and it's better to rest first."

"I'm not going to make the deadline for turning over the money, am I?"

"No. But did you really think you would?"

She had to shake her head. She'd known almost from the first moment that she was fighting a losing battle. She'd had no clue what Mr. Lyon was talking about—and she'd known Eric well enough to know that he wouldn't leave a trail of bread crumbs. Wherever the money was, she had no idea.

And that worried her deeply because what would happen when the deadline came and went? She didn't think Mr. Lyon was going to take it well even if he couldn't find her or Charlotte. Would she always be on the run? Would she and Charlotte be put into witness protection, cut off from the life they knew and fearing they'd be found? She shuddered to think it.

"What can you tell me about your conversation with Mr. Lyon?" Dex asked. "Did he have an accent? Did you hear anything in the background?"

She frowned. "He did have an accent, but I couldn't tell where it was from. I didn't hear anything distinctive in the background. A television, but I couldn't tell what was on it."

"Language?"

She tried to recall the faint conversation, but it had been nothing more than gibberish to her. "I don't know. I was much more focused on what he was saying than anything else."

"Understandable. But if you remember anything, no matter how insignificant it seems, you need to tell me."

"I will."

He stood and stretched. "We'll leave at first light. I'm going to bed."

"Can I have my phone back? I'm reading a book on it."

He shook his head. "It's not safe. We don't know the kind of resources Mr. Lyon has. If he's managed to get access to GPS information on your phone, he could pinpoint your location."

"You said there was no signal here."

"There typically isn't. But all it takes is one bar for a brief moment and someone could find you. It's not a risk you need to take."

"I can't sleep yet," she said. "And if I can't read, what am I supposed to do?"

His eyes darkened for a second, and she wondered if he was thinking about the kinds of things they'd done together a long time ago. Suddenly that's all she was thinking about. Her, Dex. Naked. Bodies joining, senses exploding, pleasure pouring over them both.

Her nipples tightened and her skin prickled with remembered sensations. Dex's gaze dropped to her mouth and her lips tingled, aching for contact with his. She wanted to remember what it felt like for someone to touch her with tenderness, to care about her pleasure. Even when Dex was rough, he was gentle. He could take her hard and fast and still treat her with the utmost care. He'd been an addiction back then. After he'd shown her what sex was all about that first time, she'd never been able to get enough of him.

She'd felt like she'd loved him forever, and she'd never thought he would feel the same way she did. He'd been her best friend's big brother, and he hadn't looked at her twice—until suddenly he did. Her life hadn't been the same after that. Four years he'd been hers.

Four years.

"Dex," she breathed.

He stiffened, and she cursed herself for speaking his name. For breaking the spell. For a moment, he'd been looking at her like he used to. For a moment, she'd thought they might forget where they were and all that had gone before.

"Not my problem, Annabelle," he said. Then he turned on his heel and went into the bedroom, shutting the door behind him with a finality that told her he wouldn't be back tonight.

Dex thought about jerking off but couldn't quite bring himself to do it with Annabelle in the next room. He was hard though, and aching. It had been weeks since he'd had sex with anyone. That didn't usually bother him much. His sex life ebbed and flowed because of his job. He was used to it.

But tonight he'd give anything to sink into a woman's body and lose himself there. Unfortunately, the only woman in a twenty-mile radius was the one woman he'd never willingly touch again. Even if, for a brief moment, he'd wanted to.

Until she spoke his name. Hearing her voice had snapped him out of the spell he'd been under. And he *had* been under one—looking at her mouth and remembering how it felt on his body, how it felt when he'd kissed her.

He didn't bother undressing. He lay on top of the bed, fully clothed, and folded his arms behind his head. His gun was beside him on the table, his phone charging nearby. He didn't expect anyone to find them out here or he'd have stayed in the living room and told Annabelle to go to bed while he kept watch.

He focused on his breathing, stilling himself as he concentrated on the rise and fall of his chest. He was a master at blocking out emotion, at calming the tension and nerves, at becoming utterly still so he could do his job.

He thought of Jane, of her sleek metal casing and fiery smell. Of the way her trigger resisted him until the last second, giving way with a sweet sigh that exploded from the other end of the barrel and knocked him in the shoulder. Jane was a pretty thing, and lethal. She did as he commanded. She'd never failed him or deserted him. Jane didn't let him down.

Annabelle's movements in the other room distracted him from his thoughts. She was pulling open drawers and shoving them closed again. Looking for reading material, maybe. Guilt stung him for a second. He could have given her the phone. All he had to do was turn off the cellular data so the phone wouldn't connect to any networks. If her book was downloaded, she could read it.

On the other hand, it wasn't in his nature to trust her —or anyone who wasn't a Special Operator—when he said no calling or texting. If he gave her the phone and went to sleep, what's to say she couldn't turn the cellular data back on and make a quick call to her daughter? He couldn't risk it, so keeping the phone was the logical solution.

He sighed and sat up. There was a bookcase in this bedroom. It was the only bookcase in the house. He flipped the lamp back on and peered at the spines. He could let her come in and choose something, but then her perfume would be in his room and he'd have worse trouble ignoring her presence than he already did.

He pulled a couple of books off the shelf and stalked to the door, jerking it open. She looked up from the magazine she'd found and blinked questioningly.

"Here," he said, shoving the books toward her.

She jumped up and hurried over to take them. "You found books? Thank you!"

"Yeah. If that's not good, there are a couple more in here."

She turned the books spine up. "Hmm, Louis L'Amour and Tom Clancy—I'm guessing there's no romance novels in there?"

"Didn't see any."

She gave him a crooked grin. It was endearing and he hated it. "Then these are fine. Thank you."

"I did it because the walls are thin and I can hear you pacing around in here like a herd of cattle."

"Sorry. I'll be quiet now."

Did he really need to be such an asshole? "Do you want to look at the bookcase?"

"Do you mind?"

"No." She didn't mean anything to him anymore. He could handle her walking into his room for a few moments, especially since he planned to stay out here until she was done.

She went over to the bookcase. "Oh wow," she said. "There are a few books here, aren't there?"

"Yeah."

She selected one of the fattest books he'd ever seen. "Oooh, perfect!"

"What is it?"

She tucked the L'Amour and Clancy back on the shelf. "T.E. Lawrence. *Seven Pillars of Wisdom*."

He didn't know what that was, but it clearly tripped her trigger.

"*Lawrence of Arabia*?" she said, making it into a question. "You ever see that movie?"

"Nope."

"Shocking. It's quite the epic." She held up the book. "Based on this book here. Lawrence was a British officer in Africa and the Middle East during World War One. He helped turn the Arabs into a force to defeat the Turks. And caused quite a few problems too. Part of why we have trouble in the Middle East today comes from what the British and French did when they divided up the region and redrew maps without thought to tribal boundaries."

He'd seen that trouble in the Middle East firsthand. More often than he'd like. "If you already know those things, why d'you want to read about it again?"

She shrugged. "Because the story is more gripping than a novel, and the words are beautiful. You feel like you're in the desert."

"I've been to the desert. It's not all that great."

"Well, I haven't. This book is the best adventure story you'll ever read in your life because you know it's true—or close to true."

"I don't remember you caring about history all that much."

She laughed. "I didn't think I did—but my friend Molly is a huge history buff. She loaned me Lawrence and told me I had to read him. So I did."

Dex couldn't remember the last time he'd read a book. Newspapers and journals, yeah. But not a book. He didn't have time.

She opened the book and read aloud. *"By day the hot sun fermented us; and we were dizzied by the beating wind. At night we were stained by dew, and shamed into pettiness by the innumerable silences of stars."*

"Tell me that is not gorgeous." Her eyes burned brightly. *"The innumerable silences of stars."*

He thought about the nights spent downrange in Qu'rim and Acamar, Iraq and Afghanistan, waiting for the target to appear. The vastness of the sky, the silence of the desert, and the chill air that punched you in the gut because it was so damned hot during the day.

"I guess it's nice," he said, annoyed that he liked it. "So what?"

She scoffed. "Nice? It's poetry! Want to hear more?"

She looked hopeful and sweet. The urge to say yes swelled inside him, pushing against the rock-hard determination to say no. But the memory of standing in a Kentucky church with the rain pouring down and the guests fidgeting in their seats was a hot poker to the brain.

"Not really." Her face fell. He didn't care. He didn't have to be nice to her. He didn't have to let her get beneath his skin. This was all too close for comfort—riding in the truck for hours, eating a cozy dinner they'd made, sharing a bathroom—and now she wanted to add reading a book together?

No.

Tomorrow morning, he'd drive her to DC, hand over the computer to his team, and forget all about Annabelle Quinn. Because once he delivered the computer, he was done with her too.

"Going to bed. Enjoy the book."

TEN

WHEN DEX RAPPED ON HER door way too early, Annabelle jolted awake and stumbled into the shower. She turned the water as hot as she could take it and let it melt the ice of sleep from her veins. There was no hair dryer, so her hair hung wet and limp down her back when she was through. She yanked on jeans and a tank top, shrugged into a button-down shirt, and stumbled out for a cup of coffee. Dex handed her a granola bar. She was still choking it down when he told her it was time to go.

The air was decidedly cool in the mountains of West Virginia. Annabelle wrapped her jacket tighter and waited for Dex. When he unlocked the big Ford, she climbed inside and curled into her seat.

A yawn cracked her jaw. She should have put the book down much sooner, but it was a distraction she'd needed.

Until she'd started thinking about Dex saying he'd been to the desert. She knew what that meant. He'd been fighting in the wars in the Middle East. Qu'rim, Iraq, Afghanistan. It had never been far from her mind over the past few years that he could be in danger. She'd kept an eye on the newspaper. If Dex were ever killed in action, Briar City would know about it. Katie would make sure that Dex was given a hero's return and burial.

Annabelle shivered at the idea of Dex coming home in a flag-draped coffin. When he'd first told her he wanted to join the military, she'd been fearful of what might happen. But she'd understood his reasons—he was a farmer's kid and his dad couldn't put him through college, so he would join the military and get college money that way.

That was nearly ten years ago now, so he clearly hadn't left the Army once his initial four-year enlistment was up. She wondered if that was because of her. Her stomach cratered at the thought.

"Do you like the Army?" she asked him when they'd been on the road for an hour.

He shot her a puzzled glance. "Yeah, I do. It's been good to me."

"What do you do in the Army? You never really told me when I asked you last night."

"I fight," he said.

"Dex."

"I don't owe you any answers, Annabelle."

She sighed and sat up straighter. "I know that. I'm trying to have a conversation. Not to mention you told me, repeatedly, this is your job—but I don't know what that means. How do I know you can really find the money, or Mr. Lyon, or keep Charlotte and me safe? Because you keep telling me to trust you—and I do trust you—but you don't tell me anything else."

"I'm in Special Ops. Counterterrorism. I fight the bad guys."

He didn't say anything else after that, and she got the hint that he wasn't going to. "Thank you for that. I appreciate it."

"You'll need to keep that information to yourself," he said. "When you go back home."

"I will."

Dex was all business this morning. "You'll be briefed when we get to DC. They'll explain everything—or as much as you can know."

"So this is kind of like *NCIS*," she teased, trying to lighten the mood. "They're always doing super-secret stuff and going after the bad guys—terrorists and rogue agents and spies."

"If that's how you want to think of it."

"It is. So do you have an Agent Gibbs?"

"Who?"

"He's the guy in charge. Gray hair, badass as hell. Everyone jumps when he says boo. I kinda find him sexy."

He snorted. "I don't know how sexy he is, but we have a guy like that. Mendez."

"Will I get to meet him?"

"I don't know." His brows arrowed down. That wasn't good for her. "Look, Annabelle... when we get to DC and turn over the computer, there'll probably be other operators—agents in *NCIS*-speak—who'll take over. You'll be safe with them, and they'll make sure they get to the bottom of this."

Her heart fell. "You mean you won't be helping me?"

He looked troubled. "Do you really think that's the best idea?"

"Well, yes. I trust you. I know you, and I know you're a good man. I don't know these other people."

"They're all good people. You'll be fine."

She folded her arms over her chest. "You don't want to help me, do you? You want to get as far away as possible."

"I want you to be safe. You don't need me to make sure that happens."

"We were friends once."

"You're the one who changed that, not me."

Helpless disappointment boiled in her gut. Anger underpinned it. Sorrow bound the whole mess together into one giant ball of suck. Because there'd been a lot of sorrow for her too. He had *no* idea.

The unfairness filled her to bursting. She'd kept the truth to herself because bringing up the past changed nothing. But she had a sudden need to prick the bubble of his indifference. To make him see he wasn't the only one who'd suffered. She'd endured his anger and contempt since yesterday. She was tired of it. She hadn't planned to tell him the truth, but she could no longer hold it in.

"My parents *forced* me to marry Eric," she spat out. "To save my father's ass."

His jaw went granite-hard, his hands flexing on the wheel. His brown eyes glittered hotly as he shot a glare her way. "Don't."

She flinched. But her anger frothed anew at his attempt to shut her out. He didn't believe her.

And that pissed her off.

"Jesus Christ, Dex. You don't even want the truth, do you? Well, you're getting it, like it or not." Part of her brain said *no, no, no.* But the other part was too far over the line to care. "My dad worked for Eric's father. My parents spent beyond their means, and my dad got a little creative with the Archer books so he could siphon off money. Eric caught him. Eric's price for silence was me."

He white-knuckled the wheel. "That's insane."

"Yes, I know. But Eric was a classic narcissist. *Everything* was about him. When he decided you were the enemy, he wanted everything you had. He didn't get to be quarterback or homecoming king, he didn't get a school record or win a state championship—but he got me, and he hurt you in the process. He was pretty pleased with himself over that."

Dex's face was red and she knew he was thinking about it—and getting angrier by the minute. Hell, she was angry too. Angry and heartbroken and filled with regret for the past. And then there was Charlotte. Did she tell him about her doubts or did she leave it in the past? What good would it do to drag that up when she didn't even know what the truth was?

Dex growled and slammed a palm down on the wheel. Annabelle jumped.

"If he wasn't already dead, I'd kill him."

"You believe me then?" Annabelle squeaked.

They rolled into a town and Dex yanked the truck into the first parking lot he could find. He left the engine running as he turned to face her. Because this thing was fucking with him, and he needed to know if she was playing him. Again.

"Tell me exactly what happened."

Her chin dropped, damp strands of her golden hair spilling over her shoulders. She pushed the hair away. Her fingers trembled. He didn't doubt she was emotional over this—but what kind of emotion was it?

"I just told you. There's no more to know. I let them convince me their lives were over if I didn't do this one thing. Dad would go to jail and Mom would be destitute. She'd never had a job—she'd only ever been a society wife, and she'd be forced to go to work. Probably in a low-paying, unskilled job." She snorted. "Can you imagine my mother waiting tables? Or cleaning hotel toilets?"

"So fucking what." He said it quietly, but his stomach churned and his heart pumped. He'd never liked the Quinns. Pretentious assholes who thought they were better than everyone else. Cleaning toilets would be just what her mother deserved. Jail was too good for her father.

Her chin jerked up and she glared at him with glassy eyes. "You're judging me? What if it was your dad Eric threatened? Would you help him or would you hang him out to dry?"

He gritted his teeth. Yeah, what would he do? Most likely he'd go pound Eric into the ground and threaten to force-feed him his own balls if he didn't back off. But that wouldn't have been Annabelle's reaction.

Her parents had never liked Dex. He was a farmer's kid, and even when he'd joined the Army, he hadn't been good enough for their daughter. *When* they paid attention to their daughter, which they didn't tend to do very often.

But of course they'd paid attention when Eric demanded Annabelle in return for his silence. The fuckers had sold her out—and Dex too. They hadn't cared about her happiness or her well-being. They'd sold her out to save their own asses.

"Why didn't you tell me?"

She spread her hands. A tear spilled down her cheek. "How could I, Dex? You wouldn't have understood."

"You don't know that."

Her laugh was bitter. "Yes, I do know that. You hated Eric. You'd have gone after him—and how would that have turned out?" She shook her head. "You'd be the one in jail."

He hated to think she was right. But she probably was. He'd have killed Eric Archer for daring to threaten the woman he loved. He'd have killed him for even thinking he could touch a hair on Annabelle's head.

But Eric had done much more than that, hadn't he? They had a daughter together. A four-year-old daughter.

Acid and bitterness churned in his gut. He wanted to punch something, and he wanted to go deep into the woods and shout until he was hoarse.

He had to *think*. Yes, he was furious. The pain of that day came back to sucker punch him. It had been brutal. His entire life changed in that moment, and in all the long moments after. He'd stopped believing in anything so capricious as love. It obviously changed depending on the day, so why believe in it? Love, trust, faith—she'd taken those things from him.

He'd been defined by that day in ways that still pissed him off because he hadn't been in control of it, but he'd accepted it. Life sometimes sucked, but those sucky moments didn't have to rule you.

Now Annabelle was blowing everything he knew about what had happened out of the water. Blowing him off course and into choppy seas.

He could choose to believe she was making it all up. It would be easier that way. But the things he knew about Eric Archer told him it wasn't a lie. The dude had been obsessed when they were in high school. They'd been friends once, but it went wrong over a girl. Not Annabelle. Trisha Carpenter. Trisha had been the head cheerleader, and Eric and Dex both liked her. They'd both been on the football team, both tried out for quarterback as freshman but didn't get it.

But then the quarterback got hurt and Dex was chosen to take his place. That's when Trisha turned her attentions to him. Eric had spent weeks talking about how much he liked her, how she was going to be his girl someday—and then she'd wanted Dex. Eric had never forgiven him for it. Soon after, they'd been rivals.

"Dex?"

He focused on Annabelle. He'd loved that face. Loved that body. Believed in her with all his heart and soul. And she'd left him for that piece of shit Archer. It was a betrayal he couldn't forgive.

"You still should have told me," he growled. "You made a decision that affected me and you let me believe—" He raked a hand through his hair. "Fuck, it doesn't matter what you let me believe. You didn't respect me enough to include me in a life-altering decision that had deep ramifications for you and me."

"I'm sorry. I didn't know what else to do. I didn't think I had a choice."

He hated being so angry. Hated the way it made him feel inside. He shoved the truck into gear but didn't let off the brake just yet.

"You always have a choice, Annabelle. You made yours and it ruined us both. It's too late to change that."

ELEVEN

MENDEZ'S CELL PHONE RANG. IT was Sam, so he answered.

"I missed you last night, Johnny," she said, her voice a sultry purr.

"Sorry about that, but we had a situation."

She laughed. "You always have a situation."

"So do you. Nature of our jobs, I guess."

"Yes, that is completely true." She dragged in a breath and he heard the telltale crackle of her e-cigarette. "In fact, our situations are about to intersect I believe."

An itch started at the back of his neck. A prickly, annoying itch that told him he wasn't going to like this one damned bit.

"Oh? How's that?"

"Annabelle Quinn-Archer. We want her."

Annoyance flared in his gut. "I don't have her. Why do you want her?"

"Now, Johnny, I gave you the information about Eric Archer and his deal. You wouldn't know the origins of the money if I hadn't told you."

"I'd have found out. Maybe not as quickly, but I'd have gotten it. You forget that you aren't my only source."

"Yes, but I'm your favorite one."

"That's true," he said, thinking of the way her lips sometimes wrapped around his cock and took him to heaven. Not that he didn't appreciate all the other ways in which he and Sam took pleasure from each other because he damn sure did. Still, he didn't have the sense that if she cut him off, he'd go mad.

He'd shrug and move on, and that wasn't what she deserved. He'd been thinking about it a lot lately—of their relationship and the casual nature of it. He sometimes thought she wanted more. Hell, he sometimes wanted more—but not with Sam, and that's what bothered him.

"Eric Archer received over half a billion dollars from the Russian he met in Africa. That's a hell of a fortune— and if his wife has any clue where that money is, we want to know."

Half a billion for unproven technology? Either the Russians were stupid or Eric Archer had been the Einstein of con artists. "She's with my operator. They're coming in, but I don't know when they'll arrive."

"You'll let me know?"

"Yeah, I'll give you a call." It was a measure of the kind of man he'd learned to be over the years that he could tell her he would when he didn't know for certain it was true. He never gave his hand away, and if there was a compelling reason to keep Annabelle Quinn-Archer in HOT's custody, then that's what he'd do. To hell with what the CIA wanted. If they got the woman, they'd probably cut HOT out of the loop.

The spirit of cooperation hadn't been all that strong lately. Mendez blamed Congressman DeWitt on that score. He'd gotten the ear of the director, and he liked to bend it as often as possible. Mendez, however, was not the sort of man to relinquish the advantage when he had it.

"I'd ask if we'll see each other tonight, but I think I know the answer to that," Sam said with a laugh.

"Soon," he said. "Bye, Sam."

The minute they hung up, he stood and headed into the ops center. Time to institute the backup plan.

Annabelle wanted so badly to call Molly, but Dex had told her she couldn't turn her phone on. He'd given it back to her that morning, but he'd warned her not to power it up.

"You could bring Lyon down on us both," he'd said, his expression grave.

She might be desperate to hear her child's voice, but she wasn't stupid. Dex had gotten a message from his people that Molly and the kids were fine, so at least she didn't have to worry. What she really wanted, however, was for this to be over and everything to be normal again.

Whatever normal was these days.

She and Dex hadn't spoken about Eric or the marriage again. The truth hadn't changed anything for him. He was still angry that she'd left without an explanation.

But what if she'd told him the truth five years ago? What would have happened then? Would he have kicked Eric's ass? Probably, and she couldn't see how that would have been good for anyone.

Dex's phone rang. "Yeah? … Okay, copy that. … Another hour then. … Yeah, delta delta over and out."

"What now?" she asked, mostly because she was tired of the long drive with no sound. Dex hadn't turned on the radio. What did he think about during those long stretches of silence?

"I'm taking you to a safe house instead of HQ. My team's meeting us there and we'll try to crack the computer."

Whatever. She had no idea how any of this stuff worked. They did, which was all that mattered. "What's delta delta?"

"Me. It's the military phonetic alphabet. *D* equals delta."

"Doesn't that get confusing? What if someone else has the same initials?"

"It's radio speak. Mostly we have call signs we use."

"What's yours?"

"Double Dee."

She cocked her head. "Really? That's not too original, is it?"

He snorted. "It could have been worse. Someone wanted to call me Dee Dee early on."

She wanted to laugh. "Oh dear."

"Yeah, well, military call signs aren't always meant to be flattering. Thankfully I wound up with something not too bad in the end."

"So what are some of the names you've heard? Any funny ones?"

"We have a Flash Gordon. Oh, and one of our SEALs is named Cash, so he's Cash Money." He shrugged. "Not original, but that's kind of the point. If people got to pick their own name, they'd all be Tiger or Dragon or Eagle or some such bullshit."

"No stallions?" she asked with a grin.

"Yeah, probably some of them too."

Annabelle memorized his profile. He was as handsome as ever, but he was harder in a way too. She couldn't imagine all the things he'd been through in the military, but they'd marked him. What had changed Dex? *Besides* her, because surely she wasn't responsible for all the changes in the past five years.

"I guess you must like the military."

He glanced at her. "It's a job."

"It's more than a job, Dex. You could get a job in Briar City. But this… Well, it's you, isn't it?"

He was quiet for a moment. "Yeah, it's me."

"I was so scared when you wanted to join up. I was afraid of losing you—and I did lose you, but not the way I thought I would. Still, if I had to lose you, I'm glad it was this way and not the way I was worried about."

He scrubbed a hand over his forehead, his jaw tensing. "Can we stop talking about the past? There's nothing we can do to change it."

She folded her arms and settled into her seat to stare at the passing countryside. "Sure, if that's what you want."

"It is."

It wasn't what she wanted, but what good would it do to keep talking? Now that she'd told him about Eric and her parents, she wanted to keep talking, wanted to see if it brought any kind of healing. And maybe, just maybe, it was starting to settle in that Eric was out of her life and she could do what she wanted. No more living a lie because he wouldn't let her go. No more pretending they were a happy couple to the world when it was far from the truth.

A sigh slid from her. Maybe Dex was right and it was time to look to the future. Maybe talking about the past wasn't necessary anymore. But what *was* the future? She didn't know. Especially with Mr. Lyon in the mix. If she didn't find this mystery money and hand it over, what then?

What if she never found it? What if the money was gone? What if Eric had spent it? Or hidden it so well it was as good as gone?

A shiver skated from the nape of her neck to her toes. She hunched down in the seat as if doing so could hide her from the world. Dex and his people might not find the money—but they had to find Mr. Lyon before he found her.

The house Dex took her to was in a town, a small town on the outskirts of DC. She wouldn't have thought there was such a thing, but this place was as quaint and cute as an old town could be. There was a main street with old storefronts and a diner, and historic homes near the town square where the courthouse perched like a benign guardian.

Dex turned onto a side street and drove away from the town center, finally pulling into the driveway of a small ranch house on a street full of ranch houses. The houses were a little shabby, but the neighborhood looked clean and well cared for.

She hauled her own stuff inside, then collapsed on the couch and turned on the television, grateful to have sound in her life again. She could have asked Dex to turn on the radio, sure, but instead she'd tried to start various conversations with him. None had been all that successful.

Now she heard him on his phone, presumably letting his people know they'd arrived. It was still early since they'd left West Virginia at the butt crack of dawn, but it felt later. She hadn't been on a long car trip in years—and she certainly hadn't been on one with a silent hulk of a man whose dislike of her hung in the air like a black cloud for the entire ride.

She got up and went to the kitchen to explore the refrigerator and pantry. Thankfully, there was peanut butter, jelly, and bread. As she made a sandwich, she couldn't help but think of Charlotte and wonder what her little girl was doing right that second. Charlotte loved peanut butter and jelly. Annabelle's heart twisted and tears pressed against her eyelids. She knew Charlotte was probably happy as a clam with Molly and Becca, but Annabelle missed her.

And she was worried too. Charlotte had just lost her father a month ago. Now her mother was gone. Would she be anxious that her mother might never come back either?

She was a smart kid and the thought was bound to occur to her.

"You okay?"

She looked up to find Dex watching her. He slipped his phone into his pocket and hooked his thumbs through his belt like a cowboy wearing six shooters. The movement popped the muscles in his chest and arms. She swallowed.

"I was thinking about Charlotte."

"She'll be fine, Annabelle."

She clenched the butter knife in her hand and gave her head a shake. "I know—but my being gone like this, well, it's like when Eric left. He never came back. She took it well enough, though she still asks about him. She's at that age where telling her someone went to heaven is a good explanation. But I worry that the longer I'm gone and out of touch, the more she might think about her father and wonder if I went to heaven too."

He frowned. And then he pulled his phone out and handed it to her after unlocking it. "Here. Call your friend. Talk to your daughter."

Her heart swelled with hot emotion. "Thank you."

"Never mind that. Call."

Dex went over to the couch, sinking down on it and propping his feet on the coffee table before picking up the remote. Annabelle called up the keypad and punched in the number, her heart starting to hammer as the phone rang.

"Hello?" It was Molly's voice and relief flooded Annabelle.

"Mol, how are you?"

"Annabelle—"

Her voice choked off and another, colder voice came on the line. A voice she recognized.

"Hello, Mrs. Archer. Where is my money?"

TWELVE

DEX ROCKETED OFF THE COUCH. He was at Annabelle's side in half a second. Her face was the color of milk. She crumpled to the floor in slow motion. He went down with her, cupping her face and forcing her to look at him. The devastation in her expression rocked him. She looked as if someone had taken the one thing that meant the most to her in the world.

Ice floated through his veins. He snatched the phone from her limp fingers and hit redial. It rang incessantly, but no one answered.

"What happened, Belle?" He grabbed her by the shoulders and shook her gently when she just blinked at him. "Tell me what happened."

"Mr. Lyon," she breathed. "He has them."

Dex shot to his feet and dialed his team leader.

"Hey, man. We're en route. Be there in another twenty-five minutes or so," Richie said by way of greeting.

"We've got a problem," Dex replied. "The safe house with Annabelle's daughter has been compromised."

"Fuck," Richie said. "I'll make some calls. Stay put. We're coming."

"Copy."

Dex turned around after he'd finished the call. Annabelle was still on the floor, her back against the kitchen cabinets. She was breathing hard, and he knew she was about to lose it. He went over and sat beside her, hauling her into his arms. She was small and seemed so fragile as he pulled her against him.

She splayed an arm over his torso and pressed her cheek to his chest. His heart throbbed. Other parts wanted to throb as well, but he refused to let them. That's not what this was about. He put a hand on her head, stroked her soft hair.

"We'll get them back, Annabelle. I promise."

"You promised they'd be safe," she said on a whisper.

Her tone wasn't accusatory, but he flinched anyway. He *had* said that. He'd believed it. How the fuck had Lyon gotten past their security? How had he even known where to look? And who the hell was Lyon anyway?

"I know I did, honey."

"Then how can you promise…?"

He squeezed her a little tighter. "Because I can. He's not going to hurt them, not yet. They're his leverage to get what he wants. If he hurts them, you won't give him the money."

"I don't have the money!"

She was starting to sound a little hysterical. He understood it, but he couldn't let her lose her cool yet. He tipped her chin up and forced her to look at him. His heart lurched the way it used to do whenever he looked at Annabelle. *Jesus.*

He didn't want to feel any tenderness toward this woman—yet how could he stay unmoved?

"We'll find the money. You've got help. You don't have to do this alone."

Her fingers curled into his shirt. "You can't leave me now. Please don't leave me—I don't know these other people."

"I won't leave you. I'm in this until we get your daughter back."

The tension in her body loosened. "Thank you."

His gaze dropped to her mouth. He wanted to kiss her, and he wanted to push her away. He didn't have to make a decision though, because she dropped her cheek to his chest and dragged in a breath.

He wasn't surprised when the first sob escaped her. He expected many more to follow, but she clenched his shirt and breathed hard, her entire body trembling. She didn't sob again, and his heart ached for her. He'd thought for so long that he hated her, but he didn't. She'd married Eric, but she'd done it for her parents.

Assholes.

Yeah, he was pissed she hadn't told him the truth back then. He could have helped her if she had. Could have helped them both. He closed his eyes and held her, his cheek on her golden head, his arms wrapped around her sweet body. He'd never thought he'd do this again. He hadn't wanted to.

But that was a lie. He did want to hold her. He would probably always want to hold her. She'd been his first love. His only love, though he didn't love her anymore.

His team arrived within minutes. Dex helped Annabelle up and set her down on the couch before answering the door. Richie Rich and Billy the Kid filed in with equipment and grim expressions.

Richie shook his head and Dex glanced at Annabelle. She was looking at them with the mile-long stare of someone who wasn't really seeing anything. He introduced the guys and she nodded, but he didn't know if she really processed it.

Dex handed over the laptop to Billy, who was setting up a command center on the dinette table in the kitchen.

"What happened?" Dex asked them in a low voice.

Richie blew out a breath. "We're still getting intel. He killed an FBI agent though."

"How did he know where to find them? Who fucked up?"

"Molly Carter took a phone call about fifteen minutes before he arrived. We've got the phone records, but the number is a burner."

"No!" Annabelle was on her feet, her face red, and he knew she'd heard. She stalked toward them, eyes flashing. "Molly isn't behind this! No way, and don't you dare say—"

"Annabelle," Dex said, wrapping an arm around her and tugging her into his side. "Nobody said that. But it's a possible connection, and we have to trace it."

Her body shook like an earthquake, her chest rising and falling too fast. He steered her down onto one of the chairs at the dinette and made her put her head between her legs.

"Breathe, Belle. It won't do your daughter any good if you fall apart."

She sucked in air and he rubbed her back. Richie lifted an eyebrow. Kid didn't say anything because he was too busy plugging things in and firing up his laptop.

"Charlotte," she said, her voice muffled. "Her name is Charlotte. Lottie sometimes."

"Charlotte," he repeated. "You have to stay strong for her. And Molly. What's Molly's daughter's name?"

"Becca."

"Right. Charlotte and Molly and Becca. So tell me about Molly, Belle. How long have you known her, where's she from—that kind of thing."

Richie nodded his approval. His arms folded over his middle. His expression was intense. His wife was pregnant. Maybe that alone let him know how desperate Annabelle must feel. Not that Dex didn't, but he didn't know what it was like to have a child or how vulnerable that could make someone. He'd once heard it described like wearing your heart outside your body.

Annabelle took a deep breath and leaned back. Her face was still red and her eyes glistened. "I met Molly in college—we were both pregnant seniors trying to make it through to graduation." She snorted. "Not that Eric wanted me to graduate. I fought him over that one. Still don't know how I won…"

Dex squeezed her shoulder. "So you've known her for five years or so?"

"Yes." She swallowed. "She's from California, but she took a job in Lexington after graduation. A couple of years ago, she started freelancing and works from home. She lives in Briar City."

"Where's the father of her child?"

"He was never in the picture. She's raising Becca alone." Annabelle frowned. "She recently started seeing a guy though…"

The hair on Dex's arms prickled the way it did when something was off. He'd learned to trust that reaction over the years. It was probably nothing, and yet he couldn't shake the feeling.

"Tell me about him."

"I… I don't know. I haven't met him yet." Annabelle's eyes widened. "You don't think he had something to do with this, do you?"

"Not necessarily," he said. "But we have to consider it. What did Molly say about him?"

Annabelle frowned. "He's a lawyer, from Europe originally. It's only been about three weeks since she started going out with him, so I don't really know anything else. She called him…" Her skin lost what little color it had. She got to her feet, grasping the table for support. "Leo," she whispered. "She called him Leo. It's the same guy, isn't it?"

Shit.

"It could be," Dex replied. There was no hard evidence linking them, but Leo was simply another name for lion. If it was the same man, he liked to play games. Not a good sign.

Tears slipped down Annabelle's cheeks freely then. Anger spun into a tornado inside him. He wanted to make this go away, but he was helpless. For what seemed like the millionth time in the past few minutes, he wrapped his arms around her. She clung to him while he tried not to think about how good she felt there.

"It's okay, Belle. It'll be okay. We'll find this bastard, and we'll get them back."

Because there was nothing else he could say. He met Richie's gaze over the top of Annabelle's head. His team leader looked grim.

Billy Blake fired up the laptop and connected a cable. He looked up then and gave Dex a hard smile. "I'll get inside this piece of shit," he said in a low voice. "And then we'll find that money."

Numbness wrapped around Annabelle. She'd thought that losing Dex had been devastating—and it had been—but losing Charlotte was a million times worse. Because Charlotte was a child. Because Charlotte depended on Annabelle to keep her safe—and Annabelle had failed. How could she have let this happen?

Blindly, she pushed herself out of Dex's arms, in spite of how warm and safe she felt being there, and groped for her purse on the table. When she had it, she started toward the door.

"Hey, hey. Where do you think you're going?"

Dex was like a massive freight train blocking the way. He put his hands on her shoulders and kept her from taking another step.

"Let me go, Dexter Davidson," she growled. "I have to help my baby."

He didn't let go, but his voice was gentle. "How are you going to do that, Belle? This man wants the money, and he's not going to take it well if you don't hand it over. He won't give you back your daughter, or your friend and her daughter, until you give him what he wants."

She closed her eyes and concentrated on pulling in one breath after another, filling her lungs. If she could just concentrate, she could calm herself. Except she felt like she was holding on by a thread and any minute she would dissolve into a pool of atoms that would never be made whole again. They'd just float away into nothingness, and she'd be stuck in this limbo forever.

"Simple encryption," the man sitting in front of the computer said.

Annabelle jerked her gaze to him like he'd thrown her a lifeline.

"You're in?" Dex asked before she could find her voice.

"Yep. Just need to hash it out with my equipment. I've reset the password so we won't have trouble getting in again."

"Is there anything there? Anything pointing to the money?" Annabelle's heart was in her throat as she moved toward the table.

The man—Billy?—winked at her. "It'll take a little bit of time to sort through everything, but I'll find it."

A phone rang and Annabelle jumped. But it wasn't her phone, and it wasn't Dex's. It belonged to the other guy—the tall, handsome one who had a Cajun accent. Matt —but Dex called him Richie.

"Girard," he said, his voice clipped. "Hey, *cher.* … Yeah, got a lot going on today. … Can you fix some gumbo? I'll call you later and tell you where to bring it, yeah?" He laughed, a rich sound filled with happiness. Annabelle envied that. She wanted to hate him for that happiness, but she couldn't. She was too numb to feel anything other than fear for her child. There was no room for anything else. "Love you too, *cher*. Bye."

"Damn. Evie's cooking?" It was Dex speaking.

"Don't worry, I'll have her bring it to HQ when we get back there later."

"Hey," Billy said, and everyone looked at him. His mouth curved in a broad smile. "Got something."

"The bank account?" Hope rode hard through the chambers of her heart.

"No… but I do have a name."

THIRTEEN

"DMITRI LEONOV," MENDEZ SAID, HOLDING up a file folder two inches thick. "Former KGB, rumored to have the Russian president's ear. It's entirely possible he was sent by the Russian government to procure Archer's technology. He's also something of a gun for hire, so he might be working for a private contractor who wanted to buy the tech for their own purposes."

"That would be some valuable technology if it worked," Lieutenant Colonel Bishop said. "Recharging spy and combat drones using radio waves? It could revolutionize warfare."

Mendez looked grim. "Whoever controls that kind of technology could crush enemy defenses with repeated attacks. No limits on flight time. Just rotate the controllers in and out back at HQ and run a nonstop campaign. Fewer drones could command the airspace. And then there are the other applications—recharging just about everything without generators, solar panels, or the need to stop and plug in somewhere."

"Sounds like a spy novel," Garrett "Iceman" Spencer drawled.

"It does, but Archer Industries purportedly figured out how to make it work. So we have a revolutionary technology, a dead American, a Russian spy, half a billion dollars in missing money, a dead FBI agent, three hostages, and no idea where the money is yet—am I right?"

The colonel sounded about as pissed off as Dex had ever heard him. Billy must have heard it too because he jerked his gaze from his computer, nodding hard. "Yes, sir, that's right. I haven't found any evidence of the bank account numbers so far."

Dex wanted to punch something. They'd left the safe house earlier and come to the Hostile Operations Team headquarters where they had better access to equipment and resources. Not to mention it was the kind of place where nobody was getting to Annabelle.

HOT HQ was located on a military base in Maryland. It was a nondescript, high-tech building sitting behind concertina wire and some of the most sophisticated security measures on the planet. Annabelle was here but in an area that didn't require a top secret security clearance to enter. Evie Girard was with her, which Dex was grateful for. Matt's wife had shown up with a pot of gumbo and a cheery smile. Somehow she'd gotten Annabelle to eat, and the two of them were talking when Dex left.

But if they didn't get those account numbers and find the money, Dex didn't know what would happen or if they'd ever get Annabelle's daughter back alive.

Mendez dropped the folder on the table and opened it. He took out a photo and passed it around. "Dmitri Leonov, aka Mr. Lyon, aka Leo. We've run a search on Molly

Carter's calls—the ones from Leonov all came from a burner, but we've got records of Ms. Carter's texts and we've pieced together that she met Leonov on a dating site. He must have targeted her because of her connection to Annabelle Archer."

"Why not just go straight for Annabelle or her daughter?" It was Richie this time. "Why target her friend on the off chance he'd need her?"

"He likes to toy with his prey," Dex interjected. They swung curious gazes his way, but he'd been thinking since Annabelle told him about the first call from Lyon. "Annabelle said that Eric was mauled by lions. This guy didn't call himself Mr. Lyon because it's an anglicized form of his own name. He did it because he's a sick fuck. The same with calling himself Leo when he met Molly Carter. It's a game to him."

Mendez nodded. "That's right. Leonov gets off on terrorizing people. It's not just about the money to him. It's about the game. Molly Carter is another form of leverage. That's why he targeted her. He might also have needed her in order to learn everything he could about his target."

Mendez sounded like a man who knew what he was talking about. Dex wondered if he somehow knew this Leonov. The guys had told him how Mendez spoke fluent Russian when they'd brought Grigori Androv into HQ last month. Shocked the shit out of all of them.

Lieutenant Colonel Bishop spoke. "If he's the one who shot Eric Archer and threw him to the lions, then yeah, it's not just about money. Though why didn't he force Archer to return the money instead of killing him that way? He could have saved himself a trip over here, right?"

Mendez had his hands on his hips. "You'd think so, but we're dealing with a madman. Wouldn't be the first time, would it?" They all snorted—except for Dex, who didn't like the idea of a madman having anything to do with Annabelle. "There's also the possibility that Archer wouldn't give him what he wanted and he lost control. This doesn't bode well for our hostages—so we need to find this asshole ASAP."

Dex's blood froze. If anything happened to Charlotte Archer, he didn't want to have to face Annabelle and tell her he'd failed. Not when he'd promised her HOT would fix this and get her child back safely.

Mendez glanced at him as if he sensed Dex's discomfort. "All right, here's what we have to do—Double Dee, he's got your number, so you're going to need a new phone for coordinating with the team. But let's leave that one on and put a tracer program on it. Let's turn Ms. Quinn-Archer's phone back on and see if he calls that number, also with a tracer. Meantime, find those account numbers, Kid. We're running out of time."

"We need a picture of your daughter," Dex said softly. "And Molly and her daughter, if you have one."

Annabelle slipped her phone from her pocket, her fingers trembling as she pulled up pictures. She'd been sitting in this room with the lovely Evie, chatting about pregnancies and kids and things she couldn't even remember, and eating some amazing food. She hadn't forgotten that her daughter was a hostage, but she'd felt calmer—and Evie had been very sweet and kind, taking her hand and squeezing it when she got upset.

Now Evie sat with her arm around Annabelle's shoulders as if they were old friends. Annabelle was glad for it because she found it comforting. She scrolled through the pictures and pulled up one of Charlotte. She was missing a tooth, her hair was wild and red, tumbling down her back, and she had freckles. Annabelle sometimes thought she looked a little like Katie Davidson, but then she told herself she was seeing things.

Dex frowned hard, and her stomach dropped. His gaze tangled with hers and held. "She has your eyes and chin."

She did indeed. She might also have Dex's cheekbones and nose, but Annabelle was never sure. Some children were spitting images of their parents. Others took time to tease out the traits. Annabelle sometimes saw Eric in Charlotte. And sometimes she saw Dex.

"She does."

He sent himself the picture. She heard it go, and then he handed her phone back.

"And now Molly and Becca."

She found a picture of them. They looked so much alike, and her pulse throbbed at the idea they were victims of Eric's greed. And her stupidity. How could she not have known what he was up to?

Dex took the phone and transferred the picture before giving it back to her. "Thanks. And leave it on, okay? Lyon might call you."

There was a commotion at the door. A woman who made Annabelle's breath stop in her chest strode in like she owned the building. After a painful moment of not breathing, Annabelle's lungs started working again. She knew this woman. Gina Domenico? The superstar? Was that even possible?

She was gorgeous and blond—and she wore a determined expression. A man entered behind her—tall, dark, handsome, lethal-looking. A bodyguard, maybe?

But no. Annabelle shook her head. The whole thing was ridiculous. What would a pop superstar be doing here? Except it was uncanny…

Gina—or the woman who looked like Gina—walked over to where she sat. "Are you Annabelle?"

Annabelle could do nothing except nod. The Gina look-alike squatted beside her chair. "Oh honey, let me hug you."

Her arms opened wide, and then Annabelle found herself enfolded in a perfumed hug. She glanced up at Dex, who looked ready to fight the world on her behalf. It made her chest tighten.

"Sweetie, I'm so sorry. And I understand, believe me. My little boy was kidnapped." She sniffled. "But these guys and gals got him back. Saved my bacon too, let me tell you. And hell, saved so many people I don't even know about. But honey, without them, I wouldn't be here to tell you any of this."

Annabelle could only gape.

"Baby," the man who'd come in with her said, "you might want to at least tell the poor woman your name."

"Oh my goodness, of course." Gina-not-Gina—because it just wasn't possible that a global superstar would be right here, right now—held out her hand. "I'm Gina Hunter."

Annabelle took her hand, still gaping, and lifted her gaze to Dex. He was grinning. "Yeah," he said. "She's who you think she is."

"Sorry," Gina replied. "Yes, Gina Domenico—that's my stage name—but Hunter is my married name. Jack"—she waved behind her—"is my husband. He was HOT, but now he's my head of security."

"Uh," Jack said. "Baby, we've talked about that. You aren't supposed to say that word."

She blinked. "What word? Oh. Oh my goodness. Right." She smiled broadly. "Anyway, this place—these people—they are the answer to your prayers. They *will* get your little girl back. And she'll be fine."

Annabelle didn't know what to say. "Thank you."

Gina hugged her again, whispering fiercely in her ear. "I know how hard this is. I really do. You are allowed to be pissed off and scream and cry—and don't let any big, muscled alpha asshole tell you what to do or think, though they will. Listen to them, but don't be afraid to speak up when they try to bulldoze you. Because they will, honey, believe me."

With a last squeeze, Gina was on her feet. She went to hug Evie.

"Thanks for coming," Evie said.

"You bet," Gina replied, smiling that famous smile of hers. "I couldn't stay away when you told me about Annabelle. No mother wants to go through this kind of hell, but if she has to, then she should be able to talk to people who understand better than anyone."

"So what's the plan?" her husband asked Dex.

"We're waiting for a call right now," Dex said. "We don't know where he is. He killed an agent in the safe house in Kentucky. We're searching security footage for any identifying plate numbers."

"He's not working alone."

"No, we don't think so either."

Annabelle snapped her gaze to Dex. "He has help?"

"He has to. Attacking the safe house and extracting the hostages took more than one person."

Her belly tightened at the thought. Right now she would give Lyon anything—*anything*—to return her child. But she didn't have what he wanted, and time was running out.

She started to say something but her phone rang. Dex's expression was serious. He nodded. "Answer it, Belle. Keep him on the phone as long as you can."

"Hello?" she said, her voice shaky. She hated that, but there was nothing she could do about it.

"Mrs. Archer—have you made progress?"

She licked suddenly dry lips. "I've managed to get inside Eric's computer—but I don't have the account numbers yet."

Dex had told her to tell Mr. Lyon the truth if he called. For now.

"That's too bad." For the first time, she could hear the barest hint of his accent. She'd thought he had one before, but she'd been too upset by everything he'd said to pay attention. Now she was listening closely—and she heard it.

It was slight but definitely Russian. There was the thickening of the voice during certain vowels, the rolling undertone.

"I need more time. I'll find it."

Her heart performed a drum solo in her chest and her throat was tight. Gina came over and put a hand on her shoulder, squeezing. It was enough to focus her on the task at hand.

"You have three hours. If you don't call me with the numbers, you won't like what happens next."

"If you hurt my daughter or my friend and her daughter, you'll never see a penny of that money." Her words were rapid-fire ammunition. She wanted them to pierce his maddening arrogance.

Mr. Lyon chuckled and her blood turned to ice. "I like a woman with fight in her," he said. "But you've inconvenienced me, Mrs. Archer. You called the FBI, and I don't appreciate that. Now you threaten me when it is I who hold all the cards. Be careful, my dear, or you will have reason to wish you were the one who is dead."

FOURTEEN

"ANYTHING?" DEX ASKED. HE'D LEFT Annabelle with Evie, Gina, and Jack, then rushed back to the secure area where his team was working. The room was a beehive of activity.

Billy looked up from the equipment he was monitoring. His fingers flew over the keyboard. "Yeah, I think so. I've found a file with numbers. I'm tracing them now, hoping for a routing number to a bank. Once I know that, I can start homing in on the account numbers." He snorted. "Eric Archer wasn't an idiot. It's all here, but it's locked down. Took me a while to break the encryption."

The door opened abruptly and someone barked, "Atten-*shun!*"

Everyone shot to their feet as Colonel Mendez stalked into the room.

"As you were," Mendez said, and they went back to work though they kept an eye on the ranking officer in their midst. "Did we get a trace on Leonov?"

Iceman cleared his throat. "No, sir. He didn't stay on long enough. But we did find the cell tower the call went through—it's in New York City, sir."

Mendez did not look happy. "So either he's moved his hostages or he wasn't in Kentucky today and someone else has them." Mendez stood there for a second, nodding his head as if he were thinking to himself. "No, I'm going with the theory he's moved them. Start planning for an extraction. The instant we get any data on his exact location, we need to be prepared to go in. Let me know the second you find that money, Kid," he finished before turning and walking out again.

Dex gaped after him. A HOT mission on US soil? That wasn't typical. They all knew it too. Gazes clashed and jaws dropped.

Richie recovered quicker than the rest of them. "All right, team. You heard the man. Time to get our shit together and prepare to infiltrate enemy territory."

Mendez's secure cell phone rang as he strode down the hall. It was Sam. He answered her with a clipped, "What do you need?"

"Well, my goodness, someone's cranky today," she said in that throaty purr of hers. "You promised me a call when you had Annabelle Archer, Johnny. I haven't heard from you yet."

Mendez rubbed his forehead as he stepped into his office and closed the door. "There were some complications."

Like finding out who the Russian was. That had been a complication for sure. On more than one level.

"Complications?" Sam's voice was cool. It managed to piss him off.

"It happens, Sam," he growled. "Not everything works out the way you expect it to."

"Don't I know that," she grumbled.

She wasn't the only one who'd sacrificed her happiness in the pursuit of this nation's ideals. It was something they all did. Something they had to do because they were driven deep down to uphold everything that mattered in this world.

"You didn't tell me the Russian was Dmitri Leonov."

Sam huffed. "I didn't think it mattered."

His gut twisted. He could almost feel his blood pressure rising. And that was something because he never got rattled. "It matters to me."

Because he knew Leonov. Quite well, in fact. He'd once worked with the man, long ago in what seemed like another life. He'd been young and filled with patriotic fervor. Leonov had been the same, only for Russia. He'd had certain ideas…

"I know he killed Valentina Rostov, or had her killed —but that's the way it worked back then, Johnny. You know that as well as I do."

Mendez hadn't heard that name spoken in years now. He still thought of her, of course—but she was gone forever and he rarely dwelt on the past. Except right now he could see her beautiful face—the cascading red hair that framed it, the piercing blue eyes, the pink lips that he knew were soft and sweet.

"He probably did. So?" It took everything he had to sound as though he wasn't affected by that name. To sound as though he didn't want to split Leonov wide open and eat his motherfucking heart raw.

She blew out a breath. "I thought you had a fling with her during the posting in Moscow. That's what I heard anyway. My mistake."

"It matters because I know Leonov and how he operates. Keeping me in the dark does neither of us any good."

"I'm not keeping you in the dark, Johnny! This isn't one of your operations. It's ours. Hand over Annabelle Archer, and we'll take care of the rest."

Mendez leaned back in his chair and propped his feet on the desk. Over his dead body. "Too late for that, Sammie. Leonov took Ms. Archer's daughter hostage. He also took a friend and her daughter. And that kind of thing is exactly how we get involved. This *is* a HOT operation now."

Annabelle's phone rang after only two hours. Dex nodded for her to pick it up. They'd moved her into the room with his teammates after sanitizing as much classified information as possible. Dex was her escort, which meant she couldn't go anywhere without him. Not even to the bathroom.

But having her with them was important because she was the one communicating with Leonov and they needed to control the conversation. A set of headphones perched on Billy's ears so he could listen to the phone call. Dex grabbed a set off the table and slapped them on.

"Hello?" Annabelle said.

"Mrs. Archer, we speak again." Leonov sounded smug.

"I still have an hour," she told him. They were all aware of how much time was on the clock. Billy had found the bank—a bank in Switzerland—and now he was running account numbers. They were almost there, but not quite.

"I've added some incentive for you."

Annabelle closed her eyes. "I told you, Mr. Lyon—"

"Yes, the mother-bear thing is all very fun, but I haven't hurt your daughter. Or any of my hostages. Yet."

His pause was long in order to spike Annabelle's anxiety. Dex hated the man. If he ever got his hands on him...

"I am very angry with Archer Industries," Leonov continued. "Your product is a sham. It does not work as promised."

"It's still in the testing phase," Annabelle said. "Eric was wrong to tell you it was finished."

He snorted. "Yes, well, it's too late for that. And too late for Archer Industries. Turn on the television, Mrs. Archer. CNN if you please."

She shot Dex a wide-eyed look. Iceman went over and flipped on the television. CNN blared to life. A building burned, the flames licking higher and higher. Fire trucks crammed the site, pumping water into the blaze, but it didn't abate.

Annabelle gasped. "That's Archer Industries!"

"It used to be," Leonov said, chuckling. "Your house is next, Mrs. Archer. And then the houses of your employees—"

"You can't do that!"

"I can. I will. Unless you give me what I want, this will never end. I'll take everything you love—and every*one* as well. Including that handsome military man who rescued you yesterday."

Dex wasn't surprised that Leonov knew he was military. All it meant was that Leonov was too, or had been. Like recognized like. He wasn't worried about the threat. It was meant to rattle Annabelle, but the likelihood of Leonov actually finding him was low. And even if Leonov did, Dex welcomed it. He'd kill the motherfucker and be glad.

Billy looked up and punched a fist in the air. "Got it," he mouthed.

"Goodbye, Mrs. Archer. I'll be in touch."

"No!"

But Leonov was gone.

"I fucking got it," Billy exclaimed. "There are five accounts, not just one. Each account has one hundred million dollars. Holy shit, that's a lot of money."

"We have to give it to him," Annabelle said, her eyes glistening with tears. "I'll call him back and—"

"No, Belle," Dex told her. "We can't do that."

She shot to her feet, her eyes flashing. "Why the hell not? You see what he's capable of. He'll kill my daughter and my best friend and her daughter. He'll raze everything to the ground if he doesn't get what he wants. We *have* to do it."

Dex gripped her by the shoulders. "Honey, if we do that, he'll have no incentive to return the people you love. He *will* kill them and then he'll dump them and you'll never see them again."

"You don't know that—"

"Actually, I think we do," Iceman said. Everyone turned to look at him. He was staring at his computer screen and the map on it. "He's airborne over the Atlantic."

FIFTEEN

"BUT WHAT DOES THAT MEAN?" Annabelle asked the man who'd spoken. He was big with dark hair and tattoos, sitting in front of a computer screen. Hell, they were all big men. Tattoos seemed to be a requirement for the job.

Dex touched her arm and she jerked her attention to him. "It means he's fled the country, Belle. And he didn't go alone."

Drums danced in her chest. Her lungs squeezed. She wanted to scream. Dex folded her hand in his. Didn't take a genius to figure that didn't mean good news.

"You're saying he took Charlotte with him? And Molly and Becca?"

Dex looked grim. "Yes, that's what I'm saying."

Annabelle worked to get air in her lungs. She thought about what Gina had said—about her son Eli being kidnapped and taken to an island in the Caribbean. About how frantic she'd been, and how numb at the same time.

"Trust them," Gina had said. *"They know what they're doing."*

Breathe, Annabelle. Trust. Try to be logical. "So what now?"

"We go after them."

"We have the money," Billy added. "You have negotiating power, Mrs. Archer."

Power. That's what she needed. And strength. She had to be strong if she was going to get through this and find her daughter. Stronger than she'd ever been in her life.

"Please call me Annabelle." She didn't want to be called Mrs. Archer. It made her skin crawl. All she could hear was Lyon's slimy voice saying it.

A man entered the room and everyone snapped upright. Even Dex. He'd let go of her hand. Someone barked, "Attention!"

The man who'd caused all the fuss said, "As you were," and everyone relaxed again. He was tall and handsome with salt-and-pepper hair and a tough look that said he meant business.

This was Agent Gibbs. The man she'd asked Dex if they had in their organization. He looked every bit as competent as the *NCIS* agent. Except that was television and this was real life—she hoped this guy really was as skillful as the fictional character.

"Mrs. Archer," he said, coming over and shaking her hand lightly. She appreciated that he didn't squeeze too hard. Some men thought handshakes were a strength contest.

"Please. Call me Annabelle."

His skin was warm and his grip easy. He was devastatingly handsome. Her pulse throbbed a little hotter and she couldn't think. She wasn't interested in him, but his magnetism short-circuited her brain anyway.

"I'm Colonel Mendez," he said, dropping her hand. "Thank you for coming here today and for helping us find the accounts your husband opened in Switzerland. I know this isn't easy for you."

"No, it's definitely not." It occurred to her that she'd heard a figure mentioned earlier. She'd been thinking of the fact that Mr. Lyon was on a plane, she had no idea where her daughter was, and her company was burning down live on CNN. Billy had said… what? Five accounts. One hundred million in each.

Oh dear God…

"You look pale, Annabelle," Colonel Mendez said. "Would you like to sit?"

"Yes," she breathed.

He ushered her to the chair she'd so recently vacated, and she sank down on it. Then she gazed up into those dark eyes. "Five hundred million dollars—half a billion! How did he manage it? The technology doesn't work—or not yet anyway. Not consistently."

Mendez dropped onto his haunches, bringing him to eye level with her. "I assume you have the research backed up somewhere."

"We do. Marshall—Marshall Porter, he's the lead engineer—was working on some modifications." Her eyes widened. "He's been working late the past few weeks—what if he was there?"

"I've been in contact with the authorities in Briar City. There was no one inside except for security and the janitorial firm. According to your badge reader, every employee had badged out by the time the fire started."

"Was anyone hurt?" She should have asked that first, but she was numb and trying to process everything. Her brain compartmentalized each horror rather than connecting them into one big picture.

"There was an explosion in your laboratory. One of the janitors was injured. He's in stable condition at the local hospital."

"Oh my god." She swallowed. "And he said there would be more—my house, the houses of my employees —"

"We're not going to let that happen." Mendez looked up at someone. "Get a list of employees and alert law enforcement."

"Yes, sir."

Mendez turned the force of his attention on her again. Her belly squeezed tight. "Annabelle, what else do you know about Helios?"

She had to clear her throat. "Not much. Marshall and Eric spent a lot of time on it. They'd made progress, but it wasn't working as planned yet."

"It must have worked enough to sell a prototype."

She nodded. "It probably did, so long as the buyer didn't test it extensively. But it wasn't consistent. Any hard field tests and it would have failed."

"Tell me, how much did the project depend on each man's contributions?"

"Eric was a decent engineer, but not a genius. Marshall is. Without him, there would be nothing." She lowered her gaze for a moment. "But Eric took all the credit. Marshall is socially awkward, so he didn't mind. The arrangement worked. Eric was dynamic. He could talk to people, get them to invest. But he couldn't build the technology without Marshall."

Colonel Mendez rose and she tilted her head up. "Thank you for your help, Annabelle. With this information, we'll be able to figure out how to rescue your daughter and your friends."

She could only nod and pray he was right.

Her phone rang at the precise moment the last hour was up. Annabelle answered, knowing who would be on the other end of the line.

"Did you find my money?"

She'd been told what to say to him. "Yes. I have the account numbers now."

"Then you will transmit the money to me and I will release your child along with the others."

"How do I know you'll do that?" Her stomach clenched into a fist, her pulse hammered, and her throat was tight. Her skin prickled with heat. She hated confrontation. Always had. She'd rather hide—but she couldn't, not when so much was at stake.

"Because I will kill them if you do not."

"If you kill them, you'll never get the money."

He was silent for a moment. "So we are at an impasse. What do you propose?"

"An exchange. When I see their faces and hug them, I'll have my people transmit the money."

He chuckled. "Well, well, Mrs. Archer has found her spine. But how do I know you have the money?"

"Five hundred million. It's a lot of money."

"It is indeed. Your husband could have told you that, however."

"He could have—but he didn't. The money's in Switzerland."

"Is it? Very well, we shall do an exchange. I do hope you enjoy traveling, Mrs. Archer. It will be a long trip."

"That's fine."

"Then I will be in touch with instructions. But be aware, if you are lying to me—if you hope to fool me into handing over your loved ones and you do not deliver as promised—I'll kill them one by one while you watch. And then I'll kill you."

The call ended and Annabelle sagged, her body vibrating with a cocktail of fear, rage, and revulsion. Dex was at her side, ripping off the headphones he wore.

He squeezed her shoulder. "You did a good job."

"Stellar job," Matt Girard added. "That's exactly what we wanted to happen."

"He doesn't really plan on letting them go, does he?" There had been something about his voice, something about how casually he did things like burn her company and threaten to burn houses, that told her he lacked empathy. He wanted the money, but he also wanted to kill.

"It doesn't matter what he intends," Dex said. "We don't plan based on his intentions. We plan based on the worst-case scenario. So, yeah, we're going to plan for a situation in which he intends to kill them. But we aren't letting it get that far."

She didn't know if he could deliver or not, but she had to believe in him—in all of them—or go mad. She reached for his hand, tangling her fingers in his. "Thank you."

It was a small gesture, but it felt right. For once, he didn't seem to mind the contact. He squeezed her fingers in return.

It was another hour before they wound everything up. The team packed up their equipment.

Matt said to Dex, "Take her home for a few hours. We'll get everything squared away here. We've got his signal so we can track where he ends up whenever he pings into a cell tower."

"What if he calls again?" Annabelle asked, scrubbing her hands over the goose bumps taking up residence on her arms.

"They'll be able to listen in," Dex reassured her. "Your phone is linked into the system now. Doesn't matter where you are when he calls. Same thing if he calls mine."

It took a few minutes to wrap everything up, but they finally exited the building and walked out to his truck. The night air was chilly and she shivered. It had been a long damn day, and her jaw cracked as she yawned.

Dex opened her door and she got inside. He went around and started the truck, then they backed out of the space and drove a short distance to a group of three-story buildings with stairwells on either end. Annabelle frowned.

"Where are we?" she asked when he turned off the truck.

"Home."

"But we didn't leave the base."

"No, I live in the dorms." He shrugged. "It's an option. Some of the guys do, some don't. I didn't intend to stay, but I've also never worked too hard to find a place off base."

"Am I staying with you?"

He nodded. "It's like a small apartment. There's a living room with a foldout sofa and a kitchenette in addition to the bedroom and bath. It'll be fine. Unless you prefer we go to a hotel."

"No, this is fine." They'd already stayed overnight in a cabin together. What was a night in a dorm? It would be like college all over again—except there she hadn't had a living room or a kitchenette. Or a bath, come to think of it. That had been down the hall.

They walked to the first building and she followed Dex inside. He stopped halfway down the hall and inserted a key in a lock. Music thumped from somewhere, but it dialed down considerably when they stepped inside his room and he shut the door. He flicked on a light switch and she took in the place.

Small, yes. Neat—spartan, actually. A television, a magazine on the table, some speakers, a couple of books, a laptop. The kitchenette was between the living room and bedroom. It was galley style with a stove, fridge, and a few cabinets.

She didn't know what the bedroom looked like because the door was shut. Dex went over and opened it.

"Unfortunately, the bathroom is through here, so the bedroom door will have to stay open."

"That's not a problem for me."

"I just didn't want you getting inside and locking it on me."

She blinked. "Oh—no, of course not. But I'll be on the couch, so it's fine."

"You can have the bed. I'll take the couch."

"Dex, really, it's not necessary."

"Belle, you've had a helluva shitty day. You need to rest. At some point in the next few hours, we're boarding a plane and heading for God knows where in pursuit of that fucking nutjob. As much as I don't want you along, you're going. We need you close because this fucker is too smart and he'll know if you aren't there."

Despair and weariness washed over her. "Do you mind—could I just take a shower, please?"

"Yeah, sure." He led her through the bedroom and into the bathroom. Good thing she'd wanted a shower because there was no tub. But the bathroom was spacious with white tiles and white towels, and the shower was large and glassed in. "It's not fancy," he said. "But the water gets hot quick."

"Thanks." She stood there, not knowing what else to say or do. It was as if her mind had stopped working. Just shut down and couldn't come up with a word or an action.

Dex backed out and pulled the door with him. "Let me know if you need anything. I'll be here."

It took her a long minute before she was able to move, before the idea taking a shower kicked in, and she reached in to turn on the tap. She shed her clothes and stepped under the spray. Warmth seeped beneath her skin.

Her heart hurt and numbness hung over her like a blanket. She groped for whatever bottles Dex had and found a two-in-one shampoo/conditioner. She washed her hair and then used the same stuff to wash her body.

But she didn't get out straight away. She let the water flow over her, let it wash away her fear. Except it didn't work. Nothing could warm that cold pit inside her that wouldn't go away.

She started to shake. Then she sank down on the floor as the tears she'd been holding in broke free. Vaguely, she heard the door open. The water shut off, and then strong hands lifted her, wrapped her in a towel, cradled her against Dex's chest as he strode from the bath and laid her on the bed.

He grabbed another towel and worked to dry her exposed skin, his touch sure and clinical. She didn't even care that he'd seen her naked. No man had seen her in so long she couldn't even remember what it felt like to be a woman.

Maybe, with Dex, she could.

She wrapped her fingers around his wrist and he stilled. "Stay with me, Dex. Please stay."

SIXTEEN

NOW THAT HE HAD HER in his arms, Dex was trying very hard not to look at Annabelle's body. He'd heard her crying in the shower—sobbing, actually—and he'd acted. Didn't matter that she'd ripped his heart from his chest five years ago. He couldn't listen to her sob when he knew what she was going through.

She was a mother, and her child had been ripped away. Right now, she was hurting more than he'd ever been hurt. He was rational enough to realize that.

"Belle," he said, his voice raspy with emotion. "I'm not going anywhere."

He tucked the towel over her body, hiding her from view. Then he took the second towel he'd grabbed and wrapped it around her wet hair. Her blue eyes were wide and wounded. She'd pushed herself upright to lean against his headboard. His gut clenched as she met his gaze.

"I don't want to be alone," she said. "I… I think when I'm alone."

He carefully rubbed the strands of her hair between the folds of the towel, removing as much extra moisture as he could. He'd have to find a comb next.

"You aren't alone," he said gruffly. "I told you I'm not leaving."

"Will you stay in here with me? At least until I fall asleep?"

God, what she was asking him to do. And yet he would. No matter how much he liked to tell himself he hated this woman, he didn't. She still meant something to him, though not the way she once had.

He cared because he'd known her since she was a little girl in pigtails. He'd picked her up when she'd fallen before, and he'd bandaged scrapes when no one else was around to do it for her or Katie. Later, he'd loved her with all his heart and done his best to make a life for them.

"I'll sit with you until you sleep." He stood and went to find her comb. When he returned, he started working the teeth through her hair, untangling knots and smoothing the blond hair straight.

She was still wrapped in the towel he'd put around her in the shower. It wasn't a huge towel, so consequently he could see a lot of leg and the creamy swells of her breasts. He tried not to think about her pink nipples or the shadow between her thighs. He'd seen it all when he'd put her on the bed and started to dry her more thoroughly.

Maybe he should have left her in the bathroom with the towel around her and let her take care of it herself, but he didn't think it would have worked. She'd been numb when he'd dragged her from the shower.

She sniffled. Redness rimmed her puffy eyes. *Dammit.*

"What was Eric going to do with half a billion dollars?"

He wasn't sure if she was talking to him or to herself, but he answered anyway. "He could have disappeared with money like that. Bought an island. Laid in the sun and sipped umbrella drinks for the rest of his life."

"But that's not the way Eric was. He needed attention. He needed people to exclaim over his brilliance. He could never disappear. There would be no one to feed his ego."

He knew enough of Eric to know that was true. "What about Porter? Could they have been planning to split the money?"

Annabelle frowned. Then she shook her head. "No. Marshall is a scientist. He'd care far more about the accolades from his peers. Of course, he was getting a bonus—a pretty big one—once the technology worked as planned."

"Just a bonus, huh?"

She turned her gaze to him. "He works for Archer Industries. All our employees sign paperwork that states they aren't allowed to file patents for anything they work on. It's standard procedure in the industry. He works for the company, so the company gets the patent."

Yes, it often was standard procedure since the company supplied the laboratory and paid people for their work, but it could also create hard feelings. If what Annabelle had said about Marshall Porter being the brains of the Helios project was true, it was entirely possible he was angry about not owning the rights to exploit the technology for himself. It was clearly very valuable.

Dex made a note to call his team and ask them to find out what kind of information existed on Marshall Porter. It might be nothing, but they had to follow all angles. So far as he knew, Porter was still in Briar City. He hadn't been in the laboratory when it exploded, so he was certainly somewhere.

Could he have known about the money? If he had, did he know that Eric had gotten it or did he think because Eric died in Africa that he hadn't been successful?

Dex finished combing Annabelle's hair and took the towel in to hang it over the rack. When he returned, she'd slipped beneath the covers and the other towel dangled from her fingers. He hung that one in the bathroom as well.

He tried not to think about the fact she was naked in his bed, but he wasn't doing a good job of forgetting. His balls tingled with the beginnings of arousal. If he didn't shut this down, he'd be sporting a woody in about twenty seconds.

He stared down at her, hands on hips, brain rolling with a million thoughts. "You said Eric wouldn't agree to a divorce. Why?"

Frown lines appeared on her forehead. "Control, I think. If he divorced me, I'd be free to go back to you."

"If you despised him so much, why didn't you leave anyway?"

"Charlotte. He threatened me with a custody fight."

Asshole. "So you stayed and slept in separate bedrooms. And you didn't know about the money."

She shook her head. "Not at all. I don't know what he intended to do with it, but I'm convinced he wasn't going to disappear. Buy a bigger house, a better car, more and fancier toys probably. He wanted to be a billionaire. Maybe he thought that was a good start."

Dex snorted. "Half a billion is a very good start."

She closed her eyes and rolled her head against the pillow. "All I wanted was security for my daughter. And I've managed to fail spectacularly at that."

He dropped to a sitting position beside her, squeezed her fingers in his. "You didn't fail. Eric failed the two of you. He got into this trouble and he dragged you with him. It's not your fault."

Her lower lip trembled. "I miss her, Dex. She must be so scared."

He lifted her hand to his mouth, pressed his lips to her smooth skin. It was a bad move since it sent a shudder of longing rolling through him. "She has Molly and Becca. Now, I don't know your friend, but I bet she's doing a fine job of distracting those kids from what's going on."

He hoped it was true. He'd been on missions where hostages simply fell apart. People who seemed strong in everyday life couldn't cope when faced with life-threatening danger. Not that he blamed them or didn't understand. He did. He just prayed like hell that Molly Carter was one of the strong ones.

Annabelle nodded. "Molly's amazing. She's one of the best people I know."

"That's good, Belle. Think positive thoughts."

"I'm trying to... Dex, can I ask you something?"

"Yeah, sure."

"Will you kiss me?"

Annabelle knew he wasn't going to like that request, but it was the only way she could think of to get her mind into another place. Not that she was likely to forget what was happening, because she wasn't, but a kiss from Dex had always had the power to consume her before. Would it still have that power? Would she feel more confident, more settled, if he kissed her?

He was staring at her with a hard expression. His T-shirt clung to his muscles like a lover. It had gotten wet when he'd picked her up, and now it left nothing to the imagination. Heat flashed in his eyes.

But was it the heat of anger or of desire?

She had no right to ask him to kiss her. But it seemed necessary somehow. Like she was a leaf whipping in the wind and the only way to anchor her was a kiss.

"I don't think that's a good idea," he growled.

A sharp pain jabbed her heart. Of course he wasn't going to kiss her.

"I understand."

"I don't think you do." He skimmed a finger along her cheek. "It's not that I don't want to. It's not that I hate you so much I can't bear to touch you again. I want it too much. A kiss won't be enough for me. If I kiss you, Anna-belle, I'm gonna want to bury myself inside you. But not before I've kissed every inch of your body. Not before I've spread you open and licked your sweetness until you come so hard you see stars. You're naked in my bed, and all I want is to join you there even though you're hurting and scared. All I can think about is your slick heat and the way you feel wrapped around me. That's not fair to you right now. It's not what you need from me."

Her body went nuclear. Her nipples budded so tight they ached. She was wet and hot and aroused. It had been ages since she'd been touched—and even longer since she'd enjoyed it. Five long years. She hadn't wanted a man since the last time Dex had made love to her.

Maybe he was right. Maybe now wasn't the time. She was confused and scared. She felt so damned helpless. But Dex was here, and she had an urgent need to do whatever it took to distract herself from the pain.

She didn't care about consequences.

"Maybe it's exactly what I need."

He closed his eyes. "No, honey. No. It's not right."

She surged up and pressed her lips to his before he knew what she was about. He stiffened—and then his mouth dropped open and his tongue tangled with hers. She wrapped her arms around his neck, trying to drag her body closer to his. The covers slipped down her torso, exposing her breasts to the air. Her core throbbed with heat and silky need.

The kiss was desperate and hot. Her pulse pounded in her throat, her temples. She expected him to pull away at any second. Instead, he pushed her back on the bed, his body covering hers, pressing her into the mattress. The covers were a barrier between them, but that didn't stop her from trying to rock her hips upward.

His hands ran along her arms. Gently, he pried them from his neck. She thought he would push her away, but he trapped her wrists in one big hand and pushed them against the headboard. Molten desire surged in her blood, immolating her inhibitions. She bucked upward, but he was maddeningly in control and withholding what she wanted.

He broke the kiss and stared down at her, his dark eyes troubled. "You have to know, Belle, this isn't going to rekindle anything between us. If you're thinking we're going to fall in love again and take up where we left off, we aren't."

Disappointment galloped into her soul. "Did I say that?"

"No, but you're upset and hurting. If I were any other man, would you kiss me right now?"

"No. But you aren't any other man. You're Dex Davidson, and I trust you." She sucked in a breath. "Yes, I'm upset. I don't know what to do—but I know I need to *feel* something. I need you to make me feel like there's hope, like someone in this world cares for me, even if it's not really true."

Ice crusted inside the walls of her heart. She needed warmth and he was the only one who could give it to her. If they didn't have a history, if he were a stranger to her, then no, she wouldn't want this. It was more than sex with him. It was comfort.

He sighed. "I can't," he said softly.

She pushed her hips against his. The steel in his pants told another story. "Can't? Or won't?"

"Won't. You married Eric, Belle. You had reasons, I get that, but you threw what we had away and you ended up with him. When I imagine you with him... Shit, it still pisses me off to think of him touching you. Of you letting him do the things I did."

The unfairness boiled over inside her, frothing and spilling into a sizzling mess. He had no idea. *No idea!*

"Let him? Jesus Christ, Dex, I didn't *let* him do anything! Eric raped me."

SEVENTEEN

DEX FROZE. HE WAS IN the process of lifting himself off her when her words hit him. He went utterly rigid.

What the fuck?

His vision went dark. Hot rage cascaded over the rocks of his disbelief. "What did you say?"

Her body sagged beneath him. He let her wrists go and managed to push himself to a sitting position against the headboard. She jerked the covers up and sat beside him.

"I said he raped me." She expelled a hot breath. "He came over a couple of nights after I was supposed to marry you. My parents left so we could be alone." Her bitter laugh just about broke his heart. "To talk about the wedding, for fuck's sake. I begged him to let me go and not hurt my dad, but he wouldn't hear of it. He said if I didn't marry him, my parents would lose everything and my dad would go to jail. And then he... he told me to strip or the deal was off. What choice did I have?"

What choice did she have? Jesus fuck, if Eric Archer were alive today, he'd only *wish* he'd been torn apart by

138

lions. Because Dex would destroy him as slowly and painfully as possible.

"What happened then?" He needed to know. His heart was a bruised thing in his chest, and his blood was hot with helpless fury. For her. For what she'd gone through.

"He raped me. I didn't fight him, so I wondered for the longest time if it was really rape. But it *was* rape because I didn't want it. Because he shoved himself inside me without any care. Because he—he tore things and I bled." She made a strangled noise in her throat. "Just a few nights before that, I'd been with you. I thought of you the whole time, but it didn't help—because I knew you were lost and never coming back."

Rage hammered in his temples. Dex wanted to hit things. Throw things. Kill a dead man. He wanted to take her in his arms and tell her he was sorry, and then he wanted to make everything right again. But how the fuck was he going to do that? She'd suffered, and he'd been off nursing a broken heart and feeling sorry for himself.

How had he not realized something had to be terribly wrong for her to leave him the way she had? From the first moment he'd kissed her in the hallway of his house, Dex and Annabelle had been right together. Meant to be. And it all fucking fell apart because of her parents and Eric.

Dex dropped his head in his hands and dragged air into his lungs, trying to keep himself from exploding. Trying to find the calm he typically had on a mission. The stillness that was utterly necessary to a sniper.

He couldn't. Instead, he found a pit of despair and anger. Hot tears pressed against his eyelids. He never cried. Fucking never. But one spilled over and dropped down his cheek. It wasn't for him. It was for her. For what she'd gone through with Eric Archer.

He reached for her with one arm, dragged her into the circle of his embrace, and buried his face against her hair.

"I'm sorry, Belle. Sorry for not being there."

She slipped an arm over his torso and hugged him tight. Tears vibrated in her voice. "It's not your fault. I should have told you what was happening. I should have been braver and told you the truth about why I couldn't marry you."

He crushed her to him. "Yeah, I wish you'd told me. But I think you were brave, Belle. You sacrificed your happiness to save someone else. You did what you thought was right." He pulled in a breath to steady himself. "I'd kill Eric if he wasn't already dead. It's a good fucking thing we aren't still in Briar City because I'd be kicking your dad's ass. I still might."

He had a vision of punching Jerry Quinn's lights out. It was a satisfying thought.

"As much as I think he deserves it, he's still my dad. And Charlotte's granddad, so no, I can't let you do that."

"You deserved better than what they did to you."

"I know. But my parents don't know what Eric did, or what he was like. I never told them what happened."

Of course she hadn't. They wouldn't have wanted to know. Once their miserable lives were back on track and they didn't have to worry about Eric holding Jerry's embezzlement over his head, they'd have gone about their lives like everything was perfectly normal. Even if they'd had any inkling that their daughter was unhappy or abused, they'd have shrugged it off and pretended it didn't exist. Because that's the kind of fuckwads they were.

"Do you hate them?"

Because right now he did.

She was quiet for a long minute. "I should. But hate is a hard thing to live with. I hated Eric. That's enough for me. My parents... Well, I'm mad at them. Still. But they actually love Charlotte, and they're good to her. I shudder to think of them becoming her guardians if something were to happen to me—"

The words choked off, and he knew she was thinking about her child being held hostage by Dmitri Leonov. Not that she knew Leonov's real name. It was safest for her to think of him as Mr. Lyon. She couldn't let his name slip if she didn't know it, so his team had made a conscious decision not to tell her.

He put his other arm around her and hugged her. "Don't think about it, Belle. We'll get her back. Lyon wants the money more than he wants anything else. He'll keep her safe so long as he doesn't have what he wants."

She clung to him. "I just can't bear the thought of her being scared or thinking I've abandoned her."

"I know, honey. I know."

"When I came to your dad's farm yesterday... I had no idea it would turn out like this. I keep thinking I should have gone and picked her up from preschool myself. Then she'd be with us right now."

Dex pictured the car sitting outside her house yesterday. "No, I don't think so. He'd have grabbed you both before you ever had a chance to find out where the money was. And when you couldn't produce it, he'd have probably used your daughter against you."

She shuddered. "You're saying she'd be dead."

"It's possible, yes."

"Oh God—how are we going to stop him? How will we get her and Molly and Becca back?"

"You have to trust me and my team. This is what we do. We do it often enough that we aren't afraid of failing. We'll be where he thinks we can't be, and we'll do what he thinks can't be done."

She seemed to melt just a little. He knew she wasn't going to be at complete ease until she had Charlotte in her arms again, but this was a start. He pictured the photo Annabelle had shown him. Red hair, blue eyes, freckles. So much like Annabelle when she'd been young, other than the red hair. Eric had been olive-skinned with dark brown hair. Whatever the girl had gotten from him wasn't immediately apparent, but Dex had seen plenty of kids who didn't look like their parents. Or maybe he was just bad at spotting the resemblance.

"Are you okay?" she asked, and it kinda stunned him that she was thinking of him when she had so much to think about.

"Yeah," he said gruffly.

"I'm sorry I threw all that at you. I've only ever told Molly."

He closed his eyes. They were still wet, but he'd managed to stop the tears from turning into a flood. Thank God. Last fucking thing he needed was to sob like a drunk at a funeral.

"Belle," he said, and his throat tightened. He forced the words out anyway. "Don't apologize. I needed to know."

"I know you don't love me anymore. I know too much has happened to change that. I just… I'd like it if we could be friends again. Is that possible?"

He rubbed his cheek against her hair. She smelled like his shampoo, and a flood of warmth washed over him.

"Yeah, I think we can."

Annabelle needed more, but she couldn't ask Dex for what she really wanted. Not yet. Maybe never. And really, was it possible to get back what they'd had?

Her heart said it was. Her heart said that she'd never stopped loving him, that being in his arms right now, even if it was just for comfort, made her realize how much she still wanted him in her life.

What she really wanted was to rewind the clock and go back five years. She wanted to make a different choice. She wanted to drive up to the church, even if it was all by herself, and walk down that aisle where he was waiting for her.

But what about Charlotte? What if that choice meant she wouldn't have her daughter?

Annabelle closed her eyes. She knew what she would do—she would make the same choice she'd made the first time. She'd leave Dex and go to Eric if it meant she got her baby girl.

A wave of despair hit her. Despair for her daughter and for the man she still loved. At the same time, a fierce voice blossomed to life inside her.

You know the truth deep down, Annabelle. You've just never wanted to admit it. Charlotte is Dex's daughter. No way could she be Eric's. Because you never got pregnant again.

She shook that voice away. She *didn't* know it was true. She only wanted it to be true. Wanted it so badly that she was trying to rationalize it in her mind. There were a lot of reasons a woman could get pregnant one time only. Just because Eric never managed to make her pregnant again didn't mean Charlotte wasn't his.

She couldn't go there right now, and she couldn't take Dex there either. It wasn't fair to him, not when her baby girl was in danger and he needed to have his head on straight in order to get Charlotte back.

She believed him when he said he would. She had to believe him or she would go mad.

Dex ran a hand over her hair, and her skin tingled in response. The hair on the back of her neck stood up in a good way. She liked him touching her. Liked it so much. She'd thought she'd never want a man to touch her again. Eric had only ever touched her for selfish reasons. Yes, he'd raped her the first time—and maybe the next three or four times. But eventually she'd accepted his advances because there was no other choice. Was it still rape if she opened her legs and pretended to get off so he'd get it over with?

She didn't know and she didn't have time to obsess about it. That was past. This was now. She turned her face into Dex's chest and sighed. His shirt was still wet, but she didn't want to let him go.

Desire began to buzz in her veins again. Her nipples tightened and her body grew languid as syrupy heat sank into her bones.

"You should sleep, Annabelle," Dex said. "We'll know where Lyon is soon and we'll have to be on our way. Can't promise you'll get any rest on the trip."

"I can't sleep, Dex. Not now."

Not as hot as she was. Not as needy. How was it possible to be so damned horny when her life was falling apart around her ears? She ran a hand up his chest, cupped his jaw. He turned his face into her hand, and she felt something wet. For a second she thought maybe it was water from her shower, but he'd dried her off. Her hair was damp but not drenched. He shouldn't have moisture on his cheek and yet he did.

"Are you crying?" she whispered, her heart in her throat. It beat so hard it hurt. "For me?"

"I'm pissed," he said roughly. "Pissed and so fucking sorry I can't choke the life from Eric's worthless body. I'm sorry he hurt you."

She pushed herself upright with a cry, kneeling beside him. Then she took his face in both her hands and kissed the salty wetness from his cheeks. He wasn't sobbing, wasn't leaking tears like she did when she was particularly hormonal, but he'd shed a tear or two—and they were for her. It made her ache and made the love in her heart swell until she thought it would burst through her chest.

It was dangerous to love Dex Davidson, to go out on that limb that could collapse beneath her at any moment, but she didn't much care.

"Dex. Oh, Dex."

The covers slipped off her again, exposing her naked skin to the air. And to his gaze. The room was dim since the only light came from the living room, but it was enough to illuminate her body.

His eyes dipped to her chest, to her breasts that sat up all perky-like and practically begged him to touch. He made the visual journey down her torso, down to the apex of her thighs. The sheet still covered her there, but barely. She was wet and hot and achy—and she wanted him to touch her. Right there.

Right. Damn. *There*.

"Belle," he said softly, his gaze rising to hers again. "What are you doing to me?"

"I hope the same thing you're doing to me." She took his hand and brought it to her breast. Fire flowed beneath her skin, lighting up her nerve endings with sizzle and flash. He didn't pull away.

Instead, he tested the weight of her flesh—and then his thumb ghosted over her nipple and she gasped.

"I have to be honest," he told her, and she shuddered as his thumb kept up a light teasing rhythm. "We're different people now—and I don't know what's right and what's wrong anymore. With you, I mean."

She knew what he was saying. "We used to run the gamut, didn't we? From tender and sweet to hard and fast and rough. You're wondering which of those is off-limits."

"Yeah."

She couldn't possibly love him more for caring. For thinking about it.

"I think, with you, anything is possible," she said truthfully. "But it's been a long time, so maybe not rough in this instance."

He put both broad hands around her waist and brought her body closer, her nipple to his mouth. She braced her hands against his shoulders and whimpered as the fire engulfed her. It felt so good. So right. She'd thought she was dead inside—but she wasn't. Not with Dex.

She was alive and vibrant. Filled with emotion and a desperate kind of need.

He licked her nipple thoroughly, then sucked it between his lips, nibbling the tight flesh as goose bumps rolled down her spine like a shock wave. She wanted to scream and beg. He popped the tight flesh from his mouth and blew cool air over its glistening tip. She didn't think it was possible for her nipple to bead any tighter, but it did. There was an answering ache in her pussy, a flood of wetness and heat and urgent yearning.

"How long?"

She had trouble focusing her thoughts. "What?"

"How long has it been?"

She dug her fingers into his shoulders as he dropped a finger down the center of her body. He skimmed through her curls, but he didn't touch her where she most wanted.

"How long, Belle?"

"Two years."

He stilled. "Two years? Seriously?"

She nodded. It hadn't been long enough for her. "Eric's interests moved on. He had an affair with his secretary for a while. I don't know who he was with for the past several months. I didn't care."

"Jesus."

"It was about ownership, Dex. It was never about me."

He gathered her to him and pressed openmouthed kisses to her shoulders, the curve of her breasts, before sucking the nipple he'd neglected into his mouth.

Annabelle arched her back. The ends of her hair tickled the curve of her buttocks, and she suddenly felt something she'd not felt in years.

Sensual. Desired. Wanted.

Dex pushed her back on the bed until she was beneath him, her head at the foot of the bed. He lifted himself on strong arms above her, then reached over his head with one hand and dragged his shirt off. It disappeared onto the floor, and then he glided down her body, licking and kissing a path toward the place that burned for him.

When he knelt between her legs, her heart lodged in her throat. His eyes burned as he met her gaze. His expression was filled with pain and determination at the same time.

"He wasn't fit to lick your boots, baby. The man was evil, and a fool. I'm sorry for what you went through."

"I know you are."

He lifted one of her legs into the air, kissed her ankle. She closed her eyes and gathered fistfuls of covers in preparation. Because when he touched her, when Dex finally sank his tongue into the heart of her, she was going to explode.

He took his time getting there. He worked his way down her calf, up her inner thigh as he pushed her open. Then he curled her leg around his neck and settled above her, sliding his fingers into her slick folds.

"I've dreamed of this," he said, and she opened her eyes to find him looking at her with that hot, hungry gaze. "Of you."

Her heart felt as if he'd ripped it from her chest with those words. "Dex," she choked out, because it was all she could say.

He lowered his head and swiped his tongue along her wet seam. Annabelle cried out as if she'd been touched with a hot brand. Every nerve ending she had was concentrated right there in the center of her. Her clitoris swelled almost painfully, her juices ran, and her breath came out in pants as she waited.

And then, mercifully, he licked her where she wanted him. Her body came alive with sensation. It was as if she'd only been existing in black and white but now the world was in color. Full, beautiful color that almost hurt to look at because it was so bright and perfect.

"Belle," he said against her hot flesh, "you still taste as sweet as I remember."

"Dex—oh my god, Dex." She lifted herself and grabbed his head, held him to her as he lashed her with his tongue again and again.

Pleasure built to a crest inside her, rising higher and higher until she thought it couldn't get any better. Until she thought surely she would crash over the edge and splinter apart.

But Dex knew how to work her body. He'd always known. He let her go higher, and then he backed off just enough to stop the headlong rush into oblivion. He slipped a finger into her body, worked her just enough to distract her from the main event.

"Dex!"

"Patience, Belle," he growled—and then he attacked again, taking her so high she could see the stars.

"Please," she begged. "Please."

This time, he let her fall. Annabelle couldn't stop the scream that erupted from her throat. It had been so long, so damn long, and she'd never expected to feel this way again. Never expected to be with Dex, with the man she loved, as she tumbled over the edge and came apart.

Her orgasm was long and perfect and shattering. Her toes tingled. Her legs trembled. And Dex didn't stop making her come until she was completely wrung out.

She was still panting when he lifted himself off her and stood. She looked at him through a haze of pleasure, reached for him, tangled her fingers with his.

"Don't go," she said.

His fingers flicked open the button on his jeans. "Go? Baby, I'm just getting started."

EIGHTEEN

MAYBE IT WAS SELFISH OF him, maybe he should back off and let her rest now that he'd made her come. Because he didn't doubt she'd be able to fall asleep after an orgasm like that.

But holy shit, he was so fucking hard he might explode if he didn't do something about it. And jerking off in the shower did not appeal.

He wanted to slide into her body and take them both to the edge. Repeatedly. He craved it in a way he hadn't craved anything in years. He'd been with other women, and it had been exciting and passionate and hot.

But he'd never felt this deep drumbeat of need in his soul, this driving, all-consuming desire to possess another woman's body and make a mark on her soul.

He felt that with Annabelle. And he shouldn't. Too much time had passed, too many hurts had happened—but here he was, needing her so much that the pain was physical as well as mental. The only cure was to fuck her hard and deep and long.

Annabelle came to him on her knees, reaching for his zipper. He let her slide it down, let her push his jeans over his hips until he could kick them off. His cock rose up tall and proud, and she made a noise he took to be appreciation.

Then her hands closed around him, and he hissed in a breath as the nerves in his body flared to painful life. Not that they hadn't already been alive, but there was something about her touch that made it that much more intense.

She gripped him in both hands and tilted her gaze up to his. He knew what she wanted to do. He shouldn't let it happen, and yet when she bent and swirled her tongue around the head of his cock, he didn't stop her.

He speared his fingers into her lush blond hair and held on. "Belle," he grated. "Jesus."

She moaned as she opened her mouth. Her fingers dug into his hips as she pulled him into her. She took more of him than he thought she would, and his dick jerked in response. The pleasure, the insane heat, the liquid fire rolling through his veins—it was almost too much.

When she cupped his balls, a chain reaction lit up the circuits in his body. It was all hands on deck in two seconds if he didn't put a stop to it. He stiffened, marshaling his iron strength to stay in control. When he was reasonably sure he wasn't going to blow, he eased her away.

"I wasn't finished," she said breathlessly.

"I almost was, baby."

She giggled, and the sound curled around his heart. Happiness fizzed in his veins like champagne bubbles. *Not* what he needed right now.

"Well, we can't have that," she said. "Not yet anyway."

"No, not yet." He jerked open the bedside table and found a pack of condoms. He tore one off and sheathed himself. "You sure about this, Belle?"

She'd propped herself on her elbows. Her legs dropped open. Her pussy was pink and slick, and he nearly groaned at the delights waiting for him within those magic walls.

"Yes. I'm sure."

He thought about tugging her to the edge of the bed, pushing her legs together and back until her ass was in the air. She'd be tight and the pressure would be exquisite. But it was also rougher than she needed right now.

He put a knee on the bed and sank between her legs, rolling his hand from her knee up to her wet center. When he touched her clit, she gasped.

He took his time sliding into her because it had been two years and she needed the consideration, but the urge to go faster drummed in his blood. Somehow he managed to ease into her until they were joined completely.

"You okay?"

"Yes," she gasped out. Her legs wrapped around him, her heels digging in as she arched her hips up to meet him. Her fingers pressed into his back, her nails biting sharply and sweetly at the same time.

"I never thought—" He couldn't finish the sentence. He'd never thought he'd be with her like this again. Never thought he wanted to. And he couldn't say the words because he was realizing how untrue they were—he did want to. He *had* wanted to.

"Me either."

He dropped his mouth to hers, tried to kiss her lightly and softly, but he should have known better. It was like setting a match to gasoline. Passion and lust ignited as their mouths met. Tongues tangled together frantically—and his body began to move.

He pulled his hips back, withdrawing almost to the tip, and then slammed deep inside her. She raked her nails down his back, her legs tightening around him, her body rising up to meet his.

It was every bit as good as it had ever been. Sex with Annabelle was different than sex with any other woman. They'd always had an explosive chemistry. From the first moment they'd touched, all the way up to the last, the passion had been off the charts. He'd thought that was because they were in love. He'd been wrong. He didn't love her anymore, and it was still radioactive between them.

He desired her. Obviously. Felt more for her than he liked, but that was to be expected since they'd known each other most of their lives and shared a tangled history.

His body was on fire in a way it hadn't been in years. Fire rolled and flared and rolled again. His brain beat with the command to take her, take her, take her. He pushed his hips into the cleft of her body again and again, the tempo rising as they strained toward the peak.

Her head dropped back, her body stiffening. The walls of her sex gripped him hard, pulsing as he thrust into her tight, wet heat.

His body was primed to explode, stars beginning to burst behind his eyelids—and then he let go, thrusting deep one last time. His climax slammed into his balls and splintered him apart at the same time.

Oblivion.

It took time to come back from that kind of sensual detonation. Annabelle's limbs were foreign objects she couldn't control no matter how many times she sent the signal for them to move.

Limp, languid, satisfied.

Dex pressed her into the mattress, his body quivering deep inside hers, his neck taut, the muscles corded as he poured himself into her with a groan. When he finally stirred, it was to move off her. He levered up out of the bed.

Cool air caressed her body. She hadn't realized they'd gotten so hot, or that the moisture on her skin was sweat. Just a few minutes ago, it had been dampness from the shower.

She heard him moving in the bathroom. Removing the condom, disposing of it. Like so many times before. Until she'd gotten onto the pill and they'd finally been able to make love with nothing between them. She'd been on the pill when she'd gotten pregnant. She'd had a course of antibiotics for a sinus infection a couple of weeks before Dex returned home for the wedding. She hadn't known that antibiotics could affect the pill, though it had probably been in the literature she'd gotten from the pharmacist.

It was yet another reason why she couldn't be sure if Charlotte belonged to Dex or Eric—it had all happened around the same time. Later, when she'd been married to

Eric, he'd flushed her birth control pills and torn up her prescription. She had not gotten pregnant again, something for which she was very thankful. Eric had not been a very attentive father to Charlotte. She didn't expect he would have been any better with another child.

Dex strolled out of the bathroom and stopped. His hands went to his hips as if he was thinking about something. She still lay at the foot of the bed. She needed to turn around and climb under the covers so she could see him better. Somehow she managed to make her body obey this time.

"You all right?" she asked as she slipped her legs beneath the sheets and leaned against the headboard. Because she knew this had to be emotional for him too. She wasn't the only one feeling the weight of their history.

He stalked over to the bed and sank down on it, leaning against the headboard beside her. "Fine. You?"

"I… Yes, I'm fine." And she was, but she was also feeling guilty again. How could she tell him that he *might* be a father? What if he wasn't? That wasn't the kind of thing you told somebody when you didn't have the answer. She had to get Charlotte tested first. Only when she knew the truth could she make a decision about how to proceed.

"That was great, Belle."

She pulled her knees up to her chin, feeling suddenly vulnerable and exposed. His tone wasn't that of a man who was thrilled with what they'd just done. "I thought so."

He raked a hand through his hair, but he didn't make a move to join her beneath the covers. "We can't do it again. Not once we leave this place."

Annoyance pricked her. "Well, no. We'll be traveling, won't we? And I didn't think we were going to drop everything and have sex whenever the mood struck."

He reached over and pushed her hair back, tucking it behind her ear. His eyes searched hers. "We probably shouldn't have done it this time, Belle. But I don't regret it."

All she could do was tell him the truth. "I don't regret it either."

"Thank you for trusting me to take care of you."

Her heart pinched. "I've always trusted you, Dex. You're the only man I've ever believed in. The only one who never let me down."

He got under the covers and dragged her down with him, tucking her into the curve of his body. She felt protected there. Safe.

"Better sleep now. We'll have a lock on Lyon's location soon enough, and that's when things will get crazy."

Annabelle closed her eyes. It felt so right with him. It *always* felt right with him.

But his words still echoed in her brain. *If you're thinking we're going to fall in love again and take up where we left off, we aren't.*

Mendez sat in the leather recliner in his living room, nursing a beer and watching CNN International. He'd cycle through them all tonight—CNN, Al Jazeera, BBC,

Fox—and he'd feel like he might know something by the time he went into work the next morning. Add in the intelligence briefings he got from the Pentagon, CIA, and NSA, and he was definitely well-informed.

He had to be because he had to make recommendations to lawmakers about where to use HOT assets or where the next trouble spot would be. There were a lot of trouble spots in the world, with more being added every day.

He took a swig of beer and gripped the object in his hand tightly, the smooth metal warm against his skin. He didn't often take it out, didn't examine it. But tonight he'd felt the need. He opened his fingers and stared at a locket. It was silver, engraved with a double eagle, and etched with a name on the back. He flipped it over and stared at the name.

Valentina Alexandrovna. Her first name and her patronymic name. Her last name wasn't there, but it was imprinted on his brain. Rostov.

He rarely opened it, but of course tonight was a self-torment night. The photo of the woman was small but clear. Her hair was russet and her eyes were blue. She had high cheekbones and a delicate mouth. Her nose was small and tilted up slightly at the end. She was smiling, and his heart did a slow thump in his chest.

That smile was over two decades old. The woman in the picture was nothing but bones. A shell of a woman buried in an unmarked grave in Moscow. *If* she'd been buried. It was entirely possible she had not. He'd never found the answer, though he'd asked.

He snapped the locket closed and stared at the television, his jaw clenching tight. Dmitri Leonov, of all the damned people, was sailing back into his life while Valentina was dead.

He thought back to his first posting as a young intelligence officer. The embassy in Moscow. The Cold War had been in its death throes, but there was still a job to do. He'd met Leonov there. And Valentina. They were Russian Army. Dmitri was also KGB, though Mendez hadn't known that at the time. He'd only learned of it afterward. After Valentina was lost to him and there was nothing he could do to get her back again.

He held up the locket by its chain before closing it into his fist again. He got up and went into his bedroom, put it back into its velvet bag, and tucked it into the drawer he kept it in.

There was no changing the past. But he could make sure that Leonov finally got what was coming to him.

NINETEEN

ANNABELLE WOKE EARLY, BUT DEX was already up. She heard him moving around in the kitchenette. It was still dark outside, but the smell of coffee permeated the air. She sat up and stretched, the sheets sliding against her naked skin. Her body was languid and relaxed. Her mind was not.

Anxiety crowded its way in, shoving aside the temporary respite she'd been enjoying. She got out of bed, searching for something she could put on, and found Dex's discarded T-shirt. It covered her ass, which was all she needed right now. She'd get something out of her overnight bag when she located it.

The door opened a slice and Dex and peered in. Mussed hair. Shirtless. Sexy as hell. Loose sweats hung on his hips, revealing the V that made her mouth water. If the sweats slipped much farther, his cock would appear. Annabelle's belly twisted with a hunger that had nothing to do with food.

When he realized she was up, he opened the door all the way and held out a steaming mug. "Coffee?"

"Please." She wrapped both hands around the cup and inhaled the scent.

"You still take cream? I put some in."

"Yes. Thank you."

She followed him as he went back into the kitchenette and got his own cup. She leaned against the door and watched him. It felt so intimate. Like the old days when she stayed with Katie and then ran into Dex in the morning, making coffee after feeding cows. Sometimes he made her breakfast. They'd still been teenagers then, full of yearning, but they'd managed to keep their hands off each other when the possibility of discovery was so high.

Now, when they didn't have to keep their hands off each other, life had changed too much to be so free.

"Want a bagel? I think I have cream cheese."

"Sure, that sounds good."

He took a bagel out of a bag, inspected it, then popped it in the toaster. "I bought these before I had to go home for Dad's fall. They're still good though. No green spots."

"That's a relief," she joked.

He turned his head, his gaze sliding over her body, down her bare legs, back again. Heat flared in his gaze. "You look good in my T-shirt. Any panties under there?"

Fire rolled through her as she shook her head.

"Maybe after you eat your bagel, I should bend you over this counter." He said it so matter-of-factly that it made her shiver.

Her nipples beaded. She was wet instantly, her clitoris throbbing with arousal. She could tell by the darkening of his eyes that he hadn't missed the jut of her nipples against his shirt.

"You like that idea." It was a statement, not a question.

"I do," she said. "Very much."

He grinned as the toaster popped. "Then you'd better eat this bagel and prepare to hold on tight."

He slathered cream cheese on it. Instead of giving her the whole thing, he only gave her half. "On second thought, I'm going to help you eat it. We can get another one after I've fucked you against the counter and in the shower."

Her breath sat in her chest like a stone. "Why waste time eating?"

He ripped into the bagel with his teeth. "Energy, Belle. Going to need it."

When she finished the last of her half, he grabbed the hem of the shirt she wore. He dragged it over her head and threw it into the bedroom. The front of his black Army sweats tented as he grew hard. She reached for him, but he dodged her.

"No, let me look at you."

Her heart skipped as his eyes wandered over her. The harsh fluorescent light in the kitchenette didn't hide anything. She didn't look the way she had five years ago, which he could clearly see this morning. She was twenty-six, almost twenty-seven, and she had stretch marks from carrying Charlotte.

Her breasts weren't as perky as they used to be either. Nursing a baby did that to a woman sometimes.

She tried to cover herself, but he gently took both her hands and pushed them away from her sides.

"What gives?" he asked.

"I had a baby, Dex. I'm not perfect."

He made a growling sound in his throat. "Nobody is, Belle. And I think you're still as goddamn beautiful as you ever were. Take my breath away."

"You're too nice to me."

He tilted her chin up and forced her to meet his eyes. "I'm not nice. I didn't like you at all until last night, remember? We're working on being friends, so no, I'm not too nice. But you are just as gorgeous as you ever were. More so, probably."

Her pulse throbbed. "Then you're blind. You took a blow to the head and lost some visual ability along the way."

"I'm a sniper, Belle. Vision is the most important thing I possess."

He skimmed a finger over her collarbone, down between her breasts, over first one nipple and then the other. Goose bumps rose on her flesh, and she shivered pleasurably.

"You've lost your sharp edges and angles," he said. "You're lush and soft now, your promise fulfilled. I like this body. I want this body."

He turned her, stepping up behind her to palm her belly, her breasts, tugging her back against him with his other hand on her hip. His cock was hard where it nestled against the cleft of her buttocks, and she pressed backward, seeking to make him groan for her.

He growled instead, and then he nipped her ear. It was a sharp feeling, not hard or painful, but it sent more goose bumps chasing in a chain reaction down her spine.

His mouth dropped to her neck, licking and kissing. He slid a hand down her abdomen, his fingers gliding between her folds. He hissed when he found her wet for him.

"Beautiful, Belle. Hot and beautiful. You want me in here?"

His finger slipped inside her, caressing her walls, and she moaned. "Yes."

He took one of her hands in his and put it between her legs, rolled her finger over her clitoris. "Hold that thought, baby."

She stroked herself softly while he went into the bedroom. She heard a drawer open, and she knew he was getting a condom. He tore it open, walking back to her.

"Hands on the counter," he commanded. "Hold it tight."

She did what he said, arching her back and sticking her ass out. He gripped her hip with one hand—and then she felt his cock at her entrance, probing. A moment later he slid home and they both groaned.

"Jesus, Belle. You're so fucking wet."

"You make me that way, Dex."

He started moving, slowly at first and then faster, driving her against the counter. She pushed back against him, holding on tightly as he fucked her hard. She wouldn't have thought she'd be ready for this kind of sex so soon, but she was completely overwhelmed by her need for it. She loved his roughness because it was also tender. Because he cared about how she felt and whether or not it worked for her.

It definitely worked this morning. Last night it wouldn't have.

"Dex," she moaned. "Oh my god."

He slapped her ass and she squeaked. It wasn't a hard slap, but it stung. And it was precisely what she needed at that moment.

164

He came down on top of her, his front to her back, his fingers tangling in her hair and dragging her head back so he could kiss her. She moaned hard when his tongue met hers.

His body pumped into hers frantically. She shoved her hips backward, against him, taking everything he had to give her. When he reached around and fingered her clitoris, she came instantly. Stars exploded behind her eyes, and she wrenched her mouth from his so she could suck in air.

"That's it, Belle," he told her gruffly. "I love it when you come."

She was still coming when he suddenly stilled, his cock swelling inside her, a groan tearing from him as he found his own release. She gripped the counter, her lungs pumping, her heart drumming, her world shattering.

Dex slid from her body and swung her into his arms. His grin stopped her heart. "Time to shower, baby."

He fucked her again in the shower. He meant to take it easier, take it slow and overwhelm her senses with pleasure, but he had a desperate need to possess her again. Because this thing between them wasn't going to last.

Dex didn't want to start over with Annabelle. He didn't want to take up where they'd left off, or try to rekindle the love they'd once had. Life moved on, and so had he.

But holy shit she was hot, and she still managed to make him lose his ever-loving mind. There'd been a time in his life when he would have said or done anything to get inside her. He didn't feel like that anymore—and yet, when he was in her, it was hella good. Annabelle Quinn was an addiction. One taste and he needed more.

Three times in the space of a few hours. It wasn't enough though. He knew he'd want her again later. But there was no later because they were on their way to find Dmitri Leonov soon. Annabelle might be going with them, but there weren't going to be any opportunities to get her naked. She'd stay with Victoria Brandon and Lucky Mac-Donald, the two women on the team.

No more private rooms. No more chances to make love to her. Nor would she want him to once they were on their way and their heads were firmly back on the task of rescuing her daughter from a madman.

The thought of not having her again was depressing in its own way. He'd fucked many women since her, but none of them had a history with him. None of them made his guts turn inside out and his heart feel like it was being squeezed in a vise.

Annabelle did those things to him. And then, when he was inside her, stroking his way to an explosive orgasm, he felt like nothing ever had or ever would compare to the way it felt when he was with her.

She did things to him. Things he didn't like anymore. It was nostalgia and history, but it still did a number on his mind. He shouldn't succumb to the temptation of fucking her, yet he did.

Three damned times in a few hours. He dragged on his shirt and ran his fingers through his hair, his mood darkening as she hummed in the bathroom. She was in his space, imprinting herself on his memory, and there was no way he'd ever shower in that bathroom again without thinking of Annabelle on her knees, sucking his dick before he'd picked her up and shoved himself inside her while she wrapped her legs around his waist.

He'd forgotten the condom, but he'd quickly remembered, withdrawing and handing the packet to her. She'd rolled it on while he held her, and then he'd plunged into her again, groaning with the rightness of it. And with the sorrow, because being inside her bare, even for a second, had shown him what he was missing.

Still, he'd lost his mind and fucked her hard against the wall. She'd clung to him, urging him on, her legs tight around his waist and her arms wrapped around his neck. He'd sucked on her nipples, biting and licking them while she chanted his name and begged him to make her come.

He'd done what she'd asked and then he'd found his own release, pumping a load of hot semen into the condom. His knees were weak after that and he sank to the shower floor, taking her with him. They sat under the spray, holding each other and panting.

When the water started to cool, he'd turned it off. They'd gotten out of the shower, dried, and gotten dressed without saying much. Annabelle had changed into a pair of jeans, boots, and a clingy blue top that accentuated her eyes. She was gorgeous, and he found himself contemplating what it would be like to have her in his life on a regular basis.

Except that was impossible. She lived in Kentucky and he lived here. Never mind that she had a company in Briar City and a child to raise. There was nothing about this thing between them that could ever be anything but temporary.

His phone buzzed. He welcomed the interruption. "Davidson."

"We've found Leonov," Iceman said. "He's in Jorwani, Africa. The mission is a go."

"Be right there."

TWENTY

ANNABELLE DIDN'T KNOW WHAT SHE'D expected, but a private plane hadn't been it. She leaned back against the seat and watched the activity around her with hooded eyes. There were nine men and two women, Victoria and Lucky, on Dex's team. Both women looked tough as nails. They chatted together easily. Once in a while, a couple of the men came over and ran intimate fingers down one of the women's arms or exchanged meaningful looks. Whatever else was going on here, those four were couples.

Not quite what Annabelle expected on a military operation. Then again, she didn't know what to expect. These guys didn't even look like they were in the military. They wore civilian clothes, and other than a certain bearing they had, it wasn't clear they were in the Army at all.

But she knew they were because she'd spent time with them in that brick building with all the razor wire and intricate security measures. She'd had to sign documents in order to access certain parts of it.

Plus the Gibbs guy—Colonel Mendez—wore a uniform. Dex had taken her into a different area this morning.

Everyone was there, and then the colonel came to talk to them.

They'd boarded a bus and driven to a nearby airfield. A plane sat with engines humming. The name of a cargo company was emblazoned on the side, but it wasn't a cargo plane. Or not strictly a cargo plane. Equipment and supplies probably took up the luggage area, but the rest of the interior was almost ordinary.

The seats were spacious, but that was because the rows weren't crammed together like in a commercial plane. It wasn't a fancy private jet, but it was roomier than a typical carrier. There were still flight attendants who walked up and down the aisles, asking if they would like something to drink or eat.

"You okay?" Dex asked, settling in beside her after talking to some of his guys.

She shrugged. "Okay, I guess. Why hasn't Lyon called back yet?"

"I'm not sure. He might be making you sweat."

"He's doing a good job of it." She'd worried there might be more reports of things burning down during the night, but there hadn't been. So far it was only Archer Industries that had suffered any damage. She'd called her secretary this morning when she'd finally been allowed to do so.

Archer Industries was shut down for the foreseeable future. The lab was destroyed beyond repair. The projects? Ruined, of course. And Marshall Porter?

Unavailable. Lucy had been calling his number, but he hadn't picked up. He wasn't in the lab, that much they knew, so Annabelle wasn't worried he'd been killed. But where was he?

She'd texted him, but so far he hadn't replied. She couldn't decide if that was a normal thing or a suspicious thing. Marshall was an extreme introvert, and it wasn't unheard of for him to disappear for a weekend. Since this was a Saturday, it was possible he'd gone on a trip and had no intention of returning until Monday morning.

But why wouldn't he answer her texts? She'd never gone without an answer before.

"He'll call."

He meant Lyon. The aching in the pit of her stomach wouldn't go away. "I hope so."

Dex curled his fingers into hers. "He wants the money, Belle. Don't forget that. Without you, he doesn't have it. And without your loved ones, he doesn't have you."

She squeezed his fingers in return. She knew he was right. Logically.

But Mr. Lyon didn't strike her as completely logical. He seemed vindictive and impatient.

"Is he still in Jorwani?"

"Yes."

Jorwani was an African nation that bordered Kenya on the north and Somalia on the east. It wasn't a good place to be. Not these days. There had been fighting between the government troops and opposition forces who called the government corrupt. A charismatic man named Zain Okonjo was the opposition leader, and the conflict was escalating.

"Why would anyone want to go there right now?"

"If they're the kind of person who profits from war, it's precisely where they'd want to be."

"You're saying he's profiting off the conflict?"

Dex nodded. "Probably. He wanted your drone recharging technology. That's not the kind of thing you sell to someone for giggles. There's a need for it, and Lyon intends to deliver."

"Are drones really a big business in Jorwani? It seems too poor."

"I imagine Lyon was planning to sell it to the government so they could spy on Okonjo's movements at the minimum. At the maximum, they'd get an attack drone from somewhere and use it to decimate the opposition. Lyon probably also intended to sell it to everyone else who wanted to buy. That kind of technology takes time to implement. By the time he sold it to a dozen states, he'd have more than made back his money."

"I wonder how he heard of it in the first place. It's a top secret project. It's not like we advertised it in the newspaper."

He gave her a meaningful look. "There are ways, Belle."

"You're saying Mr. Lyon knew where to look? Like Eric took out a secret ad on Craigslist for spies or something?"

"There's a whole dark web out there, honey. Most people don't know about it—or don't want to know. You can buy anything there. Bitcoin is typically the currency of choice."

She shook her head. "What is that? I've never heard of it."

"It's virtual currency. Unregulated. It can be used anonymously. No names attached, no locations."

"But Eric and Mr. Lyon didn't trade in Bitcoin. Those are actual dollars in the Swiss accounts."

"Yes, they are." He shrugged. "No idea, but possibly Eric insisted on money he could move rather than a Bitcoin account. Bitcoin is trading pretty high right now, but nobody knows what could really happen to it. There are no regulations, as I said."

"Eric and I weren't precisely close, but I'd have never thought he could do something like this." She frowned. "His parents died in an accident three years ago, and he inherited the company. I thought it meant something to him." As much as anything besides his own ego could mean to Eric.

"Is this the kind of thing someone else could have involved him in? What about Porter?"

"But why? Wouldn't Marshall sell the technology himself if that were the case? Why involve Eric? It's not like a fund-raiser where he'd need Eric's ability to talk to people. Especially not if it started out on this dark web you mentioned. He could do all his talking in messages."

Dex expelled a breath. "Unless Porter didn't want to negotiate the deal at all. But if he's the one with the brains, he'd have known how to do it—and he'd have probably traded in Bitcoin and then sold it on the open market. Harder to trace. Besides, if he *was* involved, why is the money still in Eric's accounts a month later?"

"Maybe someone else on the project involved him in it. But I don't know who." There were other engineers who worked on the testing, but none of them stood out as potential traitors to their nation. Not to mention that until Helios worked as it was supposed to, it wasn't worth the risk to try to sell it.

Which brought them back to Eric and Mr. Lyon. "If Eric really went to Africa for a safari, it's entirely possible he bragged to the wrong person about Helios and got himself tangled up in something he couldn't get out of."

"He'd have had to have something to sell though. He didn't go to Africa without that. And then there's half a billion sitting in Switzerland."

That number made her belly clench. "Yes, that's true." Which put them back to square one.

Her gaze slid over Dex's profile. After the way he'd rocked her world last night and this morning, she couldn't stop thinking about how much she wanted to do it again.

And again.

There was no hesitation with Dex. No fear. She wanted everything he could give her and more. When he'd slapped her ass—oh, a bolt of lightning sizzled into her core just thinking of it—she'd only wanted more of the same. Not the slap necessarily, though that would have been fine, but more intensity. More Dex.

All of Dex.

She was hopeless over this man. Always had been. She'd thought she'd grown numb over the years, that her love had subsided into something else. It hadn't. She still loved him fiercely, craved him fiercely, and wanted all he had to give.

He did not want the same. Anguish gripped her in its talons. She swallowed it down.

"You said you were a sniper. This morning."

His dark gaze settled on her. "Yes."

"What does that mean?"

Something passed over his face. Something cool and detached. "What do you think it means?"

"I don't quite know. You sit on rooftops and shoot the enemy, I guess."

"Yes. Sometimes. But there's more to it than that. Sometimes a dangerous target has to be eliminated. We get into position and… wait."

She shivered. He was talking about assassinating people. Not just shooting an enemy who also had a gun, but waiting for a designated target who might not be armed. It wasn't what she'd expected, and yet it made a terrible kind of sense.

"I… Wow. I'd have never guessed. You were so out-going in school, so happy—"

"I don't have to be unhappy to do my job. It's a hard job, but a necessary one. And yeah, I learned stillness and inner reflection after you left me. I had a lot of time to think. I was angry."

Guilt perched in her soul like a malevolent crow. Sorrow for all she'd lost with him took up residence beside it. Dex wrapped her hand in his, startling her. Her gaze met his. Her heart thumped extra hard at the heat in his look.

"It's not your fault, Annabelle. I'm responsible for my own emotions and my own choices. The path I went down was the path of my own choosing. I could have chosen another one."

"Why do we make the choices we make then?" She'd been asking herself for the past two days why she hadn't told him what was happening five years ago. Why she hadn't trusted him enough to involve him. Why she'd taken it all on herself. It was like she'd had a martyr complex or something.

"Because it's who we are," he said softly.

"You get anything on Marshall Porter yet?" Dex asked Richie.

Richie and Kid were sitting at a table with Iceman and Chase "Fiddler" Daniels. Kid was on the computer and the others had grim faces.

Dex had left Annabelle reading and come over to talk to the guys. They still had several hours to go and a lot of intel left to obtain before they could plan how to get the hostages back. He needed to get involved in work. Sitting with Annabelle, talking about the past—well, that wasn't good for him. Especially not now.

He'd told himself that last night and this morning was it, the end of their reunion. They'd talked, they'd fucked, and there was nothing left for them. Whatever they'd once had was in the past, in spite of what happened to make them split up in the first place.

It was just better this way. Cleaner.

Richie's gaze was troubled when it met his. "Not much. MIT grad. Honors. He's from Lexington. He worked in DC for a while, but he went home when his mother got cancer. She died six months ago now. He stayed in Kentucky, working for Archer Industries."

Dex studied them. No one but Richie would look at him. "So what's going on? Why does everyone look like they just got bad news?"

Richie cleared his throat. "We can't find Porter. He was at the lab last night, but he left before it blew. He's not been seen since. He didn't go home. We're waiting on credit card info to track his movements."

"So he could be on the road somewhere. Or Lyon could have gotten to him if there's no paper trail."

"Yeah."

"Is that all?"

Richie frowned. "You should probably talk to Annabelle."

Dex felt his brows arrow down. What the fuck? "I've been talking to Annabelle. What more do you want me to ask her? Was she fucking Porter?"

A weight sat in his gut at the thought, but hell, maybe she was. Maybe she'd lied about it being two years since she'd had sex. Maybe she'd wanted to see if he'd fall for it.

Deep down, his instincts told him it wasn't true, that last night had been the first time for her in a long time. His baser mind was busy conjuring all sorts of reasons for him to be wrong. He'd been burned by her and he was wary, no matter what she said about the reasons for it.

"No evidence of that," Richie said. He cleared his throat. "Has she said anything about Charlotte?"

"She's said a lot about Charlotte."

Richie's gaze strayed over Dex's shoulder, and he knew the other man was looking over to where Annabelle sat. "Has she told you that Eric Archer isn't Charlotte's father?"

Everything inside Dex went still. Like nuclear-winter still. Nothing moved. "What do you mean he isn't her father?"

"We've got, uh, a DNA test here in her records that was initiated by Eric Archer. They're not related."

Dex's temples started a drum solo. Charlotte Archer was four years old. Four. If she wasn't Eric's... Holy fuck.

He spun on his heel and stalked over to where Annabelle sat with her book. She looked up, a little bit startled, a little bit confused. And then her expression fell and she surged out of her seat. Too late, he realized she must think something had happened to her child.

"Charlotte," she gasped as he caught her by the arms and held her tight, cursing himself for scaring her.

"She's fine," he managed to get out.

Her wide eyes searched his. "Then what's wrong?"

"You tell me," he said as evenly as he could. He yanked his phone from his pocket, found the pictures and hit the one of Charlotte. Red hair, freckles, blue eyes. She looked familiar to him, but he'd thought it was because she reminded him of Annabelle. It was a blow to realize she also reminded him of Katie.

He turned the phone to her, his heart beating harder than it had ever beat in his life. "Who's the father, Belle? Eric? Or me?"

TWENTY-ONE

ANNABELLE'S INSIDES DISSOLVED. DEX'S FACE showed his emotions. Betrayal. Hurt. Disbelief. Rage.

She didn't blame him. She went limp, sinking against the seat even though she didn't sit down.

"I don't know," she said softly.

His eyes flashed. "Goddamn." He shook his head as if to clear it of something horrible. Then he wrapped his hand around hers and dragged her toward the back of the plane. Opening a door, he pushed her inside and slammed it shut. They were inside a small conference room with a table and chairs.

He was studying the picture on his phone. "She has Katie's expression."

Annabelle folded her arms over her chest to stop the chills rushing up and down her spine. It didn't work. "I've thought so sometimes. I was never sure."

"Jesus Christ, Annabelle!" Dex threw his phone onto the table and advanced on her like a bull attacking a red cape. She'd never seen him look so angry.

"I wasn't sure, Dex. I'm still not sure—but yes, I

think she's yours. I never had her tested—"

"Eric did."

Her stomach lurched. "What? He never told me."

Eric had seemed less interested in Charlotte over the past year than he ever had before. He'd pretended to care when she was younger, but lately even the pretense had been gone. She'd been relieved rather than alarmed, even if it was hard to watch Charlotte seeking her daddy's attention and not getting it.

"That's all you have to say? He never told you?"

She sank down on one of the chairs and put her elbows on the table, dropping her head in her hands. "I don't know what else you want me to say."

"You were on the pill the last time we were together. How…?"

She looked up. His eyes were hot, shining with emotion. But which emotion? Anger? Sadness? Fear? Love?

She didn't know.

"Antibiotics. They make the pill less effective. I was with you and then I was… *with*..." She couldn't say the word rape right now. "Eric. I found out I was pregnant after Eric and I had been married for almost three months. I hadn't had a period, but I'd thought it was stress—but there were other things that happened, and I took a home pregnancy test. When it was positive…" She shrugged. "Eric had been in my bed nonstop for quite some time at that point."

Dex seemed to deflate. He sank into a chair and closed his eyes. Then he shook his head and didn't say anything for a long while.

"I have a daughter. With you."

Her heart was a wounded thing in her chest. Because

Dex was hurting. Because, once more, Eric and her parents had exacted a high price for her cooperation with their agenda. "It would seem so, yes."

"When were you planning on telling me you had your suspicions? Or were you going to tell me at all?"

"I thought I'd have her tested after we got her back safely."

He smacked a hand on the table, and she jumped at the violence. His nostrils flared as hot color flooded his face. "You should have told me, Belle. All this goddamn time—you should have told me!"

"Told you what?" she yelled back, the restraints on her emotions falling away. "That you *might* be a father? That I had suspicions but didn't know for sure? Did you want to know those things right now, when her life is at stake and she *might not ever* come back again? How would that have made you feel to think that *maybe* you were the father of a child who is right now depending on you to bring her home safely?"

She was on her feet, leaning across the table, her hands flat on the surface. Fury swam across her vision. Her heart beat a staccato rhythm. She wanted to scream until her throat was raw.

Dex's eyes widened. He rose in one smooth motion and wrapped strong hands around her forearms. Gently, he pushed her down until she was sitting. He dropped into the chair across from her, his hands still on her arms.

"Breathe," he commanded.

She dragged in a breath and then another and another, willing her reckless heart to calm down. She needed to focus. Calm dripped into her veins, taking its sweet time. Fury and fear swirled into a toxic stew in her belly until she thought she might be sick with it.

Dex must have thought she was gaining control because he let her go and sat back. She pushed a shaky hand through her hair.

"Better?" he asked.

She nodded but didn't look at him.

"So now we both know something we didn't know before. I'm Charlotte's father. Care to tell me when you first thought it was a possibility?"

Her voice was like razor blades in her throat. "I hoped so from the beginning, but it didn't seem very likely. I think I started to suspect around her first birthday. She didn't have any of Eric's features—but then his mother produced a baby picture of him and there seemed to be similarities. So I dropped the idea."

"Eric must have suspected something. He had her tested."

She was furious that Eric had done it without her knowledge, but she wasn't surprised. "Probably because I didn't get pregnant again. He was suspicious because I never conceived even though he threw away my birth control. That's when he started saying she was yours."

Dex's expression clouded. "He threw away your birth control?"

She nodded, remembering those dark days. "Oh yes. He was determined we were going to have more children." She couldn't stop the bitter laugh that escaped. "I don't know why. He didn't seem to like the one he had very much, even when he thought she was his."

"Jesus, what an asshole."

"Well, men are the head of the household. Wives are property. You know the drill."

"That's bullshit. Only men without balls who want to control women because they're scared of their power think that way."

"Bingo."

"Whether you like it or not, I *am* kicking your father's ass when we get back," he growled. He pressed his palms to his temples and leaned back in the chair. His gaze fixed on the ceiling.

She felt like they were at an impasse, and yet they had to move forward. Dex was Charlotte's father. That knowledge both cheered her and terrified her.

What if he wanted to battle for custody? Or what if he wanted nothing to do with Lottie? Because that was possible too. He might not want the responsibility.

"Now's not the time to figure any of this out," he said. "But I'm going to be a part of her life, Belle. You aren't keeping me out of it. I want her birth certificate changed to reflect the truth too. She's going to know who I am."

Annabelle swallowed. "I wouldn't dream of keeping you out of her life. But Dex, we have to go slowly. She believes Eric was her father. I need time to prepare her for the truth."

"I get that. But we aren't going to spend a year doing it, you got me? Soon. She's a kid, but she's still young enough that she can handle this kind of thing with a simple explanation from the adults in her life."

There was a knock on the door. Dex got up and jerked it open. Lucky MacDonald was on the other side, holding out a phone.

"Your phone's ringing, Annabelle."

TWENTY-TWO

DEX'S LIFE HAD JUST HAD an IED thrown into the middle of it. Since Annabelle had arrived on his doorstep two days ago—Jesus, fuck, was it only two days?—everything he thought he'd known had been blasted all to hell. Each new blow packed more punch than the last.

She'd confessed that Eric had blackmailed her into marriage, with her parents' help and cooperation. She'd followed that up with the bombshell that Eric had raped her. On a personal level, Dex discovered that he still responded to Annabelle in a way he didn't with anyone else.

Now this. He was a father. He had a child. He was simultaneously pissed off, hurt, and stunned. He wanted to be angry with her for not telling him she'd had suspicions —but what could she have said? Should she have called him up outta the blue and said, *Oh, hey, I had a baby, and I'm not sure, but you might be the father? Though my husband could be the father too, but I don't know, so maybe you could send me a DNA sample?*

He was realistic enough to know how that would have gone. He'd have told her to fuck off, no doubt about it.

She held the phone determinedly as they moved back into the main passenger area, her brows arrowed down in concentration and her eyes flashing with annoyance. Dex wasn't listening to the exchange this time because Kid was recording the call. They'd listen in after the fact.

"Yes, I understand," she said. "Go to Jorwani and check into the Royal Cape Hotel in Cape Lucier. Wait for your call." She paused for a long moment. "No, I can't come alone. Jorwani is dangerous, so I'll be bringing a bodyguard. … I'm sorry, Mr. Lyon, but if you want the money, that's the way it has to be. One bodyguard to help me carry luggage and protect me from the crime that's rampant there these days. … Yes, I'll see you tomorrow."

She ended the call and dropped the phone to the seat beside her. Lucky picked it up and double-checked that the call was ended. Kid looked up from his computer and nodded.

Dex almost dragged Annabelle into his arms, but he stopped himself. She met his gaze first, before anyone else's, and his gut tightened. The fear in her eyes was stark, but she'd handled Leonov like a champ.

"Great job," Lucky said, giving Annabelle a quick squeeze on the arm.

"He makes my skin crawl."

"He's supposed to," Victoria said, sauntering over. "He's an asshole."

"You got him to agree to a bodyguard," Dex said. "That's huge." He shot a look at his team gathered around. "That's my job, in case anyone's wondering."

Nobody argued. A couple of the guys shrugged. Richie frowned but said nothing. They all knew what he'd just been talking to Annabelle about. The fact they'd known the truth before he did rankled. But hell, they'd known it before Annabelle too. The only one who'd known it before they all did was Eric, and he hadn't said a word. Evil, rotten bastard.

"We need to go over the plan," Richie said. "Meeting commencing right damn now. In the conference room."

"Not you," Dex said when Annabelle tried to follow.

She frowned as he put his hands on her shoulders. "I have a right to know what's happening."

"When the plan is firm, you'll know about it. Until then, you need to read your book and leave the details to us."

She looked militant. "Dex—"

"Shut up, Belle. This is my job, not yours. Even if Charlotte wasn't my daughter, I'd do everything in my power to get her back again."

Her eyes searched his. "I know I said I suspected she was yours, but I'm as shocked as you are. This wasn't how I wanted any of this to happen."

"Eric's been dead for a month. Maybe you should have done something about it before now."

Her eyes reflected a wealth of hurt and sorrow. "I've been dealing with a lot of crap since then. Did you want me to take my confused child into the doctor and have her cheek swabbed when the man she'd thought was her father wasn't even cold in his grave?"

He didn't know what he wanted. He only knew that his life had changed profoundly over the past few hours—and it wasn't ever going back again. He was a father. And if he didn't get this right, he might not ever get to know the child who was depending on him to save her life.

He might lose her before he ever met her.

Cape Lucier, Jorwani, was a city of contrasts. There was a wealthy class and a very poor class. Zain Okonjo battled the government forces over those contrasts, claiming to be a man of the people.

The conflict hadn't reached Cape Lucier, though the city was still affected. Cars sat abandoned in the poorer quarters due to lack of fuel. Okonjo might be a man of the people, but his cause was hurting the very people he claimed to want to help.

Donkeys pulled carts piled high with vegetables and goods. The smell of cooking meat filled the air near the markets. Mercedes Benzes glided down the streets beside the donkeys while upscale shops sat next to open stands, contrasts that stayed in Annabelle's mind long after they'd arrived at the hotel.

The Royal Cape Hotel was built in the Arab style, with arches and colonnades that surrounded a central courtyard. Palm trees stood in the courtyard, beneath the glass of the domed ceiling. It was meant to be grand, and yet there was something slightly shabby about it.

Annabelle waited in the lobby while Dex secured their room. For Lyon's purposes, he was her bodyguard, the man who toted her luggage and watched her back. For the hotel stay, they pretended to be honeymooners here for an African safari.

The rest of Dex's team was nearby, but they were paired off and pretending not to know each other. Some of them were coming in later so they didn't all show up at once. And some wouldn't come at all, going instead to other hotels. Less safe hotels, to be sure.

The other two couples—married couples, she'd learned—were here too. And two of the other guys were pretending to be a gay couple. She didn't know why she found that amusing. Gay men were capable of being big and bad and tough. But the one they called Iceman and the other—Flash?—were about as far from gay as you could get. Still, they pretended.

Well, maybe not quite pretended. Until Flash put his arm around Iceman and gave him a big smack on the cheek. Iceman appeared to blush, which was quite a feat for a man as big and tough-looking as he was. They got a few looks from the other patrons of the hotel, mostly westerners who were either reporters or disaster tourists.

Dex wandered back over with a key dangling from his hand. An honest to goodness key, not a key card. He also had his bag slung over his shoulder and he picked hers up too.

"We're on the third floor, baby," he said. "Ready to go?"

"Yes."

He put a hand on her back, his fingers lightly resting against the base of her spine, and her body responded in spite of her wish that it would not. This wasn't the time or the place.

They'd been in the air forever. Getting into the country hadn't been a picnic either. The authorities at the airport scrutinized everything. Their passports were fake, provided by Dex's people, and she'd been afraid that something would go wrong.

It didn't, but it had certainly taken long enough for the Jorwani authorities to let them into the country.

And now they were here, taking a rickety elevator to the third floor and hoping to find a decent bedroom to crash in. Annabelle was tired, though she'd slept some on the plane. But she'd been on edge, both from Mr. Lyon's call and from the knowledge that Dex was really Charlotte's father.

How many more surprises could she take?

She hoped there were no more surprises. Please God, no more.

Dex led the way down the dark hall. He slid the key into a lock and pushed open the door. A queen-sized bed greeted them. It perched against the far wall, its four posters draped in mosquito netting. There were two narrow windows with shutters that were closed to keep out the heat, and a door that she presumed led to a bathroom.

Dex waited for her to step inside and shut the door behind them. When she would have spoken, he closed the distance between them and put a hand over her mouth. Shock and desire managed to mingle in an electric sizzle that shot through her nerve endings.

"Not a word," he growled in her ear. "No idea who's listening."

Carefully, he pulled his hand away, and she nodded.

"Why don't you take a nap, baby doll?" he asked as he walked over to the dresser and felt along its length. "It's been a long trip, and we don't want to start our honeymoon off with you getting sick."

"I'm all right, honey," she said. "I slept on the plane. I'd rather go for a walk with you."

189

His eyes flashed. He moved on to the nightstand, feeling his way around it. Looking for listening devices? "Maybe later. We've got that safari trip tomorrow, and you want to be rested up."

There was no safari trip, but this was supposedly where Eric had been taking his. He met the tour company in the lobby and went off on the trip. He never returned.

"How about some food then? Room service?"

The look he gave her was inscrutable. "I don't think they have room service, baby."

"Then maybe you could go and get us a snack."

He arched an eyebrow. Then he walked over and grabbed her, tugging her against his body. "I have a better idea."

Her heart throbbed. She thought he might kiss her, but he lowered his mouth to her ear again, his breath hot against her skin. "What are you playing at?"

"Nothing," she mouthed when he pulled back to look at her face.

"No, baby," he said. "I can't be away from your side for even a moment."

He let her go and finished his circuit of the room. Then he took something from his bag and set it on the dresser. It looked like a little speaker. Once he did that, he turned to her again.

"What the fuck, Annabelle?"

She jumped. "So we can talk now?"

He tipped his head toward the speaker. "It's a signal jammer. If there's a listening device nearby, it won't pick us up."

"Then why didn't you set it up to begin with?"

"Because I still had to check for devices. Now what the hell are you up to?"

She stuck out her lip. "I'm not kidding, Dex. I'm hungry. It's not a game."

He dug around in his bag and fished out a package, tossing it at her. "We'll get dinner later, once I know it's safe. Eat these."

She caught the crinkly package. "Peanut butter crackers?"

"You aren't allergic to peanut butter."

"You know I'm not."

He frowned suddenly. "Is Charlotte allergic?"

"No, she's not. She has a pretty strong constitution actually. Hates brussels sprouts, but who doesn't?"

He looked a little bit lost. Then his expression hardened. "Yeah."

She opened the package and took out a cracker, feeling guilty that she knew everything about Lottie and he knew nothing. "Want one?"

"No." He raked both hands through his hair and went to peer out the window.

She sat on the bed, practically wilting into it. She'd lost track of how many hours they'd been traveling. Mr. Lyon hadn't called again. And Marshall hadn't answered any of her texts. She was actually getting worried about him.

"Anything on Marshall yet?"

Dex swung around to look at her. "Nope."

"He'll turn up soon. He sometimes disappears for the weekend."

"I'm sure you're right."

"So what happens now?" she asked. "Do you know where Mr. Lyon is? Where he's holding Charlotte and Molly and Becca?"

"We have one shot at this, Belle. We have to make sure he's where we can get him—and we need a location on the hostages. My team's working on that right now."

Frustration beat against the wall she'd tried to erect. "That sounds very vague."

"It's not. The less you know, the better."

"I don't really like that option."

He sauntered over to the bed, fingers hooked into his belt. "Too bad. This is the way it works."

"I know you're mad at me, but you don't have to be an asshole."

"Jesus, Belle. I'm mad, yeah. But I'm also focused on the job. Nothing is more important to me than rescuing our daughter. If I need to tie you to the bed to get it done, then that's what's going to happen. Got it?"

TWENTY-THREE

SHIT, WHY HAD HE SAID that? Of all the damned things. He pictured her tied to the bed, legs splayed, arms above her head. Body utterly naked. And, yeah, it made him hard.

Her eyes were hot—but was she angry or needy?

"You'd like that, wouldn't you?"

What sense was it to lie? "Yeah, I would. But maybe now isn't the time."

"No, probably not." Her voice was firm—and yet it broke at the end, as if she were thinking about the heat between them too.

"What about you?" he asked, and she cocked her head to the side.

"What about me what?"

He couldn't believe he was going there. "Would you like it? Being tied to the bed, I mean."

Her gaze dropped. "I feel like I shouldn't answer that."

He sank down on a chair beside the bed and put his head in his hands. "I don't want this," he said fiercely. "I don't want to want you. I don't want to go down that rabbit hole ever again. But how the fuck am I going to get out of it now?"

She didn't say anything for a long moment. "Is it that bad for you? Do you hate me that much?"

Her voice was small and it pierced his heart.

"No, I don't hate you. It would be better if I did—but I don't."

"You're the only man I've ever loved, Dex." She said it softly, but each word was like a bullet to his heart. It sank in deep, made him bleed like he'd never bled before.

"I don't think that's enough, Belle. We're different people now."

"You can't ever forgive me?"

Could he? Maybe. But was it wise? Probably not.

"It's not about forgiveness. It's—Hell, life has changed. We've moved on. That couple we were—we aren't them anymore. I don't feel the way I once did."

"Well," she said after a long moment, and he could hear the unshed tears in her voice. "I guess that's it then. No second chances. No future. Other than the future in which you're a father to Charlotte. We'll figure it out. Visitation, custody arrangements. All of it. I won't fight you unless you try to take her away from me. Then I'll fight dirty."

Pain gripped his heart. "No, there's no need for that. I think it's been dirty enough between us. We'll do it right. We'll put her first."

"I know you think I've done everything wrong, and maybe I have, but I'm glad you're her father, Dex. I'm glad you're the one she'll grow up knowing—"

Her voice choked off, and he knew she was thinking what if Charlotte *didn't* grow up because he failed to rescue her? Hell, he was thinking it too. And that wasn't the way he was wired. He was wired for utter confidence in his team and their ability. But when the hostage was precious to you? Jesus, he'd never experienced that before.

He didn't even think about what he did next. He just went over and dragged her into his arms, holding her tightly against him. Her hands splayed against his chest, fists curling into his shirt. Her breath was hot through the material. He knew she was squeezing her eyes tight and trying not to cry.

"She will, Belle. She'll grow up and she'll make us proud to be her parents."

It was odd to think of himself as a parent. But he was. He experienced a moment of rage for all he'd missed, but he swallowed it down and concentrated on the woman in his arms. She didn't need that rage right now. Maybe she'd handled the situation differently than he would have liked, but he was trying to see it from her perspective. Young, frightened, and married to the kind of man who took away her birth control and would have forced her to get pregnant if he could have. At what point was she supposed to call Dex up and tell him he *might* be a father?

He hugged her hard. He should let her go, but once he had her in his arms, it was nearly impossible to push her away. In spite of himself, his dick started to make its intentions clear. Annabelle's breathing changed and he knew she'd felt it too.

The baser part of him wanted to say to hell with it. He could strip her and fuck her until they both passed out from exhaustion. But where did that leave them?

Same damn place, same tangled-up emotions. He set her away from him and took out his secure cell phone. Iceman answered on the second ring.

"How's your hubby?" he asked, and Ice snorted.

"Enjoying this way too much, actually."

Dex wanted to laugh. Flash was a joker and Ice was typically as serious as a heart attack. Flash would push the whole couple thing as far as he could just for giggles.

"You aren't worried, are you?"

"No. Why would I be? Gay isn't contagious. Besides, I'm secure in my manhood. But you know Flash—he likes to push the envelope. I'll spank him later and he'll quiet down."

Dex almost choked. Ice wasn't a joker, but when he zinged you, it was usually with a deadpan delivery. "Oh hell, I'd pay to see that."

"Spank me, motherfucker, and I'll divorce your ass," Flash yelled in the background.

Dex shook his head. They made him laugh, and that was a good thing right now. "Any info on the surroundings yet?"

"Vic and Brandy are scouting."

"Do we have a pinpoint on the target?"

"Nope. We know the vicinity from the cell tower he's pinging, but not the exact location. He's not using the same phone to call Annabelle that he uses for his business. He's been shutting it down."

"So he's onto us."

"Maybe. Or maybe he's just paranoid."

"No, this guy is smart."

"But not so smart he was able to stop Archer from transferring that money."

"What do you mean?"

Dex had been thinking about it for a while. "Do you really think Lyon initiated a transfer when he had no idea if the technology worked as described? He'd have wanted more than test results. He'd want proof. Until he had that, he wouldn't pay that much money into Archer's accounts. And why five accounts anyway? Why not one?"

"So what do you think happened?" Ice asked.

Dex shot a look at Annabelle. She was watching him with a curious expression.

"I don't know. But I mean to find out."

"You think Eric had help."

Dex shrugged, his dark eyes not giving anything away. "I'm not sure. But it seems likely." He spread his hands. "Look, we both knew Eric. He was a rich kid, a bit spoiled, good at math and science but not a genius. He must have had help, Annabelle. Unless you think he'd gotten so damned brilliant he could outsmart this guy, he had to have a partner."

"Not necessarily. Eric wasn't a genius, but he was manipulative. He could play people. I don't doubt that he could get Mr. Lyon to give up the money through sheer bullshit. Then, when Lyon discovered he didn't have a working product, he killed Eric. Now he wants the money back."

"And Marshall Porter?"

"He never left the States. I saw him while Eric was gone. He doesn't have a twin. He can't be in two places at once."

"He only needed to handle the money, and he could have done that from Briar City."

"True, but if he handled the money, why is it still there? Why is he still working at Archer Industries? He could have bought an island, as you so wisely pointed out, and disappeared."

"Has he answered your texts yet?"

"No. But it's still Sunday in the States. He'll answer in the morning when he returns to work."

"You really trust this guy?"

She didn't know who to trust anymore. Well, other than Dex and his people. Life was crazy these days, and people were crazier. "I did trust him, yes. You're making me doubt myself, but I honestly don't know why he'd still be in Briar City if he knew where the money was. He could take *one* of those accounts and disappear."

"How do we know he didn't?"

"There's half a billion sitting there. Do you think there was six hundred million? Or some other odd number?"

"That's a good question." Dex picked up his phone and dialed. "Hey, Kid," he said. "You see any evidence of money moving out of those accounts lately? Or any evidence there was more at one point? … Yeah, if you could let me know."

Outside, the Muslim call to prayer echoed from the city's mosques. Jorwani was primarily a Muslim country, though there were pockets of Christians throughout. The country was ruled by a secular government, though Zain

Okonjo wanted to change that. Annabelle walked over to the window and peered through the shutters. She reached up to open them so she could see more, but Dex stopped her.

"Not a good idea, Belle."

She dropped her hand away and squinted through the cracks. Most of the men wore white robes. Colorful robes adorned the women. Almost all wore hijabs over their hair. She hadn't worn one into the country because it wasn't required, but there were those who thought Jorwani was headed that way if Okonjo's forces won. Subjection of women was always the first step in any move toward authoritarian government.

Take away the right to drive, the right to work, the right to have access to birth control and reproductive care —it was a slippery slope that always began with something small and then snowballed. She should know. She'd had her own rights curtailed when Eric and her parents forced her into marriage.

And then he'd thrown away her birth control, as if she had no right to determine when or how she got pregnant. Yes, she'd still been able to drive and work, but her reproductive rights had been decided by someone else. She still felt the unfairness of that down to her bones—and she would fight hard so that other women didn't suffer the same thing.

"It's lovely, isn't it?" she asked without looking at Dex.

"What is?"

"The call to prayer. So melodious."

The mullah's voice rose and fell as he performed the ritual chant. It was exotic because it was different from her experience, and haunting when she considered all the connotations—both real and imagined—that accompanied it.

"There are those who are frightened by it," Dex said, as if he knew what she was thinking. "Because it's Islam. Some people think all Muslims hate everyone who doesn't follow their religion."

"Do you believe that?"

He stilled for a moment, head up, listening. "No. I've spent a lot of time in Muslim countries. They're people, like us, and they have a lot of the same desires and wants. I didn't realize it for a long time. But the military changes you, exposes you to things you never knew existed. So no, I don't believe they all hate us."

"I imagine most people just want to make it through the day," she said. "Go home at the end of it and have dinner with the family. Look forward to the weekend so they can sleep in."

"That's pretty much true. But there are always people in this world who want to harm us—harm our country—for being who and what we are. That's why I joined the military. So I could stop it."

The thought of him on the front lines somewhere, camo paint on his face and grenades dangling from his belt, always made her shiver. She pictured bullets flying all around him as he led the charge into the unknown.

Annabelle shook herself and walked away from the window.

Dex was busy inspecting his weapons, and she had a moment where she did a double take at the variety on display. She hadn't realized he'd brought his own personal arsenal with him, but she should have known.

"How did you get those guns into the country?" She didn't remember him going through customs with a case like the one he was looking at right now.

He opened it and ran a hand over a smooth black barrel. "Best you don't know that."

She sighed and went over to where he was eyeing a rifle snuggled in foam. It was sleek and shiny.

"This is Jane," he said.

Annabelle started. "Your guns have names?"

"Jane does. She's the only one."

"Why Jane?"

"Because she's incognito. Because she's going to do damage when she's called upon to work, but she's not leaving behind a name. *Jane Doe was here*."

Annabelle frowned. "That's kind of weird, Dex."

"Any weirder than your boy T.E. Lawrence and his adventures in that giant book you tried to get me to read with you?"

She couldn't help but grin. "No, not really."

"That's what I thought." He shut the case and loaded a pistol, tucking it into a holster inside his waistband. He tucked another gun into an ankle holster.

"What about me?"

"What about you?"

"You know I can shoot. You taught me yourself."

"True, but you aren't getting a gun. I'm the bodyguard here, remember?"

There was a knock on the door, and Dex put a finger to his lips. He ghosted over on silent feet and flattened his back against the wall. There was a pistol in his hand before she'd even seen him draw, and she took a step backward, her heart thudding.

"Yeah?" he asked loudly enough for whoever was on the other side to hear. The door was wooden, but there was no peephole.

"It's Brandy and Vic," came the answer.

Dex holstered the pistol and yanked open the door. The gorgeous redhead entered first, her husband on her heels.

"What d'you have?" Dex asked.

Victoria grinned. "We think we've found where he's keeping them."

TWENTY-FOUR

THE REST OF THE TEAM gathered in Dex and Annabelle's room in the Royal Cape Hotel. They had to wait for the others to make their way over from their various locations, but once they were all assembled, the planning began in earnest.

Dex shot glances at Annabelle. She seemed to be handling it well enough, but when Vic had first announced they'd found the hostages, Belle cried out and demanded they go and get them right that minute.

Dex had taken her by the shoulders and told her they had to be more deliberate than that. Her eyes had been wide and frightened, but she'd nodded and let him guide her over to the bed to sit down. She was still there now, chewing her lip and hugging herself.

It was a risk for everyone to be here, but time was of the essence. If Leonov had anyone watching the hotel, they were waiting for Annabelle and her bodyguard to exit, not necessarily watching for others to enter. Though of course they were looking out for anything unusual. Fortunately, HOT had plenty of experience in counterintelligence and evasion. The guys had various lengths of hair, and a couple sported a few days' growth of beard.

They didn't look like military guys, and that was important. The presence of the women helped since women weren't typically Special Operators. The times were changing though, and there were more women in spec ops than was commonly known. In HOT, that number was still small, but it was going up as Mendez brought in the best of the best from wherever he could get them.

Billy the Kid had his computer out, and he was going over the schematic for the place they thought Charlotte was being held along with Molly and Becca Carter. A concrete wall topped with razor wire surrounded the compound. Guards patrolled each section, but HOT didn't know how many were inside. Yet.

They would once they got close enough with their night vision goggles. The NVGs were equipped with a thermal mode that would display the heat signatures of all the people residing behind those walls. Since Vic and Brandy had been on a reconnaissance mission to find the place, they hadn't taken much equipment. Not to mention it was daylight and too much high-tech stuff would peg them for what they were.

"We need confirmation on those hostages," Richie said. "Just because Lyon's cell pinged out of that compound doesn't mean the hostages are actually there."

"Lyon will call soon," Dex said. "Belle will get him to put Molly on, even if only for a moment."

Once they had confirmation, they would launch. If they'd had more time, they could have confirmed it without waiting for Lyon. But they hadn't arrived as early as they'd wanted to. Their plane'd had to land in Djibouti for a couple of hours, and that had cost them time. Still, they'd managed a lot in the limited time they'd had.

Having the signal from Lyon's cell phone helped them triangulate his position down to a particular quarter within the city. They'd systematically combed it until they found him. A little CIA intel from the colonel, and they knew they had their man. They just weren't sure about the hostages.

"Half a billion is a pretty large incentive to do what she asks," Kid said.

"You get any of that information I asked you about earlier?"

Dex had told his team what he wanted to know. They'd agreed with the need to research it.

"No other money. Not in or out. No other accounts connected." Kid's computer started to beep. He tapped a key, his eyes widening. "What the fuck?"

His fingers flew over the keys, his gaze glued to the screen in front of him. Whatever was happening, he didn't look happy about it. Dex's gut churned. Whatever it was, it wasn't good. He shot a glance at Annabelle. She was frowning, but she had no idea what this could mean or she'd be a lot worse off.

"No, no, no, no!" Kid shouted, slapping keys and leaning into the computer. Then he sat back, shoved his hands through his hair, an explosive "*Fuck!*" filling the air.

"What happened?" Richie asked.

Kid's eyes were wide as he lifted his gaze. "The accounts... They're empty."

"What do you mean, empty?" Dex growled.

Annabelle gravitated to his side, her heart detonating in her chest. He put an arm around her and gave her a squeeze.

"The money's gone." Billy Blake looked about as shocked as she felt. He stared at his computer screen, his hair standing on end, his expression one of complete disbelief. "I tried to stop it but… Jesus, this guy is good."

"Leonov?" someone said.

Annabelle blinked. What was Leonov?

Dex made a frustrated sound beside her. "Lyon, Belle. Think of him as Lyon," he muttered.

All she could do was nod.

"Possible, but I doubt it. He could have done that days ago and saved us all the trouble." Billy swore. "One minute the money was there, and then it started to move out of the accounts, one by one. I tried to tack a tracer onto it, but I don't know if it worked."

"How soon before we know?" Matt Girard asked.

"Minutes… or hours. If nothing pings back in twenty-four hours, I failed. It should happen faster than that, but twenty-four at the most."

Annabelle's breath stopped. Her lungs were dead-weight. Five hundred million dollars. Gone. Charlotte and Molly and Becca's lives. That's how much they were worth to Lyon—Leonov?—and now she had nothing to bargain with.

She wanted to scream. Dex tightened his arm around her as if he sensed it. She turned her face into his chest. She had no choice if she wanted to keep it together. Her eyes squeezed shut and she breathed him in—the masculine scent of him, the familiar scent of him—and willed herself to *think*.

"So if not Lyon, who? Who else knew about the sale?" It was Dex talking.

Annabelle's phone dinged in her purse. Dex let her go so she could retrieve it.

Sorry I missed your texts. Went hiking in the Shenandoahs. Just got back. Everything okay?

"It's Marshall," she said as Dex came up behind her. He took the phone from her and read over the texts before handing it back to her. "Text him back. Tell him about the explosion. Tell him you're in DC but you wanted to make sure he secured the research."

Annabelle nodded and did what he'd said. Her fingers trembled and her pulse raced a mile a minute. She'd said that Marshall couldn't be involved—but what if she was wrong? Marshall would have the know-how. In fact, Marshall was the only one who knew all the pieces of the puzzle. Marshall and Eric.

Except Eric was dead. There hadn't been much of him left though. What if he'd faked it? What if he'd fooled her so badly that she'd been blinded to the idea of him being behind everything? He'd been an egomaniac and a bastard, but was he that diabolical?

Marshall: *Wow! Was anyone hurt? Should I go over to the site?*

Annabelle: *Roy Jenkins is in stable condition. If you go over, send me a picture, okay? I haven't seen anything this morning. Been in meetings. Don't want to turn on the news.*

Marshall: *Definitely. Let me know when you get back.*

Annabelle set her phone down on the bed. It rang. For a second she thought it might be Marshall calling. But it was the man of the hour. Lyon.

Bile rose in her throat, and her stomach twisted. The money was gone, but she had to act like everything was normal. In fact, she had to act like she held all the cards. When she looked up, Dex's gaze was on hers.

"You can do it, Belle. I believe in you."

She nodded and answered the call. "Hello?"

"Ah, Mrs. Archer—are you settled into your suite yet?"

Hardly a suite. "Yes. But I don't intend to stay. Come to the hotel lobby with my friends and daughter and we can make an arrangement."

His laugh slimed its way down her spine. "I call the shots here, not you. We will meet where I say. Do you have a pen?"

"Is your place public?"

"It is."

"So tell me." He said an address and she repeated it. Billy Blake typed it in, nodding when he had it. Annabelle pulled in a deep breath even though her stomach threatened an assault on her throat. Time to play hardball. "I need to speak to Molly."

"I don't think so."

She looked at the people watching her so intently. They checked their equipment, trying to get his location. And they needed to know if the hostages were with him or not. It was the only chance they'd get to rescue her loved ones. She wouldn't fail.

"Five hundred million dollars, Mr. Lyon. If you want it, I need to hear Molly's voice. I need to know she's okay and that the children are okay."

He let out a long-suffering sigh. "Fine, if that's what you wish." She heard the echo of his feet along stone floors, and then he spoke to someone in Russian.

"Annabelle." It was Molly's voice. She sounded calm, but Annabelle knew she was probably terrified. She'd been warned not to let Molly know that rescue was imminent. It broke her heart, but she had to be strong if she wanted everything to work out.

"Molly, thank God! How are you? How are the girls? Are they with you?"

"Yes. We're fine—"

"That's enough." It was Lyon's voice again. Angry tears pricked Annabelle's eyes. "You will come alone, in fifteen minutes, and you will bring the account numbers. Once the money transfers successfully, you will be free to go. You will be given the address where you can collect your child and friends. This is nonnegotiable."

"Unacceptable. How do I know you won't hurt them once you have what you want?"

"I will have no reason to hurt them then, will I? And I will let you speak to them before the transfer is made.

Fourteen minutes, Mrs. Archer. See you there."

Before she could say anything else, the call went dead.

"Got him," Billy said. "He's in the compound."

Dex closed his eyes, stark emotion rolling over his features. Annabelle wrapped an arm around him, uncaring who saw them. She loved him in spite of herself, and he was dealing with his own chaotic emotions over the knowledge he had a daughter who was in danger.

"Then let's go get that motherfucker," Dex said, squeezing Annabelle tight before setting her away. He checked his pistol and reached for the rifle case. "We don't have a lot of time to get into position."

TWENTY-FIVE

MOLLY HUGGED HER ARMS AROUND herself as Leo ended the call with Annabelle and gazed speculatively at her. The girls were still in the room next door. She could hear them crying for her, and it broke her heart.

"This is about money?" she spat. Maybe she shouldn't say a thing, but he'd romanced her under false pretenses. A lawyer, her ass!

He backhanded her so casually that she didn't see it coming. Her head snapped sideways. Shock scalded her as she clutched her cheek and turned back to him. He was tall and handsome and somewhat older than she'd first thought. He'd said he was thirty-five in his online dating profile, but he was probably ten to fifteen years older than that.

He had hard, cold eyes. How had she not realized it before?

"Everything is about money, darling," he said. "It's not personal."

He spoke so indifferently, as if he hadn't kidnapped her and the girls. As if he hadn't killed the woman who'd been with them at the safe house. Guilt rolled through her at that thought. It was her fault they'd been found, her fault someone had died. Because she'd answered Leo's calls. Because she'd flirted and made plans to see him once everything was normal again.

Because she'd thought *he* was normal.

God, would she never learn that men were pigs? Becca's father was useless, having skipped out as soon as Molly told him she was pregnant. None of the men she'd tried dating in the years since had been any good.

And then she'd gone out with this psychopath. To think she'd let him kiss her—it curdled her stomach.

"How much money?" Because she wanted to understand.

Leo's eyes glittered. "Eric Archer stole a fortune, Molly. Once I have it back, you and the girls can go home."

She didn't believe him for a second. Why bring them to Africa if that was his intent? He wasn't planning to let them go. He was planning to kill them. Dispose of them.

A cold dread settled in Molly's stomach. Eric had died on a safari. Torn apart by lions. Was that what Leo planned for them too?

He flicked imaginary dust from his dark polo shirt. "This will all be over soon," he said coolly, as if he weren't a cold-blooded killer.

Alpha Squad split into two teams. One team would head for the compound, and the other would go to the market where Leonov had told Annabelle to meet him. It was an outdoor market, but under roof. There was a coffee stand at one end with tables. That's where Leonov wanted to meet Annabelle.

It was within walking distance of the compound, which meant Leonov would likely arrive on foot. They would watch for him and try to intercept him before he ever reached the coffee stand—but only if the hostages were safely extracted first.

Dex didn't want Annabelle anywhere near the operation, but he'd been voted down. Even by Annabelle, who'd told him with flashing eyes that she was going and he could stick Jane up his ass if he didn't like it.

Dex had to leave Jane behind, but he had his pistols and his knife. He sat with a thigh pressed against Annabelle's leg as they rode through the streets of Cape Lucier in a taxi. Iceman was with them, which meant his thigh was pressed to Annabelle's other leg. Dex didn't like that at all.

But Iceman was happily married and totally in love with his wife. That helped, though not as much as it should.

Because Dex didn't know what he felt—or should feel—for the woman sitting beside him. He'd loved her once, and then he thought he hated her. He had a child with her and he was still reeling from that fact. Truthfully, he didn't know how he felt about anything right now except that he wanted this over with and he wanted his daughter and her mother safe.

He'd figure his feelings out later. Annabelle was back in his life for good, so it was important that he think about how he was going to see her on a regular basis and not feel chaotic inside every time he did.

"We're in position." Richie's voice came through the in-ear device and Dex shot a glance at Ice. The other man nodded to indicate he'd heard too.

The teams needed to know what each was doing, so they were all linked up. Dex touched the microphone clipped inside his shirt. He spoke low enough to keep his words from reaching the driver. "Copy that, Richie. Team Bravo is almost to the market."

Team Bravo was Dex, Iceman, Flash, and Fiddler. Flash and Fiddler were in a taxi behind them.

"Copy that."

"Any sign of Leonov?"

"No—Shit. Yeah. He just walked outside. There's a black SUV parked on the street. And he's got Molly Carter with him."

"Shit," Dex said. Ice's expression was hard, and he knew it was probably an echo of his own. Change of plans if Leonov was bringing a hostage to the meeting.

Annabelle whipped around to look at him. "What's happening?"

He put a hand on her knee and lightly squeezed, warning her to be quiet. She bit her lip, but her eyes flashed furiously. He knew she didn't like being told what to do when her child was in danger, but she also knew that the only way his team was getting everyone back alive was if she did what she was told and let them operate. They'd impressed that upon her very strongly at the beginning of this mission and again in the hotel before they'd split up.

Annabelle was smart enough to get it, thank God. He'd wanted to leave her behind, out of range of Leonov, but he'd been overruled. She had to be there for the hostages' sake.

"They're getting into the SUV," Richie said.

"What the fuck is he up to then? Where are the girls?"

"No sign of them. Goddammit!" That was Big Mac's voice.

"Team Alpha is a go," Richie said. "We're going in for the girls. Team Bravo, get Molly Carter. And Double Dee, Mendez wants Leonov alive. Don't get an itchy trigger finger. Ice, see to it he doesn't."

"Copy," Ice drawled as if he were strolling through a park somewhere instead of preparing to capture a Russian agent.

Dex wasn't promising anything, so he didn't say a word. He'd try to do what the colonel wanted, but if that son of a bitch tried to hurt Annabelle or Molly, all bets were off.

"I see the SUV moving toward me," Victoria Brandon said. She was on overwatch duty outside the market, perched on the roof of a neighboring apartment building, her rifle trained on the road. "ETA in two minutes."

"We've reached the market," Dex said as the taxi halted. They got out and he took the briefcase that held Eric's laptop from Annabelle. She was supposed to take it with her to the meeting place and sit with it. If Leonov got as far as the meeting, meaning they hadn't grabbed him beforehand, she was supposed to use it to pull up the accounts. They were dummy accounts on a dummy page since the real accounts were now empty.

Billy had mocked it up as fast as he could—but if they got to a point where Leonov demanded she press the button to transfer the funds, they were in big trouble. Billy still didn't have a ping back on the tracer he'd attached to the packets, so they had no idea where that money had gone.

Or who had taken it. Clearly not Leonov or he wouldn't have called Annabelle after the money had disappeared. It could be Marshall Porter. It could also be Sam Spencer's people interfering since the CIA had been following Eric when he'd met with Leonov. Richie had a call into Colonel Mendez on that score, but they had no answer yet.

Whoever had it, they'd certainly made the job a lot harder, if for no other reason than it was a blow to Annabelle's confidence. She'd had something Leonov wanted, and now she had nothing.

"I'm going to need that," she said.

Dex took her by the arm and started hustling her toward the meeting point. Ice melted into the crowd along with Flash and Fiddler.

"Plan's changed," Dex replied. He touched his mic. "I'm going with Annabelle. It's too dangerous to let her go alone."

"Negative, Double Dee." It was Ice's voice, hard and commanding. So much for strolling through the park. "That's not how we planned this. You have to let her go alone."

"We didn't plan for him to split up the hostages either."

Annabelle made a noise, but he propelled her forward.

216

"Stick with the plan, asshole, or you're going to get yourself killed."

"I don't care."

"Double Dee. Let her go in alone. That's an order. Stand down."

"Ice, I love you like a brother, but no. Would you stand down if it was Grace?"

Ice cussed a blue streak then. Annabelle was still hurrying across the market with him, but he could tell she was mad. He shouldn't have said anything about the hostages being split up, but it was too late now.

"If you get out of this alive, I'm going to kick your ass," Ice said. "Count on it."

"Deal."

"What do you mean the hostages are split up?" Annabelle demanded.

"He's bringing Molly with him. Now focus."

Her jaw hardened. He knew that wasn't the end of it, but they had so little time. If they got out of here alive, he'd hear about it later. He'd gladly let her chew him out if that was the case.

It was dusk and the market was crowded with people who'd come out after their prayers to shop or eat. Dex escorted Annabelle over to the coffee stand. He seated her at a table in the middle, then he went and got her a coffee, setting it in front of her while he took a seat at a neighboring table. Leonov would make him, of course, but he thought he should at least pretend to observe Leonov's order that she come alone.

She had the laptop on the table and she stared at the aisles of the market, probably wondering which way he would come.

"Coming in from the east," Flash said. "He's got Miss Carter with him. Looks like a gun in her back. We can't grab him just yet. Too many people and too much chaos."

Fuck.

Dex got Annabelle's attention and pointed. She nodded. Then she took a sip of the coffee, gripping the small glass with both hands. It would be strong coffee, flavored with cardamom, ginger, and saffron. She didn't react the way he thought she might. Instead, she took another sip.

Dex faced the east aisle and waited. He had a hand on the table and an arm draped on the back of his chair, his fingers within reach of his pistol. He wished he had Jane, but she was a little too obvious for something like this. Not to mention she'd blow Leonov's head clean off his shoulders. That wouldn't make the colonel happy apparently.

A white woman emerged from the corridor, a man walking directly behind her. Annabelle stiffened but, bless her, she didn't move. Leonov and Molly walked over like they were on a Sunday stroll.

"Hello, Mrs. Archer," Leonov said. "I brought you a surprise as a show of good faith."

Molly kept her head turned as Annabelle reached for her hands.

"Are you okay, Mol?"

"Yes," her friend said quietly, dropping her head as she did so. Dex frowned. Was that bruising on her cheek? No wonder she wouldn't look directly at Annabelle.

"Yes, such a sweet reunion," Leonov said. He scanned the tables, stopping when his gaze landed on Dex. "I see you didn't obey my instructions, Mrs. Archer."

He jerked Molly back, out of Annabelle's grip, and Dex got to his feet.

"I don't know my way around, Mr. Lyon," Annabelle said. "My bodyguard does."

"This man is military," Leonov said, practically spitting the words. "Special operations, unless I've grown rusty."

"Used to be," Dex said. "Now I'm a soldier for hire—and Mrs. Archer hired me to protect her. That's what I'm doing."

"If you make a move," Leonov said, "I will shoot Miss Carter."

Fury rolled through Dex, but he managed a shrug. "I'm here to make sure you don't shoot Mrs. Archer... or renege on the agreement."

Leonov's nostrils flared. "And yet if I shoot her, I think Mrs. Archer will be furious with you. Gun on the table where I can see it. Slowly."

Dex eased his pistol from the holster and laid it on the table. He could still get to the one in the ankle holster if need be. People at nearby tables scattered at the sight of the gun.

"Step back," Leonov said.

Dex obeyed. It was a gamble to do it this way, but in his gut he knew it was right. If Leonov was focused on him as the threat, he wouldn't think there were others. Because he surely hadn't expected Annabelle to come alone. If she'd been sitting here by herself, he'd be twitchier than he already was.

Leonov took a piece of paper from his pocket and thrust it at her. "The money, Mrs. Archer. You will send it. *Now*."

Annabelle opened the laptop. "Give me a second. I have to power it up."

"Don't try to cheat me. When the money hits the account, I'll get a text. If I don't get that text within five minutes, my men have orders to kill your daughter and her friend."

TWENTY-SIX

ANNABELLE KNEW SHE HAD TO be cool. Inside, she was hyperventilating. Outside, she was the picture—she hoped—of cool restraint. The market was still noisy, but it was like they were in a bubble here. The tables were deserted, and the window had slammed shut on the coffee stand. She booted up the computer and waited. She considered stalling on the grounds her Wi-Fi wasn't working right, but Lyon would see through that excuse. He already knew the signal in the market was good or he wouldn't have set up the meeting here. He'd planned it carefully.

She didn't anticipate him handing her a Wi-Fi device. "Plug this into your USB drive."

She hesitated. Would he be able to tell that the bank page was a dummy with that thing? "Why?"

"Because it will provide a secure and fast connection. Trust me, you want fast right now." He looked at his watch. "Only three minutes left, Mrs. Archer."

She plugged the device in. She didn't look at Dex, though she badly wanted to. But looking at him might give her fear away. She couldn't do that. She hated that Lyon had Molly hostage. She hated that Molly was scared.

And the girls—oh God, the girls. She had to believe that Dex and his people were going to save the girls. If they didn't—

No.

She couldn't think that way. She couldn't think about anything except the next few minutes. Dex was here. He'd put his gun on the table, but he had another one. His team was here too. Lyon didn't have the advantage even if he thought he did.

"You might wish to hurry, Mrs. Archer."

"I'm working on it! It's not like this is the fastest connection speed, by the way." She held up the paper he'd handed her and waved it. "I have to get the numbers right. Stop making me nervous."

The market detonated before she could do a thing. A shock wave of sound exploded through the aisles and ripped into Annabelle's ears. She was too stunned to scream. Her eyes shot to Dex—he was on his feet, shouting at her, his gun pointing toward where Lyon stood. Annabelle turned to see where Lyon and Molly were—and her head yanked backward as her hair was ripped out by the roots.

She was hauled out of her chair, slammed against a body. An arm wrapped around her throat and hot metal gouged into her cheek. She tried to drag air into her lungs, but she was being squeezed so hard her vision tunneled and blackness swam at the edges.

She tried to choke out Dex's name, but she couldn't get anything past the brick wall in her throat. The grip on her eased only enough to let air in, and she gulped it like she might not get another chance. She searched frantically for Dex—and found Molly, lying sprawled on the ground, her body strangely still. Annabelle's gut twisted. Tears sprang to her eyes.

"Let her go, Leonov."

Annabelle knew that voice. Relief overrode fear as her gaze slammed into his. Dex stood there like an avenging angel, gun pointed, face hard, eyes promising retribution. Red blossomed through his shirt sleeve. Rivulets trickled down his arm. Her belly dropped.

Dex was hit. Molly was so still she might be dead. Fury clawed like flaming dragon talons through Annabelle's insides. She would tear this man apart with her bare hands if she got a chance.

Lyon—Leonov—snorted disdainfully. "Can you make the shot, soldier? It's tricky business to fire your weapon just right. You have to avoid her and hit me between the eyes before I can pull the trigger and take her with me. Do you want to take that risk?"

Dex's granite expression didn't waver. She loved him more in that moment than she ever had. He would fight for her and their daughter. He would never give up. He was the best man she knew.

"I'm a sniper. I can make this shot with my eyes closed. Do *you* want to take that chance?"

Lyon scoffed. "If you could do it, you would. Why discuss it with me?"

"It's called mercy. You might try it sometime," Dex growled.

"Mercy? More like weakness." Lyon's grip on her throat tightened. "I have not received my text, Mrs. Archer. It is time for your child to die."

No!

The thinking side of Annabelle's brain shuttered. Every thought she'd had about how to stay alive shut down as the animal side roared to life, demanding she fight. She threw an elbow backward, twisting her body in his grip. The hot metal barrel of his gun slipped away from her skull. She tried to drop but his arm tightened, preventing her escape.

Wildly, she cast about for what to do. And then she remembered something. She picked her foot up and stomped it down on his instep with every ounce of strength she could muster. She heard screaming. It wasn't Lyon though. It was her.

Lyon lifted the gun, a stream of angry Russian pouring from him, and she knew she would die this time.

A pistol exploded—but it wasn't Lyon who'd fired.

Dex. Hope sprang to life as Lyon dropped. He dragged her down to the dirt with him, his grip on her unyielding. She landed on top of him in a tangle of arms and legs. Revulsion skated down her spine as she tried to shove herself away.

"End of the road, Leonov."

Annabelle stilled. Dex stood over them with his gun aimed at Lyon's head. She'd thought he'd killed Lyon, but Dex had only wounded him. He kicked Lyon's pistol away. Iceman appeared from the shadows to bend over and pick it up. Annabelle's insides liquefied with relief. She got to her feet and Dex reached out to steady her. Her shirt was wet. Blood stained the shoulder and much of the front. She started to pat herself frantically.

"It's his," Dex said gruffly. "Not yours."

Lyon lay there with an arm over his head. The other was limp at his side as blood flowed from a wound in his shoulder. His eyes gleamed with hatred as he stared at Dex.

"You have no idea what you've done," Lyon spat. "This isn't over."

"Shut the fuck up, asshole," Dex growled.

"Molly!" Annabelle rushed to her friend's side. Her eyes blurred as she dropped beside Molly. One of Dex's teammates was there, checking Molly's vitals.

"If she's dead... Oh God," Annabelle choked out. Molly's eyes didn't open. Her skin was colorless. There was a bruise on her cheek and a cut on her lip. Annabelle shoved a shaking hand against her mouth.

"She's not dead," the man checking her said.

Flash. His name was Flash.

"But she hit her head." He turned her over. Her arm bent at a funny angle. "Her arm's broken. She might have passed out from the pain. I'll give her some morphine and we'll get her to a hospital, don't worry."

Dex pulled Annabelle to her feet. "Nobody's dead, Belle. The girls are safe. We got them out."

Her knees gave way, dragging her down to the dirt once more.

Dex didn't let her fall. "It's okay, baby. It's okay."

She clung to him, breathing, thinking. *Charlotte. Becca. Alive!*

"Is anyone hurt? That explosion..."

His fingers curled in the back of her shirt where he held her against him. He didn't seem to care that she was getting Lyon's blood on his shirt. Not that he wasn't bloody already.

Sirens pierced the air, the sound growing louder as the police moved closer to the market.

"A diversion. No one got hurt. We have to get out of here, Belle. Before the Jorwani authorities arrive."

She couldn't seem to let him go. "You got shot."

"I'm fine. Hurts like a bitch, but nothing new about that." His expression hardened again, and she shivered. "What you did— Belle, you could have died. What the fuck were you thinking?"

She hadn't been thinking. She'd reacted viscerally. Primally. She loved this man, and she loved her baby girl —and no way in fucking hell was she letting that asshole Lyon take them away from her.

"I couldn't let him win," she said. "I couldn't."

Dex squeezed her tight. "Never fucking do that again, okay?"

"Okay." It was easy to promise because she never planned to be in this situation again.

Dex made eye contact with Flash. The other man stood with a limp Molly in his arms.

"Charlotte and Becca are really okay? Really?" she asked as Dex hustled her toward the exit.

"They're at the airport now, being put on a transport to the American base in Djibouti. Which is where we all need to be. As soon as possible. We have to get out of here. Jorwani is still friendly with the US, but with everything going on in this country right now, things can get confused. It's best we aren't here in case they do."

Her legs were rubber but she forced them to move, forced them to keep pace with Dex as they strode through the market and out onto the street. There was a black SUV sitting beside the curb. The driver's window rolled down and Victoria Brandon grinned at them.

"Look what I found, y'all. Just had to take out Leonov's trash first."

Annabelle hopped into the back with Dex after he and Flash put Molly in the very back. Flash jumped into the passenger side and they rocketed down the street, but not before Annabelle got a look at a man sitting on the sidewalk with a piece of duct tape over his mouth and his hands zip-tied in front of him. Leonov's trash—the driver of the SUV.

"What happened?" Victoria asked.

"Leonov almost shot Annabelle," Flash said. "But Annabelle fought back. Dex shot him. Leonov also shot Dex, but looks like a surface wound. Not that the fucker let me doctor him yet."

"I'm fine," Dex growled. "You can get me on the plane."

Victoria glanced in the rearview and met Annabelle's gaze. "You okay, hon?"

"Y-yes." A tremor started deep inside. She couldn't seem to help it. Her teeth clattered together like small-arms fire. She tried to drop her head and hide it from them all. But Dex knew. He put an arm around her and she buried her face against his chest. He smelled like sweat and gunpowder and spices from the market. His hand skimmed up and down her arm.

"It's okay, Belle. You're safe now. Charlotte is safe. You'll get to see her soon."

She lifted her head, her eyes blurring even as her teeth continued to chatter. "I kn-know. Thank you... f-for everything."

There was so much more she wanted to say. But this wasn't the place. Not with Flash and Victoria listening in.

Not when she didn't know how Dex would react in return.

A transport plane awaited them at a small airstrip out-side town. It almost wasn't big enough for the plane to take off, but the pilots were military men who knew their jobs and could slot a big motherfucker of a beast down onto a short runway and take off again too. The plane climbed at a sharp angle once they were airborne, taking them up and away from the chaos they'd left behind.

Adrenaline surfed through Dex's veins, churning and surging and twisting him up inside. A few rows away, a little red-haired girl clung to her mother and cried. They'd boarded and Flash had insisted on cleaning and bandaging his wound while the plane charged the runway. Dex sub-mitted, but he kept his eyes on Annabelle as she rushed to the front. Annabelle and Charlotte were having a reunion up there, and he wasn't a part of it. Becca Carter was there too, also crying. Her mother was still knocked out, so An-nabelle had her hands full.

Dex wanted to help her—but what the fuck did he know about little girls? Not a damned thing.

He'd almost lost them today. Both of them. He want-ed to go up there and sweep them into his arms and never let go. He wanted to kiss Annabelle silly, and then he wanted to spank her. She'd scared the fuck out of him. He'd watched in slow-motion horror when she'd rammed an elbow into Leonov's ribs and then followed up with a stomp to his instep. Instinct took over in the split second that she managed to widen the gap between her and Leonov. Dex took the shot, hitting Leonov in the shoulder.

He'd wanted to kill the fucker, but Mendez wanted the dude alive for some reason. Not that Dex wouldn't have killed him anyway if it was the only way to save Annabelle. He'd have splattered the man's brains in the dirt and taken whatever punishment came his way.

He closed his eyes and worked on slowing his heartbeat. It didn't work.

Holy fuck, he'd fathered a little girl. A beautiful, red-haired, crying little girl. His heart clanged and his head throbbed. What the fuck was he supposed to do about it?

If he joined Annabelle up front, what would he say to his child? Would he do something idiotic like burst into tears?

He frowned. No, Jesus, he was *not* going to burst into tears. But he *was* emotional and he didn't quite know how to handle it. He wished he could call Jack "Hawk" Hunter. They hadn't served together because Dex had replaced Jack on Alpha Squad, but he knew Jack and Gina's story. Jack hadn't found out about his son, Eli, until he was three. Dex would like to know how Jack processed that knowledge and how he'd gotten past the fear of fucking up as a dad.

Dex could also ask his own father. He was lucky enough to have a great dad. Being a farmer pretty much meant Dad had to get up with the cows and go to bed with the cows. But he'd taught Dex to hunt and fish, and he'd shown him nothing but love and support every day of his life. When Mama died, he'd been a rock for Dex and Katie.

Ice got up from his seat and came over to flop down next to Dex. "You okay, man?"

"Yeah." He sighed. "Guess you're going to have to write me up, huh? I won't deny I disobeyed an order."

Ice seemed to be chewing the inside of his lip. "Nah, I'm not going to write you up. I should, asshole, but I'm not. I realize you have a lot tied up in this mission. You were right—if that was Grace, no fucking way would I have let her go alone. And if my daughter's life was at stake—yeah, someone would be going home in a body bag if they tried to stop me."

He leaned his seat back and grinned. "Besides, I disobeyed Mendez directly when Grace was involved. Remember that one?"

Dex laughed. "Yep. The night we came out of the Tidal Basin and shocked the shit out of Ian Black's men."

"But not Ian Black," Ice added.

No, because that dude seemed to know everything. "Surprised we didn't encounter him on this mission."

"I'm sure he's hiding under a rock somewhere. He'll show up again when we least want him to."

Dex scrubbed his hand through his hair. "How do you do it, Ice? How can you be a father and do this crazy job too?"

Ice shrugged. "You just do, man. What are you going to do instead? Put your whole life on hold just because you have this calling to serve your country? You can be a dad and a husband, a friend and a brother, and still go to work every day. Your chances of not coming back are a little higher than the average, but hell, man, people die in car accidents every day. *We* are what keeps our country safe and free. I'd rather die doing this than driving down the interstate in the morning on the way to a job I hate."

"I don't know what to say to her."

Ice looked toward the front of the plane. "Just say hi. That's a start. You aren't going to tell the kid the truth today. There's time for that."

Dex sat for a long minute, thinking. Then he unbuckled his seat belt. "Yeah, you're right."

TWENTY-SEVEN

ANNABELLE NEVER WANTED TO LET go of her baby. Charlotte had cried at first, but now she was lying on the seats with her head on Annabelle's lap. Charlotte sucked her thumb, a habit that Annabelle certainly didn't encourage at the age of four, but now wasn't the time to admonish her for it. She stroked Charlotte's hair and tried not to give in to the urge to drag her daughter up into her arms and squeeze her while kissing her whole face.

Annabelle's insides still shook from her close encounter with Mr. Lyon. Her shirt was dry and stiff with his blood, but there'd been no time to change out of it. Maybe once Charlotte went to sleep. Lottie'd noticed the blood and cried harder, but Annabelle calmed her by explaining it didn't belong to her. She'd grabbed one of the blankets lying on the seat and ripped it open, wrapping it around the worst of the blood until she could change.

Dex appeared in the aisle and her heart flipped at the sight of him. He was moody-gorgeous as always, but the look on his face gutted her. He looked apprehensive. Dex had never looked anything less than one hundred percent confident in the entire time she'd known him—even when he'd been staring down the man holding a gun to her head —so this vulnerability was definitely new.

He glanced at Charlotte. Her eyes were closed, so maybe she was finally asleep. Annabelle hoped so. She smiled encouragingly at Dex and he sat beside her.

"How is she?"

"Upset, but she's calming down. It's been a frightening few days for her."

"Where's Becca?"

"Victoria took her to the bathroom. I believe she may have been promised a peek into the cockpit as well."

"Richie—Matt—said they did a quick medical check of the girls. They haven't been hurt or abused in any way."

Annabelle closed her eyes, fighting down the panic and fear that welled up in response to that statement. "Thank God."

"Yep. I'd have to kill him if they had been. Orders be damned."

"Where is he?"

"There's a prison cell in the back. It's used for transporting high-value targets."

Annabelle swallowed. She wasn't going to think about movies where the terrorist got free and hijacked the plane. Definitely not thinking about that.

"Oh. Where's he going?"

Dex shrugged. "DC to start. Maybe Guantanamo. Depends on what the big guns in charge want."

"He said this wasn't over. What do you think he meant?"

"He'd say anything to get us to believe he has valuable information."

"So is this over or not?"

"Yeah, I think it is."

He took her hand in his and her brain froze. She tried not to read anything into it, though white-hot emotion surged from her head to her toes. She loved him. But he didn't love her.

"You scared the shit out of me back there."

Annabelle cupped her hand over Lottie's exposed ear. "We're going to have to work on that mouth of yours," she said, trying to inject a little humor.

He looked contrite. "Sorry. I'm not used to kids."

She desperately wanted palm his cheek and feel the stubble scrape her skin as he turned his face into it. Then she wanted him to kiss her the way he had in his room two nights ago.

"It's okay."

"The other part of what I wanted to tell you is this: you were brave, Belle. I'm proud of you."

Okay, so she'd hoped he'd been planning to say something else. She should have known better. He let go of her hand, and disappointment performed a death spiral in her belly. She appreciated his pride. She wanted more.

"I did what I had to do," she said on a shrug she didn't feel. "Same as you did."

He laughed and shook his head. "I'm a commando. You're an accountant. Big difference, sweetheart."

"But we're alive, right? It's all good."

"Yeah, it's good." His gaze dropped to Charlotte. "Lot to figure out though."

"Yes. But we will." *I love you* hovered on the edge of her tongue, but she didn't dare say it. Not only because

Lottie might hear. What if she said the words and he looked at her with pity?

"Mama," Charlotte said, lifting her head. Her little eyes squinted with sleep. They landed on Dex. She took in the bandage on his arm, the blood staining his shirt, the sweat and dirt streaking his handsome face—and burst into tears.

They'd arrived at the base in Djibouti hours ago. Molly Carter had been whisked to the hospital along with the girls and Annabelle. Dmitri Leonov had been taken separately, under heavy guard. He'd lost a lot of blood and he needed surgery to repair the damage Dex's bullet had done.

Dex and his team retreated to the HOT compound located behind razor wire and heavy security. He wanted to be with Annabelle and Charlotte while they were checked out. Wanted to know they were okay.

But there was work to do, and he needed to be here.

He rubbed a hand over the nape of his neck. He hadn't gotten off on the right foot with his kid. She'd taken one look at him and started crying. His heart froze solid in his chest. Annabelle hugged the little girl and shushed her, telling her it was okay, Dex was a friend, she didn't need to cry. She'd stopped, but she'd stared warily for the duration of the short ride.

"It's the blood," Annabelle had told him, and he'd glanced down at the red stain on his shirt. Yeah, so maybe that wasn't the best way to meet his daughter for the first time.

He stalked down the corridor of the compound and strode into the war room. His team was gathered around a table, studying reports and maps. Kid tapped his computer keys, frowning. Dex assumed that meant no signal from the tracer program. Whoever'd moved that money was damn good at what they did.

And that worried Dex. He should be happy they had Leonov, and he was, but he didn't like that the money was still missing. So long as it wasn't where it was supposed to be, Annabelle could still be in danger. He'd told her he believed this ordeal was over, but he'd said it so she wouldn't worry. He could worry enough for both of them.

HOT needed to find the money and catch whoever was playing a game of cat and mouse. Only then would they get to the truth behind everything—and find out if the Helios project was truly compromised.

Dex caught Kid's eye, and the other man shrugged. "It's only been a few hours," he said. "There's still time."

"Any word on Marshall Porter?" Dex asked.

Richie shook his head. "He seems clean. Nothing in his background to suggest collusion with Archer other than the fact he's the brains behind Helios. We've got his credit card records. He hasn't traveled to Africa. No charges over the weekend, so he must have been hiking like he said."

"Is there a woman?" Ice asked.

"The most communication he seems to have with a woman not related to him would be his texts with Annabelle."

Dex frowned. Could Porter have a crush on Annabelle? Sure, but that wasn't a reason to steal half a billion dollars. And it certainly wasn't a reason to steal it from *her* when she needed it to bargain for her life.

"None of this makes sense," Dex said. "And we still don't know if it's the CIA, right?"

"Nope. Nothing from Mendez yet."

"Shit."

"They won't tell him anyway," Ice drawled. "You know how the spooks are. If they've got the cash, we'll never see it again."

"No kidding."

Kid whooped and they all jumped. "Ha! Not true, my man. Not true." He bent over the computer and started tapping keys. "I've got a ping."

It was late when Annabelle finally got Charlotte and Becca to sleep. They'd been given rooms in a facility near the hospital. Molly was out of surgery and doing well, but she'd have to stay overnight.

Annabelle put a hand to the small of her back and stretched. She was tired, but she didn't feel like she could sleep yet. After she'd put the girls to bed, she pulled the door to, going into the adjoining room to catch up on the news. The girls were clingy, which was understandable. She'd had to tell them a story before they would sleep.

She'd told them one from memory, fudging the parts she couldn't recall.

They'd had to talk to a crisis counselor before they'd been released to Annabelle. The counselor had told her it was good for them to be together right now. It was entirely possible they'd have nightmares or full-blown panic attacks for the next few weeks. She highly recommended counseling when they got home, just to make sure they were processing what had happened, but she expected them both to be fine in the long run. They hadn't been abused by Leonov or his people, and they'd mostly had Molly to run interference for them.

Molly had made the trip into an adventure, and Annabelle teared up to think of Molly doing that. She had to have known the danger they were in, and yet she'd kept her cool well enough to pretend it was a game. Strong, courageous Molly.

Dex had said he was proud of *her* for being strong in the market, but it was Molly who really got the award in Annabelle's book. All Annabelle had to do was hang around with a group of badass military black-ops people for a few days and do what they told her to do. Molly'd had to improvise and keep it together while under the power of Dmitri Leonov.

Annabelle shuddered. His voice had reminded her of snake skins rubbing together. His eyes were even worse. He had dead eyes.

A soft knock sounded on her door and she flinched. She went and peered out the peephole. Dex stood on the other side, looking rather hot in military camouflage. That was new. They'd done this whole trip in regular clothes and now he was clad like a soldier. She'd showered and changed at the hospital, so it was reasonable to expect he would have changed too.

She opened the door and stared. He was taller than her by several inches. Broad, beautiful, strong. His muscles stretched the fabric of the camouflage, and her mouth watered.

"Just wanted to make sure everything was good," he said.

"We're fine." She glanced over her shoulder at the door to the adjoining room. "The girls are asleep finally. Molly's resting in the hospital."

"Can I come in?"

Her pulse jumped a notch. She stepped back. "Yes, please."

He walked in and turned to watch as she closed the door. With him in the room, it was suddenly a lot smaller. Everything inside her ached. She loved him so much. Still. If she'd never had to go and ask for his help, she'd never know how much she hadn't gotten over him.

She wouldn't have to go home with a broken heart. She wouldn't have to try to get through the rest of her life seeing him on a regular basis but having no right to touch him. Damn Eric—he couldn't die and leave her in peace. He'd had to put her into Dex's path in such a way she'd never be free.

She closed her eyes. That wasn't fair. Even without Eric's theft and involvement with a psycho like Leonov, there was still the matter of Charlotte.

"I'm sorry I couldn't come over sooner, but there were things to do."

"I imagine so. That was quite the adventure today. Do you have to fill out reports like the police do?"

"Not quite, but yeah, there's a mission report."

"Did you find out where the money went?"

"Almost. The Kid's tracer finally pinged him back. We don't know precisely where the money is, but he's working on it. Someone is covering their tracks pretty thoroughly."

Annabelle shook her head. "Wow. I guess people will do almost anything for half a billion dollars. Steal, lie, kidnap, murder."

"Most would. That's life-changing money, Belle. It's freedom and security and so many other things."

She cocked her head. "Are you envious?"

"No, I'm not. But that's what money represents. You know it as well as I do. Hell, with even a hundredth of that, I could make sure my dad lived in comfort and kept his farm. I could hire people to take care of it and him. But that's not my lot in life. I'm not going to be a millionaire. Not unless I win the lottery."

She couldn't help but laugh. "Do you even play the lottery?"

"Sometimes I remember to buy a ticket. Mostly no."

"So no ideas about who took the money?"

"We looked at Marshall Porter. You knew we would. He seems clean. So somebody else must have known what Eric was doing and helped him get the money in the first place."

"I honestly don't know who else it could be. Archer Industries is filled with engineer and programmer types. Some of them are brilliant. It could be anyone, I suppose. Though I have trouble believing any of them would betray their country."

"If you have any names, that would help. Otherwise we'll look at them all."

Annabelle sighed and rubbed her hands through her hair. "God, there's so much to do when I get home. Figure out where the business stands, deal with the insurance, try to get us up and running somewhere else. Oh, and scrutinize all my employees to decide who's a traitor, right?"

He nodded gravely. "Sounds about right."

Her throat tightened. "And then there's us. You and me and Charlotte."

A flash of something that might be panic passed over his features before it was gone again. Was he thinking of running away from the responsibility?

As soon as she thought it, she was ashamed. No, Dex Davidson would never run from responsibility. He was too loyal and too proud to do such a thing. She knew his family, and she knew what kind of people they were.

"Yeah, I guess there is."

"Have you been thinking about it?"

"Yeah."

He went over and folded himself into the single chair in the room. Then he rubbed his hands down the length of his thighs. In anyone else, she would say it was a nervous gesture.

"And?" she asked.

He gazed at her for a long moment. "I think we should get married."

TWENTY-EIGHT

ANNABELLE'S MOUTH DROPPED OPEN. DEX had expected that. He hadn't decided on this course of action until after he'd left the war room and started over here. There'd been so many damned things going on the past few hours, and he hadn't been thinking straight since he'd found out the truth.

But he knew what he had to do. He'd been thinking about being a father, thinking about all kinds of things, and it hit him forcefully that the right thing to do, the thing that had always been drummed into him, was to marry a girl if you got her pregnant.

And maybe Annabelle wasn't a girl, and she wasn't pregnant anymore, but Charlotte was still his. He had a responsibility. He'd failed Annabelle five years ago when he hadn't rushed over to her house and demanded answers. She'd married Eric, and the asshole had abused her.

He owed her for that. And he owed Charlotte a life with two parents, not with a full-time parent and one who only came for visits. He couldn't leave the military right now even if he wanted to. His enlistment wasn't up for another two years, so they'd have to find a place in DC while he continued to work for HOT. They could talk about what came next when the two years were up.

"I, uh... Wow, where did that come from?" she finally managed.

"It's the right thing to do," he said firmly. "The only thing to do."

She folded her arms over her chest and cocked a hip. That was his first inkling that maybe she wasn't precisely thrilled with the suggestion. Which confused him because she was the one who'd as much as admitted she still loved him.

"Is that the only reason? It's the right thing to do?"

His brows slashed down. "What other reason is there? I'm her father. You're her mother. We'll get married and I'll provide for you both—"

"Now you wait just a minute," she said, stalking toward him with a finger wagging in his face. "I don't *need* anyone to provide for me. I'm a successful accountant, and I'm the owner of Archer Industries since Eric's death. I have a company to run. So if you're trying to suggest that I marry you and stay home to clean house and cook, you are sadly mistaken in your opinion of me."

He wanted to grab that finger and bite it. Instead, he got to his feet and glared down at her. "You said I was the only man you'd ever loved. You seemed upset to think there was no future for us. That was fucking yesterday, Belle—are you telling me you've changed your damned mind already?"

She popped a hand over his mouth, startling him. "Quiet or you'll wake the girls."

He nodded, though he was fuming, and she pulled her hand away. "You're giving me whiplash, Belle," he growled.

"And you're missing the point. The point being that, yes, when you said we were different people and we could never be what we once were, *that* upset me. We were crazy for each other back then. So if you think I'm going to settle for a bastardized version of what we used to have, you're nuts. I've already been married to one man who despised me—I won't marry another one who can't love me, even if he thinks he's doing the right thing by asking."

Hot emotion swirled in his gut. He wanted to grab her and kiss her just to remind her what it was still like between them—and he wanted to storm out and go punch something in the gym. He needed to expel some of this frustration.

She got inside his head and churned his brains to mush. She also made him crazy with need. Not that it meant anything to want her. It was a physical reaction based on familiarity and history.

Except that, hell, when he'd been inside her, there was no other place he'd wanted to be. She did things to him that no other woman could do. Still.

But that was sex, not love. He wasn't going to make the mistake of thinking it was love just to make her happy.

"I don't despise you," he growled, picking up on that phrase rather than the part about love. "Hell, I think I proved the other night that I'm still attracted to you. I want you and you want me. We can be good together, and maybe one day it'll turn into love."

She didn't look mollified. In fact, she looked angrier than ever. She poked him in the chest. Hard. "No."

He blinked. "No? No what? We aren't good together, you don't still want me?"

"No, I'm not marrying you."

Disbelief rolled around in his brain. His heart squeezed. He couldn't say why. He was doing the logical thing. He expected her to be logical too.

"Why the hell not? It's the perfect solution."

If she'd looked angry before, she looked ready to burst now. She made an explosive noise and turned away, putting distance between them before whirling around again. "Why not? Why *not?* I've already told you why not —I won't marry you if you don't love me, and I won't be guilted into it either. If you try to use Charlotte to make me say yes, you're almost as bad as Eric and my parents. They didn't care what happened to me so long as they got what they wanted. Well, I won't do it again. Not for you, not for anyone."

He was stunned by her speech. And stung because, dammit, he wasn't like Eric or her parents.

"I'm nothing like Eric," he grated. "Nothing at all. And you know it. I'm trying to do the right thing for all of us."

She folded her arms over her chest again. Her eyes flashed and her cheeks blazed with color. "Nobody asked you to be in charge, Dex. You don't have to make decisions for all of us. We'll do what's best for Charlotte, but I won't marry you. I know you're her father, I know you're a good man—but she's already had one father who was never interested in her, even before he had her tested, and I won't suddenly subject her to another man who doesn't even know what being a dad is going to entail."

The urge to punch something at the gym was gaining strength. "Are you telling me that you think I'm going to suck at being a dad? That I'm going to abandon her because she's four and probably a handful and I know nothing about kids? Are you really telling me that?"

She had the grace to look sheepish. "I didn't mean it like that."

"Yeah, you did."

She sank onto a chair, her urge to fight deflating before his eyes. "Fine, maybe I did. I'm sorry. But goddammit, Dex, this is a lot to process right now. I'm about as emotionally drained as a person can be."

His own urge to fight ebbed. She'd been through a lot, and he needed to give her a break. At least for tonight.

"I won't abandon her, Belle. She's mine and yours together. I'm overwhelmed and, yeah, even a bit scared." He pressed a fist to his gut. "But here, deep down, I'm so committed to her happiness and well-being that I can't even think of abandoning her. I'd lay down my life to protect hers. *And* yours. If that's not enough for you— Jesus, I don't know what is."

What had she done? That was the refrain echoing through her brain on the long plane ride home. Dex had basically been offering up her fantasy—a life with him like they'd once planned—and she'd told him no. It was almost like she'd been an observer, watching some other woman wreck her chance at happiness with the man she loved.

She'd also practically accused him of being prepared to abandon his responsibilities at the first sign of trouble. Definitely not cool. That wasn't Dex, and she knew it.

But how could she say yes? It *wasn't* the life they'd once planned. In that life, Dex had been crazy in love with her. He'd believed in her—and in them as a couple. He didn't believe anymore. He'd said he would lay down his life for hers, and she believed him. But that wasn't what she wanted out of him.

She wanted *him*. His heart. His soul. She wanted what she'd once had with him, and if that made her crazy and idealistic, then so what? Life was too short to spend it shackled to someone who would never be what you needed. She'd already been there, and she wasn't going back.

She looked up a couple of times and caught him looking at her. But they didn't speak. He made no moves to sit with her or to talk with Charlotte. It broke her heart in a way. She blamed herself.

They made it to DC, and she didn't see him again. She'd gone into a room with Colonel Mendez and a woman named Samantha Spencer and told her version of the story. They'd warned her that she couldn't speak of it—any of it—to anyone else once she got home.

A night in DC and then she was on a small plane with the girls and Molly, heading for Lexington. The girls chattered nonstop and played games on the entertainment devices installed in the seat backs. They didn't seem tired at all, yet Annabelle thought she'd never get the grittiness out of her eyes. She was perpetually tired after the past few days. Whirlwind trip to Africa and back again, not to mention a car chase, a kidnapping, and having a gun shoved against her skull.

Briar City would be positively dull after that. Thank God.

Molly sat beside her while the girls sat across the aisle. Her arm was in a cast and a sling. Annabelle still felt guilty for involving Molly. She'd apologized so much that Molly had forbidden her to speak about it again.

Molly turned from where she'd been looking out the window. The wan look on her friend's face pained her.

"How are you, Mol? In any pain?"

Molly smiled. "No, I'm fine. They gave me good drugs. How about you?"

"I'm fine."

Molly didn't miss a beat. "I don't think you are."

Annabelle blinked. "What's that supposed to mean?"

"Dex. You're right about how seriously sexy that man is, by the way."

"Of course I am."

"You also aren't over him."

She dropped her gaze to her lap. "I know."

"So what are you going to do about it?"

"Do? There's nothing I can do." She lowered her voice after glancing at the girls. She'd told Molly about Dex being Charlotte's father. Her friend had taken it in stride. In fact, she'd been thrilled. "*Much better than that asshole, Eric,*" she'd said. Annabelle took a deep breath before saying the words that she hadn't stopped thinking about. "He said we needed to get married."

"So when's the wedding?"

"I refused." She spread her hands on her lap. "You know what it was like with Eric."

"Dex isn't that kind of man, is he?" she asked tightly.

"No, definitely not. But I got married because it's what someone else desired in order to…" She did air quotes. "…*fix* a situation. I don't want to get married again just to fix something."

Molly grasped her hand and squeezed. "Oh, honey, I get it. But if he's still the man you want, shouldn't you at least entertain the idea? Nobody says it has to happen right away. Give it time, but let him know you want to move forward."

Annabelle groaned. "God, I'm so bad at this. All I could think was that I didn't want to go into another marriage for reasons other than love. I can't back down now that I've told him that."

"No, probably not. But Belle, you have to try to move forward. He's her father, and he's going to be involved."

She nodded. "You're right. I know you are. After we get home and I figure out what kind of a mess I have to clean up at Archer Industries, I'll call him."

Molly smiled. "I think it'll all work out. It's just going to take time."

"I hope you're right."

Dex knew that Annabelle had boarded a plane with Molly and the girls and that they were currently on their way to Kentucky. He'd wanted to go with her, but there were things to be done here. He'd head out to Kentucky in a few days. Give her time to deal with Archer Industries and figure out what they were going to do first.

Give her time to think.

He was still pissed that she'd refused his proposal. Except he hadn't exactly proposed, had he? Shit no. He'd told her they should get married for the sake of the kid. That wasn't precisely the way to handle it. He knew it but he'd done it anyway.

So now he had to deal with the fallout and hope he could make her see reason in a few days. He'd go tell Katie and his dad about Charlotte too. It would be an adjustment for everyone, but they'd figure it out.

He punched in his access code and headed into the secure area of HOT HQ. He loved this place. Just fucking loved it. But he'd give it up if he had to. For Charlotte. And hell, even for Annabelle. They could build something good with time.

He busted into the war room and found some of his guys sitting around the conference table. Kid was projecting his laptop on the overhead, and everyone's attention was on the screen.

Dex stopped. "What the fuck is going on?"

"Welcome to the party, Sergeant Davidson."

Dex hadn't noticed the colonel until he spoke. Because the fucking lights were dim and his attention was on Kid's display. "Sir," Dex replied crisply, snapping to attention. "I didn't mean—"

Mendez waved him off. "Save it, son. Sit."

Dex sat. Ice arched an eyebrow at him and grinned. Yeah, that was a close one all right. He had to get back on his game. Soon.

"I've found the money. It's in the Cayman Islands," Kid said. "It bounced through three other accounts around the world before ending up in one account."

"So who owns the account?"

"That's what I'm working on." Kid tapped a few more buttons and waited. Dex didn't doubt he'd figure it out. Kid was one of the best hackers in the business. Add in the fact he was a black-ops badass, and you just didn't get any more methodical and tough when it came to chasing down obscure facts.

"Hey," Victoria Brandon said, walking into the room with a sheaf of papers in her hand. "Got something here."

"Just a sec," Kid said.

A name popped up on the screen.

"Holy shit." It was Victoria. They all snapped their gazes to her.

She held out the papers. "Found another credit card connected to Marshall Porter. It's not in his name though."

"What's the name?" Mendez asked.

She nodded at the screen. "That one. Harold M. Proctor. And Harold traveled to Grand Cayman over the weekend."

TWENTY-NINE

AFTER THE EXCITEMENT OF THE past few days, it was strange landing in Lexington to a fairly normal level of activity. Annabelle kept looking around her, searching for the anomaly. The man with dead eyes who was about to pounce.

Molly gave her a strange look as they piled into the private car waiting for them at the airport. Annabelle smiled even though her heart performed jumping jacks and adrenaline surfed through her veins. What the hell? Leonov was in custody. He wasn't coming for her or her loved ones.

Was this what PTSD was like?

She swallowed and hoped the trembling in her fingers didn't migrate up her arm and into her teeth. Charlotte and Becca were subdued, for which Annabelle was thankful. It was late afternoon, and they'd gotten up early and taken no naps.

"It's going to be all right, Belle," Molly said, squeezing her arm. "You'll have Archer Industries up and running again in no time."

"I think I should go by there," she replied. "See the damage for myself."

"Why don't you drop me and the girls at your house then? We'll have dinner ready when you get home."

"That would be great. Thank you."

Maybe she shouldn't push it, but she felt like she needed to do something. She'd been gone for a few days, and her company had burned. Her employees were in limbo, and she couldn't let that continue. Eric hadn't been insured, the cheap bastard, but the company had a policy. She needed to call the insurance company and find out exactly what she had to do—but first she had to see the building with her own eyes.

She dropped Molly and the girls at home, promising to return soon. When she settled in the car again, her phone beeped with a text.

Dex: *When you get this, go to a hotel. Take Molly and the girls with you. Don't communicate with anyone other than me.*

Her heart dropped to her toes and her lungs pumped in air at an alarming rate. She gripped the armrest and took deep, slow breaths.

"Excuse me," she said to the driver.

"Yes?" He'd been nothing but polite since he'd picked them up. He wasn't too tall or big, which was reassuring right about now.

"I need to change the plan. I have to go back home—and then I'm going to need you to take us to a hotel."

The man smiled at her in the rearview. "Sorry, Mrs. Archer, but that's simply not possible."

They went wheels up in fifteen minutes. That might have been a record, even for HOT. They didn't typically operate within the United States, not a full team with weaponry and official transport, but there was no time to get anyone else up to speed. Besides, the mission involved Russian agents and could be classified as ongoing. It hadn't ended when they'd set foot in DC because they hadn't found the end of the money trail.

Now they knew where the money was—and who the major players were.

Dex read over the file Mendez had given Richie earlier.

There was a reason Marshall Porter hadn't disappeared with the money yet. It didn't belong to the Russian government. Instead, it belonged to Zoprava, the Russian tech firm HOT dealt with a month ago when Grigori Androv had tried to kill Sophie Nash, Fiddler's woman.

Leonov worked for Zoprava. He'd done the buy for Androv, who was now dead. God only knew why Zoprava wanted it. Maybe they didn't. Maybe it was for Open Sky, the shadow hacker group that Androv also financed. They had their fingers in a lot of illegal stuff. Revolutionary battery-recharging technology could have a lot of applications beyond the one it was being designed for. It could also be highly lucrative on the dark web.

Neither HOT nor the CIA knew what had gone wrong with the original transaction. Whatever the case, Porter had the money in an account under Harold M. Proctor's name and Leonov was the hired gun sent to get the money back for Zoprava.

Androv's successor, Sergei Turov, was every bit as ruthless as Androv had been. Since Turov didn't have the money, Annabelle was still in danger. And Turov had entered the US two days ago, ostensibly to buy a racehorse in Kentucky. Since he didn't currently have racehorses, it was concerning.

It was a little over an hour to Lexington, but they made it in record time. You could do that when you had a pilot willing to put the hammer down and a colonel who could get priority clearance for landing.

Alpha Squad was on the ground and piling into two big black GMCs about an hour after Annabelle had landed. Dex checked his phone for messages, but there was nothing. She hadn't replied to his text. Worry ate at his gut like battery acid.

He called her home number. Molly Carter answered within two rings. "Hey, Molly. It's Dex," he said, trying to sound light and breezy when he was anything but. "Can I speak to Annabelle?"

"I'm sorry, but she dropped us off and went over to look at the building. Did you try her cell?"

He didn't want to upset her. "Not yet. I thought she might not answer if she saw it was me."

Which was a distinct possibility considering how pissed she'd been at him. But she would have answered that text. Annabelle might be angry, but she wasn't stupid or vindictive.

Molly laughed. "I think you might be surprised. Go ahead and give it a try. If she doesn't pick up, I'll tell her you called."

"All right. Thanks."

Richie shot him a look. "We'll send over a squad car to watch the house. No sense uprooting her and the girls again when Annabelle's the one the Russians want."

Dex nodded.

Kid had his combat laptop open. "We should be able to track her using the program I installed on her phone to listen to her calls."

Dex could have kissed Kid for not removing the program once they'd returned Stateside. "Can you turn her microphone on too?"

Kid lifted an eyebrow. "Does a bear shit in the woods?"

THIRTY

ANNABELLE'S RIBS TOOK A BEATING as her heart tried to claw its way free. The acid taste of fear clogged her throat. She'd tried to open the car door and break free when the driver came to a stoplight, but the door wouldn't budge. She'd peppered him with questions about who he was and where he was taking her, but he'd answered none of them.

And now she was here, in a hotel suite at the Lexington Hilton, pacing a room that had been carefully stripped of anything she might use to escape. She could look out the window and see all of downtown, but she couldn't get there.

Not unless she grew sticky cups on her hands and feet like a lizard.

The door swung inward and she ceased pacing, suddenly rooted in place like a rat in a glue trap. Three men walked in. Or, rather, two men carrying a third between them. He slumped in their grip, his feet dragging the floor. The men dumped him at her feet, and she yelped when she recognized him.

Marshall Porter peered up at her through eyes that had gone six rounds with a heavyweight boxer. They were puffy, red, and slitted. Blood trickled from one corner of his mouth.

"Hi, Annabelle," he scratched out.

"Marshall—oh my god, what have they done to you?"

Another man entered the room. He had his phone to his ear. Russian poured from his lips as silky smooth as water from a spout. She was beginning to hate the sound of Russian.

"Ah, Mrs. Archer," he said, pocketing his phone. "How lovely to finally meet you."

"I…" What did one say to that? "Who are you?"

"You may call me Sergei." He was all affability and good humor, which was somehow worse than the dead eyes of Mr. Lyon. This man… *this* man was the real danger, the unseen puppet master pulling the strings.

Marshall groaned and her attention dropped to him. Sympathy punched her. She wanted to wrap him in a hug and tell Sergei to leave him alone. A mom response that wouldn't work with a bully this big.

"My dear Mrs. Archer—you have my money. I want it back."

Annabelle gulped. The fear she'd experienced whenever Lyon called her and said those words was amplified a thousandfold now. They were more terrifying when delivered with a good-natured smile than when growled threateningly.

"I… I don't have it. I mean, I did have it…" Oh God, she was babbling. "B-but it disappeared. Someone hacked into the accounts and transferred it all. It's gone."

Sergei's expression didn't change, but the feeling in

the room did. The temperature dropped several degrees even as fire snapped in his gaze. Ice coated her body, freezing her limbs. Death perched nearby, waiting to pounce.

She wasn't getting out of here alive. Not unless she could produce half a billion dollars and hand it over to this Russian in the next five minutes.

Stop that. Think. You aren't dying. You have too much to live for.

And yet she didn't know how she was going to survive. Or how she was going to get Marshall out of here with her.

"That is too bad, Mrs. Archer. Mr. Porter doesn't have it either. Very disappointing." He tugged a cuff into place as if it were displeasing him when in fact he looked impeccable. He twisted the cuff link, apparently preferring it to face a different direction. When he finished, he repeated the process with the other cuff.

He turned and snapped his fingers at one of the men who'd carried Marshall into the room. The man produced a laptop and handed it to Sergei, who opened it and set it down on the nearest table.

"One of you—and I do not care which one—is going to transfer that money into my account in the next half hour. If I return and it's not done, you will both die." He paused and goose bumps chased down her spine. "You may think death is a sweet release from the hell you currently find yourself in, but be aware that I plan to make it as slow and painful as possible. Then I shall kill your families, though you won't be around to see it. I will still not have my money, this is quite true—but I will be satisfied that you won't either."

He strode from the room, the two goons on his heels. The door clicked behind them, and Annabelle was still frozen in place. The spell snapped and she dropped to her knees, rolling Marshall toward her. His face was a mess. Fury swirled, devastating everything in its path.

Concentrate.

"Marshall, I can't do this alone. You're going to have to help me."

He groaned as he pushed upright while she hooked an arm under his and tugged. When he was standing, she herded him to the bed and put him down on it. Then she rushed over and picked up the computer.

She set it on his lap carefully.

"I'm not transferring the money," he said. "It's mine."

Shock scalded through her like icy fire. "It was you? You're the one who took the money?"

"I thought you'd figured that out. What did you expect me to do with this?" He stabbed a finger at the computer.

She waved her hands, thinking of Billy Blake and his dummy bank page. "I thought you could fake it somehow! Make him think we'd done it. But instead you actually *know* where it is. You're the one who took it when I was in Jorwani!"

Anger glowed like hot coals in her belly. She wanted to kill him.

"There was a breach in my security protocols. I had to move it."

He'd taken the money when she'd needed it most. He'd known the *entire time* that he was sitting on half a billion dollars that someone was willing to kill for. And he'd known that everything pointed to her being the one who had it. She could hardly wrap her mind around it.

"You and Eric conspired to *sell* a top secret program for profit. That's treason, Marshall!"

"I would *never* betray my country!" he screamed. "And I would never give up what I've worked so hard to create. Helios is *mine.*"

She reeled. There was something unhinged about him. Had it always been there and she was only noticing it now? "But you gave Eric *some*thing to sell. You must have. What was it?"

Smugness tightened the corners of his mouth. "A fake. It looked right on paper. All the test results, the schematics, real video of the flights. It was enough."

Numbness wrapped around her and squeezed. She'd hated Eric but she hadn't wished him dead so much as out of her life. "You had to know they'd figure it out and Eric would be the target of their anger."

His eyes gleamed with hatred. "I knew."

"You sent him to his death. And maybe you set me up too. Because when I couldn't produce the money, Leonov would kill me and you'd be free to take it and disappear. Is that what you planned?"

"You stole Helios from me. You made me give up my rights. You deserve whatever happens."

If the Russians hadn't already beat him, she'd slap the shit out of him. "I don't care about Helios! You can have the whole damned thing—but without Archer Industries *paying* for your time, *giving* you a laboratory and expensive equipment, not to mention numerous opportunities to beta test, you wouldn't have a goddamn product in the first place. Do you think you could have done it on your own?

261

With what resources?"

"It was my idea. You had no right."

Fury cascaded from her scalp to her toes. Her body was on fire with it. "Transfer the goddamn money, Marshall. If you don't, I'm telling him when he comes back that you know where it is."

He snorted. "He won't believe you. They beat me and I didn't confess, so what makes you think he'll take your word for it?"

Ice skidded down her spine. She'd liked this man at one time. Thought he was harmless and sweet. She'd been so wrong. "If you don't transfer it, he'll kill us both. It's hard to enjoy that kind of money when you're dead, don't you think?"

He snorted. "He won't kill me. He needs me. You, on the other hand…"

"Why does he need you? You've convinced him you don't have the money."

"I can fix Helios for him."

Annabelle blinked. He either had the balls of an elephant, or he was seriously deluded. "You said you aren't a traitor. How is fixing Helios for a Russian not betraying your country?"

"I didn't say I would fix it, only that I *can*. It's called buying time."

The door swung open, and Annabelle squeaked in surprise.

"My meeting is over faster than I expected," Sergei said. He strolled casually into the room, his hulking men bringing up the rear. "And still no deposit in my account."

He *tsked* as one of the men drew a pistol and cocked it. "Who wishes to die first?"

THIRTY-ONE

"GOT HER PHONE," KID SAID. "Calling up the coordinates on GPS. Activating the microphone."

Dex's heart tattooed a steady beat against his ribs. They would make it. They had to make it. He pictured Annabelle, her golden hair hanging over her shoulders, her smile lighting up her face—and something punched him in the gut. Hard.

He couldn't lose her. Not again. Not like this.

The sounds of Russian conversation flowed from Kid's speakers and filled the SUV compartment. Dex's stomach knotted. Goddammit! The Russians had taken her —but what could they hope to gain? She didn't have the money. Porter did.

"They would have confiscated her phone when they took her," Richie said. "They wouldn't let her keep it."

"Got 'em," Kid whooped. "Downtown. Hilton. Top floor, corner suite."

Richie relayed the message to the vehicle behind them and they raced down Lexington's streets, skidding around corners and slaloming between cars. The only reason no police sirens blared behind them had to be Mendez. He was working it from HQ as hard as they were working it here.

They skidded into the parking lot and shot from the vehicles like bullets aimed at a target. They weren't dressed in tactical gear because that would be too obvious —and too disturbing to the guests of the hotel. But they were as armed and dangerous as only Special Ops soldiers can be. They split up, going in the service entrance to take opposite stairwells to the top floor. Kid stayed in the SUV. He would take care of temporarily jamming the elevators, and he'd monitor Annabelle's phone for movement.

Dex pounded up the stairs with his guys, pulses racing, breaths razoring in and out, legs aching with the speed and effort. They hit the top floor, sweat popping out of their pores and rolling down their foreheads, and Richie motioned them to halt behind him.

Big Mac's voice came through the mic in their ears. "Team Bravo in position."

"Alpha leader copies. Kid, anything?" Richie asked.

"You need to go in *now*. Sergei Turov's in there, threatening to kill Annabelle and someone else. Not sure who. He hasn't said a name…"

"Shit," Richie swore. "Let's go, boys."

Kid interrupted. "Mendez's orders are not to kill Turov unless there's a clear and present danger. I think we all know why."

Red swirled across Dex's vision. Yeah, they all knew why. Grigori Androv had died within hours of being released from HOT's custody a month ago. If the man who'd inherited the business also got tangled up in a HOT operation, there would be questions.

Questions that might land Mendez before a congressional committee.

But if the motherfucker was threatening Annabelle, Dex didn't care about congressional hearings or any other goddamn thing.

"Everybody got that? Good. Mission is a go. Alpha leader over and out."

They burst into the hall on separate ends. Dex's team was closest to the corner room and reached it first. They flattened themselves on either side of the door. Team Bravo came ghosting down the hallway, moving fast and silently hustling stray guests back into their rooms. Richie gave the signal and Dex and Flash moved together, drawing pistols and busting through the door. They didn't have the luxury of using a flashbang in the hotel, so they made it up with the element of surprise.

Two men rushed at them through the door of the adjoining room, weapons drawn. But they weren't fast enough for HOT. Before either could get off a round, Dex threw himself at the closest one, knocking the man's weapon up and into his nose before snatching it from his grip. For good measure, he kneed the guy in the balls. Dude went down gasping and clutching at his groin.

The other Russian went down as Flash tackled him. Flash knocked his head against the floor a few times and the dude went limp. Then Flash zip-tied him with steel-reinforced cables while Dex left his Russian for someone else to bag and tag.

In the adjoining room, Sergei Turov pressed a gun to Annabelle's skull. She sat on the bed, eyes wide and blinking, her hands clenched together. A man lay on the bed, his face bruised and beaten, a computer open on his lap. Took a minute to realize it was Marshall Porter.

Dex didn't know why the asshole was here or what was going on—and he didn't care. So long as he got Annabelle out of this alive, that was all he needed in order to keep breathing.

"I will kill this woman if you take another step," Turov said.

Dex growled. This man was *not* taking Annabelle from him. She was his one, his only. His always. He protected what was his—and to hell with orders. He squeezed the trigger and the Sig exploded, sending a bullet straight through Sergei Turov's torso. Turov dropped like a stone, gasping as blood gushed from the wound and spread over the carpet.

Annabelle's eyes widened. She turned her head, but Dex stalked over and gripped her chin, preventing her from looking at Turov writhing on the floor, covered in blood.

"Dex?"

"Yeah, baby," he said softly, "it's me."

She flung herself into his arms. He closed his eyes, breathed in her shampoo, a bubble of deep emotion welling like a geyser inside him. Any damned second and he'd blow. God, what a fucking idiot he was. He'd thought he didn't love her anymore. He'd been horribly, stupidly wrong.

"Oh Dex. Oh my god, Dex. I didn't think I'd survive this one—"

He palmed her cheek and tilted her head back, crushing his mouth down on hers with all the need and fear he'd held in check. She melted into him like sugar liquefying, so sweet and hot. Her mouth opened and she licked his bottom lip. He slipped his tongue inside, delved deep. He didn't think he ever wanted to come up for air.

His skin flamed. Desire tap-danced its way along his spine, into his balls. He couldn't get enough of her—and yet he had to stop and push her away. They had more immediate concerns to deal with. He hustled her toward the adjoining room.

"Goddamn it, Double Dee," Big Mac said. "You shot the fucker."

"He would've killed Belle. I had no choice."

Big Mac grimaced. "I know, man. I know."

"Hey," Richie called from the entry. "Gotta bug out. Let's move. Kid, release the elevators—and call 911. We've got a tango down."

"Copy that," Kid said.

Ice grabbed Marshall Porter and hefted him over his shoulder. Then they hightailed it to the elevators. Dex kept his hand wrapped around Annabelle's. He didn't want to let go. Couldn't let go. She was his, and he'd do whatever it took to keep her safe. To keep *her*.

They piled into the SUVs and squealed tires the hell out of there. Dex had an arm around Annabelle. There was so much he wanted to say to her, but this wasn't the time. His teammates crowded around them, and the tension was ratcheted on high. They'd just infiltrated a US hotel and he'd shot a Russian national.

But Annabelle was alive. That was all that mattered to him. He'd take his licks from the colonel.

And if the consequences were more dire than an ass chewing?

He'd take that too.

THIRTY-TWO

ANNABELLE YANKED THE HOSPITAL GOWN over her thighs. She was not a happy camper right this second. She didn't need to be in a hospital, but Dex and his team insisted she had to get checked out. So here she sat, in a private room in a DC hospital, waiting for the doctor to say she could go.

She'd called Molly and told her what happened. Well, as much as she could anyway. Annabelle rubbed a hand over her forehead and worked on calming her racing heart. She had no idea how Dex did what he did. She'd had enough danger and drama to last her a lifetime. If no one ever pointed a gun at her again, that would be just fine and dandy with her.

The door opened, but it wasn't the doctor who walked in. It was Dex. He hulked into the room, exuding testosterone and worry. His dark eyes raked over her and a little thrill shimmied along her nerve endings. She hoped he'd come and take her in his arms, but he stood several feet away, legs spread, arms folded over his chest, looking big and mean and ready to tear something apart with his bare hands. After the way he'd kissed her earlier, his aloofness confused her.

"How are you, Belle?"

"I'd be better if I could put my clothes on and go home."

"Soon. But we had to have you checked out first."

"In DC?"

He shrugged. "This is a no-questions-asked kind of place. Besides, we had to get Marshall Porter back here for questioning."

"And? Did you learn anything?"

"A few things. He's down the hall, but my colonel's in there with him."

She quirked a brow. "Agent Gibbs, you mean?"

He snorted and a trickle of warmth dripped into her. Maybe he wasn't still pissed at her for turning his proposal down.

"Yeah, Agent Gibbs. He's putting the screws to Porter now."

"What's going to happen to him?"

"If he turns over the money, he'll probably get a lighter sentence. If not, he's going away for a long time."

"He didn't actually kill anyone. And he didn't really turn over Helios to a foreign power."

"He didn't turn over Helios, but he compromised a top secret project by sharing what he did. Those test videos are classified. So is the existence of the project. It's still treason."

"Why did the Russians have him? Leonov didn't seem interested in him. He came after me instead of Marshall."

"They knew Eric had a partner. Took them some time

to figure out that Porter was the inventor of Helios though. He'd erased his name from every document he sent over. Turov must have decided that the two of you were the ones most likely to have the money."

"Wow. They beat him and he didn't confess. Turov must have *really* thought it was me at that point." She dropped her head. The sympathy and fury in Dex's gaze was suddenly too much to bear. "Thanks for saving me. Again."

He crossed the room and tipped her chin back. A shiver rocked her at the skin-on-skin contact, even though it was so small. His fingers. Her chin. Three or four points of contact and her entire body was on fire with want—and a wild, impossible love.

"I'll always save you, Belle. You've been in my blood since I was a teenager. I don't think you're ever getting out."

Her heart thumped. "What does that mean, Dex?"

"It means I've tried to get you out of my heart for five years. Even thought I'd done it." He brought his other hand up and cupped her cheeks in both palms. "I was wrong."

Annabelle sucked in a breath and bit down on her lower lip to keep from bursting into tears. She'd been through too much to cry now. Besides, what if she was hearing him wrong? What if he wasn't saying he loved her at all?

"I don't know what that means," she whispered past the knot in her throat.

"Means? Jesus, Belle. It means I love you. It means I never stopped, even when I thought I hated you. I love you. I loved you so much it almost broke me when you left. I had to think I hated you in order to survive it. I've been cold and dead inside, pretending not to care about anyone. But I want you in my life. You and Charlotte both. I want to marry you and make more babies with you—if you want more babies. I want to be a dad and a husband, and I want what we should have had for the past five years. Fuck Eric. Fuck your parents—though I promise not to say that to their faces if you don't want me to. Fuck them all. But please, give me another chance. Marry me and let me show you how good it can be."

Shock froze her brain. Her tongue wouldn't work. Words wouldn't form.

Worry clouded his handsome face. "Belle, baby. Say something."

"I... Dex." She curled her fists into the black T-shirt clinging to his muscles like a lover. He was warm and hard, and she loved him so much she thought she might die of it. "Kiss me."

He crushed his mouth to hers, and she threw her arms around his neck, arching her body into his as tongue met tongue. The kiss was velvety perfection, a hot, wet, arousing combination of tongues and lips and teeth. Dex fisted the hospital gown, his knuckles brushing the groove of her spine. Desire spun out of control, electrifying her skin, making her wet and tingly and achy. She needed him—his hard cock thrusting into her, his mouth on hers, his hands touching her.

Her fingers flew to his belt buckle and he stiffened. "Wait. Baby, no," he said, pushing her gently away.

Her nipples poked through the thin layer of cotton, and her body ached when he stepped back.

"I need you," she rasped.

"I need you too, but baby…"

"Lock the door, Dex. It's a private room."

There was a knock on the door and they split apart like wet paper.

"Ms. Quinn-Archer?" A woman entered with a stethoscope and a chart.

Annabelle nodded.

"I'm Doctor Howell." Her gaze skipped to Dex and back to Annabelle.

Annabelle cleared her throat. "This is my fiancé." Happiness fizzed and popped in her veins.

"Dex, ma'am," he said, offering the doctor his hand.

"Nice to meet you. If you could give us a few minutes, I need to examine Ms. Quinn-Archer. You can come back in when we're finished."

His gaze slid to hers. "If you want me to stay, Belle, I will." She liked that he gave her the power to decide.

"It's okay. Can you get me a coffee from somewhere?"

"Yeah."

He walked out of the room and her heart went with him.

"Wow," Doctor Howell said. "That is one gorgeous man. Congratulations."

Annabelle couldn't contain the smile that felt as wide as the sun. "Thank you. I'm a lucky woman."

"Sergeant Davidson."

Dex spun to find Colonel Mendez approaching. He swallowed. He'd hoped this shit train could be avoided for a few more hours, but he'd known it was impossible.

"Yes, sir," he said, snapping to attention. Not easy when holding a cup of coffee, but he did it.

Mendez strode up to him and stared him in the eye. The colonel was a big man, tall and broad and badass as hell. He hadn't done fieldwork in years, but Dex imagined tangling with him was still a master class in how to get your ass kicked.

"Son, you've caused me trouble. A lot of trouble. At ease."

Dex relaxed only marginally, ready to snap-to again should the colonel decide to deliver an epic ass chewing here in the hospital. This was a secure wing, used only for the most high-value prisoners and personnel, so there was a good chance he might not wait until they were back at HOT.

"Yes, sir. Sorry, sir."

Mendez waved as if dismissing a fly. "You took the shot. Your teammates tell me it was necessary. What do you think?"

"I think, sir, that maybe I could have aimed a little better."

Mendez snorted. "Better how? A kill shot or a shot that did less damage?"

"I preferred the kill shot—but I would have rather done less damage for HOT's sake."

"I wish you had too. But it's done. You shot the CEO of Zoprava—he's in ICU in Lexington, by the way. He survived the surgery. He may never walk again though."

Dex gritted his teeth. He didn't like having caused that kind of damage. But it was also the nature of the job. He'd take the shot again if it meant Annabelle would be in his arms unharmed.

Mendez put a hand on his shoulder and squeezed. "This is what we do, son. We protect civilians and we save the world for another day, if at all possible. I wouldn't have wanted you to sacrifice Annabelle or even that low-life Porter just to make my job easier. I'll deal with the fallout. I didn't get where I am by taking the easy road."

Relief and respect were a double tap to the brain. He'd have taken the ass chewing and the disciplinary action, but goddamn did he love this man right now.

"Take your girl to a hotel for the night. We'll have her back in Lexington tomorrow. You'll be at HQ at 0600 along with everyone else. We've still got cleanup to do."

"Sir, yes, sir."

Mendez strode away and Dex let out a breath. *Close one.*

They barely made it into the hotel room before they were ripping at each other's clothes. Annabelle's heart raced furiously as she yanked Dex's pants down his hips. He tugged off her jeans and panties, dropping them on the floor and attacking her mouth again.

She threw her arms around his neck. "Where were we when the doctor interrupted?" she purred.

"Here." He lifted her and she wrapped her legs around his waist. Her pussy rode the ridge of his cock, her legs tightening around him as she worked herself against his body.

"You're making it hard to concentrate, baby," he groaned.

"No concentrating. Only feeling." She leaned back and ripped her shirt over her head. She was wearing a bra, but he took care of that in short order. He feasted on her nipples while she moaned her approval.

She was so wet. She wanted him inside her. *Now.*

"I'm on the pill, Dex. You know I've been with no one else but you in two years."

"I'm safe," he growled. "If you trust me."

It wasn't even a question. "I do."

He took them down to the bed and slid deep inside her in one smooth thrust. Her breath stopped as he filled her. So good. Always so good.

He wrapped his fingers around hers and lifted her arms above her head. She arched her back, flexed her hips, brought him deeper inside her. He made love to her, stroking into her slowly and deliberately, taking her higher.

"Dex," she gasped as the pressure built. "More. I need *more.*"

He fucked her harder then, pressing her into the mattress with his big body, driving her against the headboard. And then it hit her, a nuclear detonation that stole her breath and dissolved her muscles. Dex came with her, groaning out her name.

They stilled, breaths sawing in and out, bodies spent. He managed to roll to his side, taking her with him. She wrapped her arms around him and pressed her lips to his chest.

This was love. Love and belonging and rightness. Tears pricked her eyes and she bowed her head, hoping he wouldn't see.

It was a vain hope. "Baby, are you crying?"

"I love you, Dex. I never thought I'd have this with you again."

"Look at me." He waited until she did. "We're meant to be. From the first moment I kissed you in my dad's house, you were mine. I let Eric steal you away, and I'll always regret that. I was a jackass, Belle. I should have come after you. I should have demanded the truth and fought for you."

Hot emotion welled in her chest, punched her in the gut. "It wasn't your fault. You don't have to apologize."

Her voice grated like sandpaper scraped over a raw wound. It hurt to speak. To feel. To *be*.

Their gazes clashed. Raw, aware, nothing left to hide.

"I love you, Belle. I never stopped."

Her heart broke open. Hot tears scalded her cheeks.

"I hate making you cry." His voice was a ragged whisper.

She laughed through her tears. "It's a good cry. I promise."

"I was angry for so long," he said, his voice raw. "I took it out on you. I told myself I hated you, but I didn't. I couldn't. You're my other half. Always have been. I fuck-ing hate that I had to live without you for five years. I don't want to live without you for another day, but I know we have to take it slow for Charlotte's sake."

"She's resilient, Dex. She'll love you like I do."

"I know there's a lot to consider. You have Archer Industries, and I live in DC. I have two years left on my enlistment. But we'll make it work. I'll fly to Lexington on weekends and I'll take leave—"

She pressed a finger to his lips. "I had an offer to buy Archer Industries after Eric died. I know we lost the building, but there's insurance. If the buyer's still interested, I'm taking the deal."

"You'd come to DC?"

"Home is where you are. I'd have followed you around the world when you asked me to marry you the first time. I still would."

He kissed her until her toes curled. "I love you, Annabelle Quinn. Always have. Always will."

"Always is a long time," she said.

"No," he told her. "With you, it's not nearly enough."

THIRTY-THREE

"SO WE MEET AGAIN, VIPER. How are you?"

Mendez stood with his legs spread apart, his arms folded over his chest, trying not to glare at the man seated at the table. Dmitri Leonov hadn't changed much. More lines around the eyes and mouth. No gray, but he probably dyed his dark blond hair.

He still had an arctic stare that made lesser men tremble. Mendez had perfected his own arctic stare over the years, so he wasn't much bothered by this man's. He knew what lay behind eyes that dead. It wasn't the kind of thing that made you think of puppies or kittens—unless you thought of someone doing unspeakable things to them.

"I'm good, Dmitri. You aren't though." It was two days since Alpha Squad had brought the man in. Two days, and Mendez had sent his best intel officers to find out what Leonov knew about Sergei Turov and his plans. He'd said nothing useful. Sam was on Mendez's back to turn the man over to the CIA. He was going to have to do it—but not quite yet.

Dmitri shrugged. "This is a temporary setback. I will be out…" He consulted his wrist. There was no watch there. Not anymore because it had been confiscated. "…in approximately six months. Fewer if my government is exceptionally good."

Mendez strolled the perimeter of the room. Dmitri stiffened when Mendez stopped behind him. Good. Let the fucker think Mendez wouldn't follow the law. That he would attack when Dmitri's back was turned.

That's what Leonov did. He waited until his prey was at its most vulnerable. Then he struck.

Mendez's blood was thick and cold in his veins. Like an ice floe moving inexorably toward a goal. This man chilled him. Infuriated him. Cost him everything he'd once cared about. The heat of anger flared, but he stamped it down.

Mendez circled and stopped in front of him. "It's possible," he said. "It's also possible that some mischief will occur and you won't make it to six months. Have you considered that?"

Dmitri snorted. "Ah, you threaten me. You have always been a by-the-book kind of guy, John." He shook his head. "No, I do not believe you."

"People change. Perhaps I've decided that your way is better."

Dmitri slouched lazily in the chair, as if trying to prove he was unfazed. He tapped two fingers against the hard plastic surface of the table. "Do you still wonder, John?"

He knew what this man wanted to hear. He wouldn't give him the satisfaction. "I wonder nothing. Moscow was a long time ago."

"You do not think about her? About Valentina?"

He shrugged. "She was beautiful and smart, but she's been dead for twenty years. No, I don't think about her."

"I do." His smile was a serial killer's dream.

Mendez's heart punched his ribs. *Goddammit!* "Then you'll have a shitload of time to think about her in solitary confinement."

Leonov spread his hands. "I have done nothing wrong. Or nothing wrong for which you can hold me."

"Receiving state secrets, killing an American citizen —I'm sure there's more." Mendez would fucking find more, because Leonov was not getting out of a US prison alive. "You're a danger to the American way of life. We don't like that kind of shit around here."

"Six months," Leonov said. "Mark your calendar, John Mendez."

Mendez turned to give the sergeant standing guard outside the room a signal. Keys rattled in the lock.

"There is one more thing," Leonov said as the lock's tumblers fell into place.

Mendez held up his hand and turned back to the smirking Russian sitting across the table. "If it's not about Turov's plans, or something equally interesting that I can use, then I don't care."

"You will care about this."

He paused for dramatic effect. Mendez snorted and turned away. The door swung inward.

"Valentina did not die twenty years ago," Leonov said. "In fact, she did not die at all."

Three months later...

"AGAIN, PAW-PAW!"

Dex watched as his dad made a quarter disappear and then pulled it from behind Charlotte's ear. She clapped and laughed and begged him to do it again. Which of course he did.

Katie handed him a fresh beer. She was grinning ear to ear. "She's precious, Dex. And I think she's good for Dad."

Dex took a swallow of beer while his chest swelled with happiness. "He has your two boys. They're good for him too."

"Well, of course they are. But he needed a grand-daughter too."

Dex let his gaze sweep over Katie's backyard. She and Jessie had bought a house on a rolling three-acre lot. There were trees and a pond, a swinging bench under a tree, and a small barn that housed Jessie's lawn tractor and other equipment. No cows, thankfully.

Annabelle stepped out of the house and wandered over to where he stood with Katie. His heart leaped at the sight of her. Every day he loved her more. They were managing well, he thought. They'd told Charlotte he was her father within a month of Annabelle properly introducing him to her. Two days after that, they'd gotten married in a civil ceremony at the Briar City courthouse. Charlotte took to him like a pig to mud, and his life had never been so full.

"I'm glad you're together again," Katie said softly as Annabelle approached.

Dex reached for his wife's hand. She came into the circle of his arm and wedged herself against his side. He loved that. Within a week after Annabelle had said she would marry him, she and Katie got together and talked. Dex didn't know everything they'd said, but Annabelle told him she'd held nothing back. Katie forgave her, and they'd been rebuilding their friendship.

Even better, Molly Carter was a part of their circle now. Molly, Katie, and Annabelle got together every time Dex and Annabelle returned to town. Girls' night, they said. Dex didn't care, though he often wondered what the hell they talked about. Especially since Annabelle always seemed to come home and rip his clothes off after.

Not that that was a bad thing. But what they hell did they discuss?

"Molly and Becca will be here in about twenty minutes," Annabelle said. "Molly had a phone meeting go a little long, and she forgot the casserole and had to turn around and go get it."

"Oh heck, she didn't need to do that," Katie said. "We have plenty."

"You know Molly."

"True."

Dex had no idea what they were talking about.

Life was good and he was fucking happy. Dad was doing well. He'd sold the farm and moved into Katie's guesthouse. He kept threatening to move to a retirement community, but so far it was just talk. His rehab on the leg had gone well, and his cholesterol and heart function were under control.

Annabelle had sold Archer Industries to a company who wanted to expand it. They were building a new facility in Briar City and another in DC. She'd sold the monstrosity of a house she'd lived in with Eric too. They'd bought a house in Maryland in a nice neighborhood with good schools and a huge playground. Charlotte had already made friends.

On the business front, HOT was still doing a bang-up job of extracting hostages and kicking terrorists' asses around the globe. So far, there'd been no congressional committee subpoenas over Sergei Turov's shooting. Turov had survived and returned to Russia under some sort of deal with the US government. Dex didn't know what kind of deal, though it sometimes pissed him off if he thought about it.

Marshall Porter was undergoing trial for treason, and the Helios project was on indefinite hold. Marshall had apparently been falsifying more than just the files he'd made for the Russians. Helios didn't work on the scale he claimed it did, and it would take far more time and money than anyone was willing to spend to make a functional product.

The US government had taken possession of the half billion dollars. Dex had no idea what they'd do with it. Probably use it to pay off contract fighters in places like Qu'rim and Afghanistan.

His team was doing well. He was the last man on Alpha Squad to get married. Some had children on the way, others were still enjoying the honeymoon stage. The SEAL

Team that had recently joined HOT often worked closely with Alpha Squad. Only one of those dudes was married, so that would be fun to watch.

And then there was the colonel. The rumor was that he had an on-again, off-again romance with the sexy CIA agent Samantha Spencer. But Dex had seen them together, and he wasn't convinced it would ever amount to anything more than that.

Some dudes just never found the one for them. Annabelle laid her head against his chest as she stood in his embrace, and his heart skipped and sang like some dang cartoon bird in a sappy story about a princess.

"Daddy, Daddy!" Charlotte came running over and he handed Annabelle his beer before bending down and scooping his daughter into his arms.

"What, sweetheart?" God, the singing in his chest was out of control. He didn't always get it right, but he was taking to this daddy thing like a fish to water.

"Paw-Paw showed me a trick! I'm going to do it for you."

She produced a quarter. But she didn't hide it. She just put her hand up to his ear and pretended to drag it out.

"Wow!" Dex said. "That was amazing, baby girl."

She giggled and squirmed and he let her down again. She ran back to his dad, shouting, "I did it, Paw-Paw!"

Annabelle's eyes were misty when he met her gaze. He had a dark urge to kiss the hell out of her right then and there, but he held it in check. Because the urges beneath that were even darker and more sensual.

"Told you I could rock this dad thing," he said.

She giggled. "Yes, you did."

"Soon as I get you alone, I'm going to rock your world too."

"I hope so."

"Mommy!" Charlotte waved furiously for Annabelle to come over and see something. With a quick squeeze of his hand, Annabelle strode off to join their daughter.

Dex stood and watched them as the damn birds kept flying and singing in his chest. His girls. The women he loved. The two beauties who made his life into something he'd never thought he'd have.

He was addicted to this rush of love he felt every waking hour. Addicted, fulfilled, and completed.

Not a bad way to go.

ABOUT THE AUTHOR

LYNN RAYE HARRIS is the *New York Times* and *USA Today* bestselling author of the HOSTILE OPERATIONS TEAM SERIES of military romances as well as 20 books for Harlequin Presents. A former finalist for the Romance Writers of America's Golden Heart Award and the National Readers Choice Award, Lynn lives in Alabama with her handsome former military husband and two crazy cats. Lynn's books have been called "exceptional and emotional," "intense," and "sizzling." Lynn's books have sold over 2 million copies worldwide.

Connect with me online:
Facebook: https://www.facebook.com/AuthorLynnRayeHarris
Twitter: https://twitter.com/LynnRayeHarris
Website: http://www.LynnRayeHarris.com
Newsletter: http://bit.ly/LRHNews
Email: Lynn@LynnRayeHarris.com

Join my Hostile Operations Team Readers and Fans Group on Facebook:
https://www.facebook.com/groups/HOTReadersAndFans/

21571957R00173

Printed in Great Britain
by Amazon